Cereal Killer

*Also by G. A. McKevett
in Large Print:*

Cooked Goose
Death by Chocolate
Just Desserts
Sugar and Spite

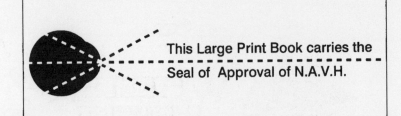

Cereal Killer

A Savannah Reid Mystery

G. A. McKevett

WHEELER
PUBLISHING

Published in 2004 by arrangement with Kensington Books,
an imprint of Kensington Publishing Corp.

Wheeler Large Print Softcover.

The text of this Large Print edition is unabridged.
Other aspects of the book may vary from the original edition.

Set in 16 pt. Plantin by Carleen Stearns.

Printed in the United States on permanent paper.

Library of Congress Cataloging-in-Publication Data

McKevett, G. A.
    Cereal killer : a Savannah Reid mystery / G. A. McKevett.
      p. cm.
    ISBN 1-58724-681-3 (lg. print : sc : alk. paper)
    1. Reid, Savannah (Fictitious character) — Fiction.   2. Women
private investigators — California, Southern — Fiction.
3. Models (Persons) — Crimes against — Fiction.   4. California,
Southern — Fiction.   5. Overweight women — Fiction.
6. Women cooks — Fiction.   7. Large type books.   I. Title.
PS3563.C3758C47 2004
813'.54—dc22   2004043043

LP
F
Ma

For
Gwendolynn and Bobby
Whose love continually warms and inspires us.
You've found each other . . . at last.

As the Founder/CEO of NAVH, the only national health agency solely devoted to those who, although not totally blind, have an eye disease which could lead to serious visual impairment, I am pleased to recognize Thorndike Press★ as one of the leading publishers in the large print field.

Founded in 1954 in San Francisco to prepare large print textbooks for partially seeing children, NAVH became the pioneer and standard setting agency in the preparation of large type.

Today, those publishers who meet our standards carry the prestigious "Seal of Approval" indicating high quality large print. We are delighted that Thorndike Press is one of the publishers whose titles meet these standards. We are also pleased to recognize the significant contribution Thorndike Press is making in this important and growing field.

Lorraine H. Marchi, L.H.D.
Founder/CEO
NAVH

★ Thorndike Press encompasses the following imprints: Thorndike, Wheeler, Walker and Large Print Press.

Chapter
1

"I'm not going to eat another bite of food in this filthy jalopy of yours until you clean it out," Savannah Reid said as she glanced over the seat into the rear floorboard of the battered old Buick. The sight of wadded burger wrappers, mustard-stained napkins, and assorted taco trash was enough to put her off the double chili cheeseburger and super-sized fries in her lap.

Secretly she had to admit that this principled stand of hers had more to do with the double scoop, rocky road, hot fudge sundae she had consumed half an hour ago than it did with the mess in the back of Dirk Coulter's old Buick. The biohazard landfill site that he affectionately called his back seat had been irritating her for years. And since that massive sundae had taken the edge off her hunger, she figured it was a better time than most to launch a protest.

"I never thought I'd see the day when you'd threaten not to eat," Dirk said as he pulled the Skylark out of the Burger Bonanza's drive through and entered the midday traffic on Vista

Del Mar. "What'd you do . . . pig out on something before I picked you up back at your place?"

If there was anything that irked Savannah more than Dirk's filthy car, it was his ability to read her with uncanny accuracy. She wanted to chalk it up to his finely honed skills as a police detective — and that might have had a little to do with it — but mostly it was because the two of them had spent far too much time together over the years.

Most married couples spent less so-called "quality" time together than they did.

Now *there* was a scary thought.

"What makes you think I ate something before you came by?" she asked.

He continued to drive as he fumbled with the Styrofoam burger container in his lap. "Easy. You had chocolate breath when you got in the car. And you've got something that looks like a piece of walnut between your front teeth."

She quickly flipped down the visor and studied her reflection in the mirror on the back. "I do not have anything stuck in my teeth!"

"Lemme see."

She peeled back her lips and gave him a gruesome grin.

He shrugged. "It's gone now. What was it? Snickers bar?"

"Ice cream sundae. Breakfast of champions. And it was probably a pecan you saw stuck in my teeth. Us Georgia girls don't eat walnuts," she added with her best Southern drawl.

He chuckled as he lifted his burger to his mouth and took a hearty bite. Ketchup oozed out the side of the sandwich and dropped on the front of his Harley-Davidson T-shirt.

"Watch it. You're dribbling on yourself there."

He glanced down. "Naw, that's spaghetti sauce from last night's dinner."

"It's ketchup. I just saw it drop. What do you mean, last night's spaghetti? You're wearing the same shirt you wore yesterday? And you're calling *me* gross because of a little nut between my teeth?"

"Hey, I sniffed it before I put it on. It was clean. I only wore it half a day yesterday. I had to change in the afternoon after that drugged-out perp bled on me."

"A perp bled on you?"

Dirk grinned. But it was a nasty smile, not one to warm the heart. "Yeah. Me and him had a little disagreement."

"I guess if he was the one who sprang a leak, that means you won the argument."

"I always do."

Savannah decided not to mention that she had seen him lose a few "disagreements" in years gone by, when he had wound up shedding more blood than the perps he'd caught. Dirk liked to think he was quite the bad ass, and he was a lot easier to get along with when she didn't contradict him. Besides, for the most

9

part, she was glad she was his friend and not his enemy. She had to agree; he *was* pretty bad . . . and frequently an ass, too.

They drove through the main business section of the small seaside town of San Carmelita and past a park whose perimeter was lined with palms. On one side of the park a dozen children entertained themselves in the sandbox and on swings. On the opposite side stood several picnic tables and barbecue pits.

"Pull in," she told him, nudging him with her elbow. "I want to eat my lunch over there in the fresh air and sunshine."

"I got fresh air." He pointed to the pine tree shaped deodorizer dangling from his driver's mirror. "Plenty of it."

She grunted and gave him another nudge.

"All right, all right." He pulled into the only blank spot at the curb and parked.

"That's a fire hydrant," she said, pointing to the obvious.

He reached into the back seat and rummaged through the debris until he produced a police I.D. plaque, which he propped on the dashboard. "Yeah, yeah," he mumbled. "If the park catches on fire, I'll move the car, Miss Goody Two-shoes."

She muttered an abbreviated speech about "being a good example to young people" under her breath as they strolled to the nearest picnic table and found a seagull poop-free spot to spread their lunch and sit down. There was no

10

point in muttering her character improvement speeches aloud; she had been trying to civilize Detective Sergeant Dirk Coulter for years. She'd had about as much luck at that as she had at dieting away those pesky extra thirty pounds, organizing her kitchen cupboards, and halting the depletion of the ozone layer.

The older she got, the smarter she got, and the more carefully she picked her battles. Now solidly into her forties, Savannah had learned the value of conserving life energy. Once a tireless perfectionist, she had recently decided to live by a new motto: *If at first you don't succeed, try, try again. And if you still can't pull it off, give up. There's no point in being a damned fool about it.*

They were golden words to live by. She considered having them tattooed on her left buttock. Heaven knows, there was plenty of room back there — something else that might have caused her a great deal of angst a decade ago. But no more.

Savannah liked herself, her life, and her butt . . . all of it. And now that she wasn't sitting in his dirty car, she even liked Dirk. With the Southern California sunshine in her face, the ocean breeze in her hair, and a chili cheeseburger in her mouth, she was a happy kid.

"You got any jobs lately?" Dirk asked between chews.

Her spirits plummeted.

Motto number two: *Happiness is short-lived.*

Enjoy it while you've got it. Something to tattoo on her right buttock for balance.

"No. Nada. Zilch. Not one ka-ching in the old cash register in over a month now," she admitted. "Private detecting may pay more than being a cop did, but work's spotty."

"Maybe you oughta drop your standards a little, start taking on those wayward hubby spying jobs. You must get a call a day for those."

"Try two or three a day. If I wanted to hang around outside quickie motels and take amateur porno pictures with zoom lenses, I'd be rollin' in the dough."

"So?"

"So *what?* There has to be a more noble way to pay the bills than providing evidence for wives who probably knew they should leave their scumbag husbands years ago."

"You could still be a cop, rousting druggies and getting stuck with dirty needles, frisking scanky hookers and chasing scrawny crack heads through back alleys, gettin' your favorite T-shirts bled on. . . . Now *that's* noble."

Savannah looked across the picnic table at her comrade-in-arms who, in spite of the additional wrinkles and crow's-feet and the slightly thinner hairline, still had a wicked gleam in his eye when he talked about being a cop. There was still plenty of life in the old dog, and she wasn't exactly ready to lie down, roll over, and play dead either.

Besides, Dirk was never happier than when he had something to piss and moan about. He lived to gripe.

Savannah glanced around the park, enjoying the rare moment of relaxation with her old friend. Dirk seldom took a day off, and when he did, he usually spent it fishing off the end of the city pier. But the tide and the winds were high this morning, and the pier had been closed, spoiling Dirk's recreational plans and dashing his hopes of snagging a free dinner.

Hence, Savannah had been graced with the pleasure of his company. And even though his disposition might not be the rosiest or his conversation the most scintillating, Dirk was as comfortable and well worn as her blue terry-cloth bathrobe. And she loved both him and the robe, whether she would have admitted it or not.

In the middle of her savor-the-moment reverie, she heard a mild disturbance on the other side of the park, near the sandbox where the children were playing. A couple of grungy, street-worn guys were standing nose to nose, fists clenched, arguing about something. Because of the proximity of the children, Savannah studied the situation with the eye of a former peace officer. Dirk, too, had laid down his burger and was listening with grudging interest as the argument escalated to a shouting match.

More than one curse floated through the

summer air, references to unnatural sexual acts and equally unsavory intimate relationships with immediate family members.

"Damn it. Not on my day off," he grumbled, rising from the bench. "And I know one of those idiots, too. The blond one's a C.I. of mine."

Reluctantly, Savannah left her own lunch to the mercy of marauding seagulls and followed him as he strode across the grass toward the pair.

"One of your informants?" she said, running a couple of steps to catch up with him. "Did he ever give you anything worthwhile?"

Dirk snorted. "Naw. He just rats out anybody who's on his shit list, anybody he wants to get even with."

"Hmmm . . . he's not long for this world if he keeps doing that. Somebody's bound to punch his time card."

"Not soon enough to suit me."

As they reached the middle of the park, the tall, skinny blond guy spotted them and abruptly left his opponent, a husky black fellow dressed in leather garb, draped in chains, and bristling with silver studs.

"Hey — hey, you, Coulter!" the blond yelled as he hurried toward Dirk and Savannah. "Come 'ere! I got a complaint to make!"

The children in the sandbox had stopped playing and were watching with their concerned mothers as the guy ran up to Dirk and grabbed him by the arm.

"Let go of me," Dirk said, shaking his hand away. "What's the matter with you, cussin' like that in front of women and children? You got no couth?"

"He ripped me off! That dude sold me bad rocks, man. I want you to arrest him."

At the word "arrest," the dude in question began to not-so-nonchalantly stroll away in the opposite direction.

"Go get him, man! He cheated me out of fifty dollars, cuz. Fifty big ones! That's gotta be a felony, right?"

Dirk fixed him with an evil eye. "What are you telling me, you moron? That somebody sold you some bad dope? Is that what you're trying to say to me?"

Savannah grinned. Even the slowly retreating guy in leather had a smirk on his face.

"Yeah, man!" the blond wailed, holding out his open palm, which contained a couple of tiny wads of cellophane plastic, wrapped around small cream-colored squares of something that looked like soap. "He sold me macadamia nuts, man! Fuckin' macadamia nuts instead o' rocks! What does he think I'm gonna do with these . . . make friggin' chocolate chip cookies? I ain't no Mrs. Fields, man! Lock him up, detective! But get me my fifty dollars back first."

Dirk stared down at the bindles in the guy's hand for what seemed like forever. Savannah stifled a snicker.

Then Dirk growled and batted them out of his hand. The misnomered contraband sailed through the air and landed in some nearby shrubs.

"Are you stupid or just plain dumb?" Dirk asked him. He grabbed him behind the neck and gave him a shake like he was a puppy who had just piddled on the good rug. "You want me to intervene because you got ripped off in a drug deal? You expect me . . . on my day off, no less . . . to arrest some guy for selling you macadamia nuts instead of rock cocaine? Is that what you're telling me?"

"Well . . . I . . ."

"You come here to a city park, where mothers bring their babies to play, and you make a damned drug deal, and you have the nerve to complain to me when you get ripped off? Why, I oughta —"

"Actually . . ." Savannah said, stepping between them, "Dirk, you oughtn't to. Really. . . ."

She nodded toward the dozen or so wide-eyed children and their mommies who were hanging on every word.

Dirk released his informant, who seemed to quickly realize that this situation wasn't going at all the way he wanted. Not only was the police detective not interested in dispensing any justice his way, but his dishonest dealer was about to leave the park.

"I can't believe this," the blond sputtered.

"So much for 'protect and serve,' huh? So much for keeping the peace and all that crap."

He left Dirk and rushed over to the shrubs, where he retrieved his bindles. Then he hurried after the guy in the leather jacket, who was waiting for a break in traffic to cross the street and exit the park.

"Can you believe that?" Dirk said, watching him and shaking his head.

"Oh, yes. I believe anything. That was a close one, huh, buddy?"

Dirk nodded. "No kidding. If they'd actually come to blows I'd be spending my day off dragging them to the house and doin' fives. The last thing I want is paperwork when I'd rather be fishing."

"Or hanging out with me if the pier's closed."

He gave her a sideways grin. "Yeah, or hanging with you."

From the other side of the park, they could hear the blond yell, "See if I ever buy anything from you again, you asshole!"

The black man slowly turned back toward him.

"Huh-oh," Savannah said. "I've got a bad feeling about . . ."

"What's the matter, you candy-ass pimp?" the blond continued. "Did that crack-whore mamma of yours use up all of your stash? Is that why you're out sellin' macadamia nuts instead of the real thing, huh?"

Dirk sighed. "Eh, shit."

17

Savannah nodded. "Yep."

Less than four seconds later, Dirk's least favorite confidential informant was on the ground, getting the daylights pummeled out of him by an angry dope dealer who didn't seem to mind at all that a police detective was casually making his way toward him across the park lawn.

Savannah strolled along beside Dirk, her arm laced companionably through his. They looked like a couple of old folks taking their daily constitutional as a few yards away fists flew, along with colorful curses, bits of spit, some handfuls of hair, and finally . . . a bloody tooth.

"I'll help you fill out the fives," she told Dirk in her best consoling voice. "You just dictate and I'll type."

"You're damned right you will," he replied. "It was your idea to have lunch in this friggin' park instead of the safe, trouble-free confines of my car. You owe me, girl."

Sitting in her cushy, wing-back chair with its cabbage rose-print chintz, her feet propped on the matching ottoman and warmed by two black cats, one on each side, Savannah was at peace with the world. Or at least, she would have been except for the pile of past-due bills in her lap that needed attention. Unfortunately, they needed more than just her attention; they needed paying. The creditors had already sent the polite green and yellow versions. But more

18

than one of these not-so-friendly reminders bore threats in bold red ink and the occasional exclamation mark — all designed to strike terror in the heart of the delinquent bill-payer.

But Savannah wasn't terrified. When sitting in her favorite chair, feet warmed by purring, sleeping cats, the most she could muster in the way of negative feelings was mild depression and a modicum of embarrassment. Someday this private investigation business of hers would start to pay off. Someday. Some way. Somewhere . . . over the rainbow.

Looking across her living room, she watched as Tammy Hart, her friend, assistant, and crime detection protégée sat studiously at the computer on the rolltop desk in the corner and surfed the Internet. Tammy seemed to think that if she searched long and hard enough, she would eventually find some jobs for the Moonlight Magnolia Detective Agency.

Not knowing diddly-squat about the Internet, Savannah had her doubts that Tammy's efforts would pan out, but if the kid wanted to look, she was welcome to it. Long ago, Savannah had realized that Tammy didn't hang around for the occasional moneys Savannah was able to shuffle her way. Like Savannah, Tammy truly enjoyed the work, when it came along. Tracking down missing kids, locating long-lost loved ones, and occasionally getting to nab a really bad guy made the dry times worth it.

Besides the joys of nailing a bad boy, and occasionally a bad girl, the two women had something else in common — an unexpected friendship. Unexpected because they couldn't have been more different.

Ten years younger than Savannah, Tammy was a California golden girl, with sun-bleached, long blond hair and lean, tanned limbs. She was also a computer whiz and a rabid health nut.

On the other hand, Savannah had dark curly hair and a peaches-and-cream complexion and was both technologically and dietetically challenged. Savannah's definition of a megabyte was a mouthful of See's candy or a Mrs. Fields cookie. As a result, her limbs weren't particularly lean . . . or any other part of her for that matter.

Once, years ago, she had hated Tammy for wearing a size zero and a half. But Savannah had come to terms with her own overly voluptuous body and now only hated Tammy occasionally . . . like when they were trying on clothes in the Victoria's Secret dressing rooms.

"So, Dirko's coming over tonight, huh?" Tammy asked without turning away from her screen.

"Sure he is. There's a heavyweight bout on HBO at nine. He'll show up at eight, hoping that I'll feed him."

"You'll feed him. You feed every living thing within a mile of you."

Savannah chuckled. It was true; Southern hospitality demanded that nobody grow faint from hunger in the presence of a Reid woman.

"Why doesn't Dirko watch the fight on his own TV?" Tammy wanted to know. "He mooches off you too much."

"It would only be mooching if I minded. I don't mind. Usually," she added, thinking of all the times Dirk had finagled her out of a free burger or hot dog when they'd worked the streets together. "Besides, Dirk doesn't have HBO. He doesn't even have cable, for heaven's sake."

"Oh, yeah, I forgot. No-frills Dirk."

"Eh, what do you expect from a guy who thinks that the ultimate experience in fine dining is supersizing his burger and fry order?"

Tammy glanced at her watch. "Seven-thirty . . . I think I'll split."

"Don't want to hang out and watch two men beat the crap out of each other?"

Tammy shuddered. "And listen to Dirk screaming at the top of his lungs about jabs, cuts, and head butts? No, thanks."

Savannah watched her shut down the computer. "No luck finding work?"

"Not unless we're ready to become bounty hunters, chasing dirtbags who've jumped bail. There seem to be a few openings for those if your name's Bubba and you're six feet four and weigh three hundred pounds."

"Shows what you know about bounty

hunting. Sure, there are some big, nasty hunters named Bubba, but I've met others who were female and looked like you, girlie-girl. And they weren't chasing just the dirtbags. Most hard-core criminals know the drill, and they'll show up for court. They've been through it all before, done their time, got out, re-offended, and landed back in the system. It's the scared welfare mother who wrote bad checks for groceries who takes off. She's terrified, not knowing what to expect, thinking her life's over. Let somebody else track her down. I'm not that desperate yet."

She glanced down at the stack of bills in her lap, then around her modest house. The lights were on. In the kitchen and in the bathroom the water was running. The mortgage payment was only three days late, and the refrigerator was well stocked.

Something was bound to come along soon. It always did.

"Thanks for coming over," Savannah said, rising and walking Tammy to the door. "Sure you don't wanna hang around and say hi to Dirk?"

Tammy made a face, reminding Savannah of a kindergartner who had just heard the name of her seven-year-old brother mentioned. "Just tell him I said, 'Sit on a tack . . . or a railroad track.' Tell him to eat an apple with a big worm in it and chew thoroughly. Tell him —"

"Okay, okay. I gotcha. I'll give him your warmest regards."

Tammy stuck up her middle finger.

"Yes, yes . . ." Savannah sighed. "Without the sign language, though, if you don't mind. *I* am a lady."

Tammy snickered. "A lady who's not above sitting on a perp's head if necessary to hold him down or jamming her fingers down his throat to get the drug evidence he's trying to swallow."

She shrugged and grinned. "Whatever the job requires."

Just as she was opening the door for Tammy, she heard the phone ring behind her.

"That's probably Dirk now," Tammy said, "wanting to know if you'll make a pot of your homemade chili and cornbread for him."

"Hmm . . . good idea. Except for the beans. I *do* have to spend the evening with the guy."

She waved Tammy out the door, then hurried to the telephone. As Tammy had predicted, it was Dirk. But he didn't sound hungry. He sounded harried.

"I'm gonna have to take a rain check on dinner tonight," he said.

"I didn't invite you for dinner yet, just the fight."

"Whatever. I'm gonna miss that, too."

"What's up? Where are you?"

"I'm still at the station house. I was trying to get out of here after processing those idiots from the park, and I caught a case."

Savannah perked up. She couldn't help her-

23

self; it was in her blood. "What's the case?"

"Dead body. Some gal's down in one of those fancy houses on the beach. Gotta go check it out. Sounds like it was a heart attack — a fat chick who was exercising too much or something. But she's young, so I have to go down there with CSU and make sure it's nothing hinky."

Savannah bristled at the "fat chick" reference, but thoughts of watching the Crime Scene Unit technicians in action made her put the offense away for the time being. Besides, other than the occasional ill-chosen adjective, Dirk showed an endearing degree of sensitivity when it came to weight issues.

"Want company?" she asked.

"Sure. The address is number one Seagull Lane. Must be right on the water."

An overweight young woman, exercising too much, who lived at a prestigious beachfront address . . . A bell rang in Savannah's memory banks.

"The DB's name wouldn't happen to be Caitlin Connor, would it?" she asked, dreading the answer.

"How'd you know?"

Images flashed across Savannah's mental screen: a beautiful woman with long flowing red hair, turquoise eyes, flawless skin, and a dazzling smile — a full-figured woman who showed the world that beauty could come in generous packages as well as petite ones. Cait

24

Connor's face and figure had sold magazines, plus-sized clothing, makeup, fragrances, and even home furnishings for the past few years, enticing generously proportioned women to enter her world of grace and fashion.

"Caitlin's dead?" she said, still unable to believe that such beauty, such vibrancy was gone.

"Yeah, sorry. Were you a friend of hers?" Dirk asked with more compassion and warmth than he was known to display under most circumstances.

"No. I never met her," Savannah replied. "I'm just a fan. One of many." Suddenly Savannah felt older, more tired, more aware of the fragility of life. "I'll meet you there in ten," she said.

There probably wasn't a damned thing that she or anyone else could do for Caitlin Connor at this point.

But she'd try.

Chapter
2

The sun was dipping into the Pacific, staining the waves with a gold and coral patina, as Savannah drove her Mustang down Shore Boulevard toward the San Carmelita waterfront. Definitely on the "right" side of the tracks, the beach area wasn't a section of town where Savannah had spent a lot of time in her law enforcement days. Normally a person could walk their dog at two in the morning in that neighborhood without fear. And the pooch didn't have to be a pit bull either.

Savannah lived in midtown, in a moderately priced stucco house with a red Spanish tile roof. Private detectives and former police officers didn't live on the hillsides with their panoramic views. And they certainly couldn't afford to live on the beaches. In her price range, you didn't even get a one-bedroom cottage within walking distance of the water, let alone one of the mansions that sat directly on the beach.

But if Savannah wasn't the type to gripe about the extra padding on her fanny, she certainly wasn't going to complain to the universal powers that she was beachless. When the occasional Pacific storm hit the West Coast and the surf flooded the first five blocks of the waterfront and the glass-fronted houses on the muddy hills started slipping off their foundations, sliding down into their neighbors' swimming pools, she sat in her dry, stable bungalow and felt terribly superior. She was poor and glad of it.

A little pseudo-arrogance went a long way toward fostering pseudo-contentment.

The streets narrowed to little more than alleys as she got closer to the beach. With property being assessed by the square inch, parking in this area was at a premium. Large signs were posted on garage doors, at the edges of postage stamp-sized lots, and in driveways that threatened everything from towing and fines to decapitation and dismemberment if you dared to leave your family's SUV on their private property when you took your kiddies to the beach.

For the most part, those who could afford to live here amid the sand and surf had little tolerance for their nonbeach townsmen, and even less for the tourist hoards from Los Angeles and the San Fernando Valley that descended on the community every summer.

Passing street after street with their quaint, nautically themed names, Savannah quickly found Seagull Lane between Heron and Pelican. Cait Connor's house wasn't hard to spot.

On a street lined with luxury homes, it stood out for its sheer size alone. A contemporary structure, it looked more like a giant glass box, a sort of arboretum, than a private home. The ocean-facing front half of the house was constructed almost entirely of triangular panes of bronze-tinted glass.

The back half of the building was a warm, terra-cotta colored stucco, again with massive windows. The effect was spectacular as each glass pane caught the golden-red rays of the setting sun and glowed with its own individual fire.

Savannah had noticed the house before when she had visited the beach, and she had heard that Cait Connor and her husband lived on the waterfront, but she had never put the two together.

Apparently, plus-sized modeling paid well. At least if you were in the super-model category with the likes of Caitlin Connor.

She parked across the street from the house, defying a sign that threatened her not to, next to Dirk's Buick and a black-and-white patrol car. A Jaguar S-Type sat in the Connor driveway, along with a silver Maserati Coupe GT. Savannah did a quick calculation and decided that both cars cost more than her house.

After looking around for the Crime Scene Unit's van and seeing nothing, Savannah decided they hadn't arrived yet. She was glad. She liked to check out the scene before they arrived and cluttered the place with all of their equipment, disturbing what she called the "subtle, dark vibes" of the area.

Not that Cait Connor's house was a crime scene. She certainly hoped it wasn't. If there was anything worse than a young person dying unexpectedly, it was finding out that foul play was involved. That made any tragedy a hundred times more painful for the deceased person's loved ones.

Yes, in spite of the yellow tape that Dirk had strung around the driveway and across the door, Savannah prayed that pretty Cait Connor with her long red hair and turquoise eyes had died of a natural — or at worst, accidental — cause.

No sooner had she stepped over the tape and started up the walk to the front door than it opened and a handsome, uniformed officer came out. Savannah recognized Mike Bosco by the stern, terribly officious look on his young face. But the moment he recognized Savannah, he grinned broadly. "Hey, girl," he said. "Long time no see." He strode down the brick walkway and put out his hand. "Should have known you'd be along sooner or later, since Dirk's caught the case. Good to see you."

"Nice to see you, too, Mike. What's shakin', darlin'?" she asked, pumping his hand and nodding toward the house.

"Gal's down in the bathroom. Dirk's checking her out."

"She's . . . gone?" Savannah knew the answer, but she couldn't help asking, couldn't help hoping just a little.

"Oh, yeah. Has been for a while. Dirk said there's some rigor already set in."

"Mmm. How does it look?"

"No signs of violence to the body. Doesn't look like anything's been disturbed in the house."

"Were you first on the scene?"

"Yes. I've been here about forty-five minutes. Dirk just got here, had me string up the tape."

"Who called it in?"

"The husband. Called 911 about an hour ago. Says he came home from work and found her on the bathroom floor."

"Is he here?"

"Yes. He's a mess. When I first got here, I had a hard time calming him down enough to get anything out of him. I guess it was a big shock, her being young and healthy. Except for" — his eyes swept briefly over Savannah's figure — "you know . . . her being . . . chunky."

Chunky? A dozen of Cait's magazine and catalog cover shots flashed through Savannah's mind. She recalled the videos of the redhead walking a runway, modeling the latest in full-figured fashions. A lot of words came to mind when she thought of Cait Connor: graceful, sultry, feminine, lovely. "Chunky" wasn't one of them.

Mike must have read her thoughts because

he quickly added, "She had a pretty face, though."

Savannah decided to go inside before the urge to slap Mike stupid completely overwhelmed her. Anger management . . . she was getting better at it all the time.

"I'm gonna go find Dirk," she told him as she brushed by him and into the house. "Let us know when CSU gets here, okay?"

"Sure." He looked relieved. "No problem."

The moment Savannah entered the foyer of the house, she forgot all about Mike and society's insensitivity to what she preferred to think of as the "horizontally enhanced."

Caitlin Connor's seaside mansion was something else.

Savannah wasn't sure what, but it was certainly something different than she had ever seen before.

Either Cait or an overly enthusiastic professional decorator had obviously been in love with the tropics. The interior struck Savannah as a grossly overdone version of "The Caribbean Meets Las Vegas."

If the structure looked like an arboretum from the outside, it looked even more so inside. Enormous jungle plants, the size of full-grown trees, reached the three-story ceiling of the living room. After a double take, Savannah decided they were a combination of silk and plastic. Oh, well . . . everybody didn't have a green thumb.

The artificial trees were filled with colorful parrots. It took Savannah a few seconds to realize — with a shudder of disgust — that they, too, were fake. Or, at least, she preferred to think they were fake, because the alternative was to consider that they were dead and stuffed by a taxidermist. And that was an even bigger shudder.

What seemed like miles of brilliantly colored batik fabrics draped the walls and formed canopies over rattan furniture, whose cushions were also covered in eye-assaulting shades of red, turquoise, yellow, purple, and hot pink, all splashed together in dizzying prints.

Savannah thought of every TV commercial she had ever seen, designed to lure tourists to the tropics. She half expected a sexy hunk named Carlos to appear with a pineapple and rum drink in one hand and a bottle of tanning oil in the other, wearing skimpy swim briefs and a "Come to me, senorita" grin on his handsome face.

"Oh, well, the waterfall's cool," she whispered to herself. The far wall was covered in natural stone and water trickled from its highest point near the ceiling down the stones, over moss and exotic plants — probably plastic — to the shallow pond below. The soothing sound lent yet another sensual layer to the tropical fantasy.

Okay, Savannah decided, *maybe Granny Reid would call it trashy gaudy.* But she thought it was still pretty neat . . . in a gaudy, trashy sort of way.

She crossed the living room to a dining area, which was also resplendent in tropical foliage with a chrome and glass table and chairs. A carved wooden bowl in the middle of the table overflowed with beaded fruit.

Beyond the table and chairs was a glass wall, and through it Savannah could see a pool and a Jacuzzi. At an umbrella-covered table on the patio sat a large dark-haired man wearing green surgical scrubs. His elbows were propped on the table, his hands covering his face. His shoulders were shaking, and he appeared to be sobbing.

She was about to go out to him, perhaps to comfort him, when she heard a shuffling sound above her. She looked up to see a second-story mezzanine and Dirk standing on it, beckoning to her.

"Up here," he said. "She's in the john. Come check it out."

Savannah glanced at the man on the patio, hesitated, then climbed a curved staircase that led from the main floor to the mezzanine.

Half a dozen doors lined the balcony, and Dirk pointed to the one on the far left. "In there," he said.

She tried to read the expression on his face to see how much she needed to steel herself before viewing the body. But Dirk wore only two expressions when he was working a scene: grim and grimmer. Neither one told her much, and today he was somewhere between the two.

"How does it look?" she said as she walked by him, heading toward the bathroom door.

"Eh." He shrugged. "You tell me."

She stepped into the room and was surprised at how lovely it was. Mostly because, unlike downstairs, it wasn't overtly decorated. Tiles, the color of pale jade, reflected the sunlight that streamed through a large skylight, and the sink and other fixtures were the same soft color. White towels, spa-thick, hung pristinely on gleaming brass rods, and near the whirlpool tub sat a basket filled with exotic soaps and bottles of bath gels.

But these amenities registered only on Savannah's mental periphery. Her attention focused on the body in the middle of the floor.

Caitlin Connor lay on her back, her head toward the door, her arms flung out on either side of her. She was without a doubt quite dead, her eyes staring, sightless and soulless, up into the skylight. Her beautiful long red hair — once her trademark — was spread across the tiles in lank, limp strands that looked as pathetic and lifeless as their owner.

"What's that git-up she's wearing there?" Dirk asked over Savannah's shoulder. "She looks like an escapee from that old TV show, *Lost in Space.*"

Dropping to one knee beside the body, Savannah examined the metallic-looking fabric of

34

the sweat suit that the body was wearing. It looked like an exercise outfit made of aluminum foil. The one-piece suit had elastic around the neck, the wrists, and the ankles and a long zipper up the front. It was the sort of garment one might wear on a bitterly cold day and was totally inappropriate considering the warm temperature of the glass house.

"It's a vapor-impermeable suit," she told him.

"What's that?"

"They're used for rapid weight loss. You put one on, exercise like a maniac, and sweat out your body fluids. Can be very dangerous, but hell, the numbers on the scale go down. That's all that matters to some people. The all-powerful number."

"Wait a minute. I think I've heard of those suits." He walked around Savannah and knelt beside her. "Didn't some wrestler kids die from using those last year?"

"Yeah. And from using diuretics and laxatives and exercising up a storm in the summer heat — all to get down to a certain weight before a competition."

Dirk pulled a pair of latex gloves from his jacket pocket and put them on. Then he fingered the material on the suit's sleeve. "Do you suppose that's what she was trying to do . . . get down to a certain weight for some reason?"

The thought made Savannah sick as she stared down at the pretty face that looked considerably thinner than she remembered from the magazine covers she had seen. Suddenly the room didn't appear so beautiful. The marble walls seemed to close in around her, and for the first time she noticed that the room was stifling hot, much warmer than the rest of the house. Looking down at the young woman on the floor, she felt a wave of nausea wash through her.

"Lord, I hope she didn't accidentally kill herself that way," she said. "Wouldn't that be a shame? I can't imagine it. Caitlin was a plus-sized model and really proud of it. She was very outspoken about the dangers of starvation diets and eating disorders. Why would she put her health . . . her life . . . at risk like this?"

"Slenda."

Savannah and Dirk turned to see Caitlin's husband standing in the bathroom doorway. He was staring down at his wife, his eyes swollen and red from crying, his face the picture of familial tragedy.

"I beg your pardon?" Savannah said, rising to her feet and taking a few steps toward him.

"Slenda," he repeated. "It was that damned cereal. She had to lose thirty pounds in two months, and she'd only dropped twenty so far. She was worried sick about it, that she'd lose the contract. We really need the money and —"

His voice broke and his broad shoulders began to shake with sobs. He covered his face with his hands.

Savannah grabbed a handful of tissues from a dispenser on the counter and offered them to him. But he continued to cry and shake his head.

She looked back at Dirk; he had that helpless, close-to-panic look in his eyes that he got when confronted with grieving men. Women were a different matter; Dirk could handle a crying female. He performed the big brother/daddy routine just fine when called upon. Chivalry was definitely the better part of Coulter's valor.

But a weeping man made him miserably uncomfortable. The thought of actually hugging and soothing another male — it was enough to send old macho Dirko into a tizzy.

"Come along, Mr. Connor," Savannah said, taking his arm and leading him away from the door. "Let's go downstairs and get you a glass of water. Sergeant Coulter can take care of . . . things up here."

She led him down the stairs and into the kitchen, where he leaned against the counter, as though too weak to stand. She was already planning strategies for catching him before he hit the floor as she looked through the cupboard for a glass. Finding one, she filled it with water from the tap on the front of the refrigerator and offered it to him.

He shook his head. "No, thanks. That's not what I need."

He pushed away from the counter and

walked over to another cupboard. Opening it, he revealed an ample supply of alcoholic potables. As he pulled out a bottle of Scotch, he said, "Something a bit stronger than water . . . that's what I need. It isn't every day you come home from work and find your wife dead on the bathroom floor."

Savannah nodded and said softly, "I'm sure it must be just awful."

He bolted the drink in one shot, reached for the bottle, and sloshed another generous one into the glass.

Savannah stepped forward and gently placed one hand on his arm before he drank it, too. "I wouldn't," she told him. "They're going to be asking you a lot of questions in the next few hours, and you'll want to have your wits about you."

She felt his arm tense, and for a moment she thought he was going to shove her hand away, but then he seemed to reconsider and set the glass on the counter.

"Yes, you're right," he said. "Although I don't have much to tell them. She finally killed herself. I knew she was going to do it. I've seen it coming for more than a year now, and I couldn't stop it."

Outside, Savannah heard a vehicle pull into the driveway, then another. The Crime Scene Unit had arrived. Maybe Dr. Liu, the county coroner, too.

She took the husband's arm again and

nudged him toward the dining room and the doors leading to the patio. "Come on," she said. "Let's go outside and sit down. We can talk out there while . . . while they do what they have to in here."

More times than she cared to remember, Savannah had been with the next of kin when a loved one's body was carried out of the house on a gurney, face covered. It was a horrible moment, every time, no matter what the circumstances.

She didn't know if she could spare Kevin Connor that heart-wounding memory. But it was worth a try.

Chapter
3

This time Kevin Connor seemed more steady on his feet as he walked from the kitchen to the patio. Apparently the Scotch had hit his bloodstream and was doing its job. He wasn't shaking as much either, she noticed, as they stepped outside and walked over to the umbrella-covered patio table where he had been sitting earlier.

"Are you a police officer?" he asked, settling into one of the chairs at the glass and wrought iron table.

Savannah sat across from him and subconsciously switched into "evaluation" mode as she studied him. "No," she replied. "I was. Now I'm a private investigator."

"Then why are you here?"

She searched his face to see if his question was a complaint, but she saw only a vague curiosity in his dark eyes that were red and swollen from crying.

"When I was with the SCPD, I was Detective Coulter's partner. Sometimes he still invites me along on his cases. And I'm" — she couldn't

40

bring herself to say "was" — "a fan of your wife's."

"Cait had a lot of fans." He stared down at his hands that were tightly clasped before him on the table, and he began to cry softly again. "They're going to be heartbroken when they hear this."

Savannah gave him a couple of moments to compose himself; then she spoke, choosing her words as carefully as she could. "I have to say, I'm surprised that Caitlin would put herself through something like this . . . a rigorous, dangerous weight-loss program. She was so vocal about self-acceptance and sensible weight management."

"Yes, but that was before she got herself roped into this cereal contract. We needed the money, and her agent pressured her, and then the ad agency was breathing down her neck. They'd based this big campaign on Cait and a couple of other models losing a ridiculous amount of weight in only a few weeks by eating their stupid cereal."

He shook his head and rubbed his hands wearily over his face. "If I'd only known ahead of time, if I'd seen the contract before she'd signed it, I never would've let her. It even said that if she didn't drop the weight in time, they would sue her for part of the cost of the promotion. She would have been ruined, and she's worked so hard for so long to get to where she is . . . or was." Again he collapsed in sobs. "I

41

just can't believe she's gone."

Savannah reached across the table and placed her hand on his forearm. "I know," she said. "I'm really sorry."

"I don't think she had eaten anything for days," he said. "She told me she was eating, even showed me the empty food containers in the garbage. But last night I caught her putting her dinner down the garbage disposal when she thought I was in the Jacuzzi. And I know she was using laxatives and diuretics again."

"Again? Did she have an eating disorder?"

"Sure she did. She battled it for ages. But she had it under control for the past three years. She didn't fall off the wagon until this damned ad campaign."

"I noticed that she was wearing a vapor-impermeable suit. Was she exercising vigor-ously?"

"Night and day, trying to get ready for to-morrow's weigh-in at the doctor's office."

"Doctor?" Savannah's mind couldn't quite grasp the thought. "A doctor condoned that sort of weight-loss regime?"

"You'd be surprised what they'll condone when the payoff is high enough. He's on Went-worth Cereal's payroll."

She glanced up and down his greens. "Are you a physician?"

He gave a dry chuckle. "Nope. Just a lowly surgical nurse over at Community General."

"There's nothing lowly about nursing," she

42

replied softly. "It's one of the most noble occupations on the planet. Nurses are right up there with teachers."

"Along with police officers and private investigators?" He gave her a brief but nice smile, and it occurred to Savannah that Cait Connor had been married to a very handsome man. They must have made a stunning couple.

She grinned and shrugged. "Well, up there with cops to be sure."

Over his shoulder, she could see the CSU technicians through the glass wall as they filed through the living and dining areas and up the staircase to the second story of the house. Dr. Jennifer Liu, the county medical examiner, led the procession.

Kevin stopped crying long enough to follow her line of vision; he turned in his chair and watched as the team disappeared up the stairs. "Who are they?" he asked, sniffing and wiping his eyes with the back of his hand.

"That's the Crime Scene Unit," she told him.

His eyes widened. "Crime? You mean, like a homicide investigation?"

"It's perfectly routine," she assured him. "Your wife was young and healthy, and she died unexpectedly. They always do an investigation under those circumstances, just to make sure."

"To make sure of what? That somebody didn't kill her?" He shook his head in disbelief. "Cait didn't have an enemy in the world. Everybody who knew her loved her. She was the

43

best person I've ever known."

"Like I said, it's just routine. They have to rule out foul play, and I'm sure they will. From what you said, it sounds like a clear case of hyperthermia and dehydration."

A worried frown creased his forehead. "I never even considered that it could have been anything but the dieting. I don't think I could stand it if I thought somebody had actually hurt her. But who would . . . ?"

"Don't even think about it right now," Savannah told him. "There's no point in putting yourself through that on top of everything else. Just wait until the medical examiner does her job and makes her ruling." Savannah deliberately avoided using the word "autopsy" because of the painful mental pictures it would paint for him. Reality would seep into his consciousness all too quickly no matter what she withheld in conversation.

"How long will the autopsy take?" he asked.

So much for protecting the psyche of the next of kin, she thought. "A day or two."

Glancing over his shoulder again, Savannah saw a woman in a bright red pantsuit standing on the other side of the glass, watching them. Unless CSU techs had drastically changed their uniform, a civilian was on their crime scene.

Momentarily forgetting that she, too, fell into that category, Savannah rose from her chair and crossed the patio to the sliding door. When she opened it, a furry bundle of energy

44

bounded out at her. It was a golden cocker spaniel puppy with enormous eyes and a stub of a tail that wagged its entire body.

"Susie, come back here!" the woman in red shouted, yanking on the red leather leash. "Ba-a-ad dog!"

The pup slunk back to her owner and lay at the woman's feet, a vanquished spirit . . . at least for a few seconds.

"May I help you?" Savannah asked.

The woman looked about the same age as Savannah with long straight black hair that fell to a blunt cut below her shoulders. She had a dark tan and, judging from the depth of the crow's-feet around her eyes, she had gotten it the old-fashioned way — from hours on the beach.

Her suit, though a bit on the bright side, was a smart cut and expensive fabric. Savannah made a quick mental note that her high-heeled Italian sandals probably cost more than her own entire summer wardrobe . . . not-so-carefully assembled over the past twenty years.

"May I help you?" Savannah asked again, interjecting a note of "What are you doing here?" into her voice.

"Yes, you can help me. Tell me what the hell's going on," the woman demanded, matching Savannah's aggressive tone note for note.

Before Savannah could open her mouth to reply, Kevin Connor shot up out of his chair and rushed over to the open door.

"I'll tell you what happened, Leah," he said, glaring at the woman. "Let *me* be the one to tell you. Cait's dead. She died. She's lying upstairs on the bathroom floor."

The woman gasped and covered her mouth with her hand.

"That's right!" Kevin shouted at her. "She starved herself and abused herself, trying to lose your stinking thirty pounds, and now she's dead. Are you happy? Well, are you?"

Savannah couldn't help feeling sorry for the woman, who had suddenly gone pale beneath her carefully cultivated tan. Even the cocker puppy seemed to sense the distress of the humans around her and whined, gazing up at her mistress with worried eyes.

Taking a step forward, Savannah gently placed herself between them. Whatever this "Leah" had done to incur Kevin Connor's wrath, she didn't need to hear such awful news delivered in such a callous manner.

"My name is Savannah Reid," she said softly. "May I ask who you are and how you know Ms. Connor?"

The woman's eyes narrowed. "Why do you want to know? Are you a cop?"

"No, a private detective. I sometimes work with Sergeant Coulter, the police detective who's in charge of this investigation." Again she gently asked, "And you are . . . ?"

"She's Leah Freed, Cait's agent," Kevin interjected. "She's the money-grubbing bitch who got Caitlin the rotten gig in the first place and then called her every day, hassling her about how much weight she'd lost. That's who she is."

Savannah glanced quickly from Kevin to Leah, expecting her to bristle at being called a bitch and accused of causing her client's death. But her reaction was minimal. The horror she had initially registered seemed to slip off her face, which was now completely passive as she stared blankly at Kevin Connor.

"We don't really know anything yet, Kevin," Savannah told him. "Until the coroner's report we won't even know what killed her, let alone who might have been responsible."

"She's responsible." He pointed his finger, shaking it only inches from the agent's nose. "Her and that damned ad company and the Wentworths. They were willing to let Cait kill herself just to sell cereal!"

"It's premature to affix blame right now," Savannah repeated. "Really, Kevin . . . you're hurt and upset, and you're saying things you may regret later."

"No way," he said. "I'm just telling the truth, and you know it!" Once more he shoved his finger in Leah's face; then he turned around and strode across the patio to a gate in the whitewashed, six-foot-high fence that surrounded the pool area.

"I think you should stick around, Kevin," Savannah called after him. "Detective Coulter will probably need to speak to you and . . ."

But Kevin Connor already had the gate open and was on his way out. "I'm just going to walk on the beach for a few minutes," he said, "and when I get back I want *her* off my property."

He slammed the gate behind him and the sound echoed across the patio. The pup whined again and plastered herself against her mistress's leg.

Neither woman spoke for a few long, tense moments. Then Savannah quietly said, "He's distraught."

"He isn't the only one," Leah replied. Now that Kevin had disappeared, her façade began to crumble and tears filled her eyes. "Cait was more than my client; she was my friend. For years. I can't believe she's dead."

"I'm sorry for your loss," Savannah told her, thinking of all the times she had uttered those words and how it never got any easier. Being with people in some of the worst moments of their lives had taken a toll on her. Sometimes she felt like forty-something going on ninety.

Sometimes — like when a beautiful, vivacious young woman lay dead upstairs on her bathroom floor — it was hard to remember that the world was a good place to spend your allotted years of life.

A sound from inside the house caught Savannah's attention, and she looked beyond Leah Freed to see the technicians carrying a gurney

48

up the steps. In a little while, they would be coming back down with Caitlin Connor's body. And that was a sight that the victim's agent and longtime friend should be spared.

Besides, Savannah was pretty certain from the look in Kevin Connor's eyes when he left that he meant it when he said that Leah had better be gone when he returned.

Dirk wouldn't be too happy about her hanging around a potential crime scene either.

"You really shouldn't be here, Leah," she told her. "Did you see the yellow barricade tape outside when you came in?"

Lean glanced uneasily over her shoulder and shook her head. "Ah, not really. I . . . ah . . ."

"Or that big handsome police officer who shouldn't have let you in?"

"Um . . . well . . . he was busy with those guys in the white uniforms and a lady who I think might have been the coroner. I told him I was a friend of the family, and he said it was okay for me to come inside."

She was lying. After what seemed like a million years of being lied to at least fifty times a day by seasoned professional liars, Savannah didn't need any sort of lie-detector equipment to figure out when she was getting the shuck put on her.

Leah Freed had sneaked in. Pure and simple. And now she was lying through her teeth about it.

Savannah's cop radar registered a blip on her

mental screen. "Why, exactly, did you drop by?" she asked the agent.

"What?"

Stalling for time, Savannah thought. *When you can't think of anything to say, ask a question.* It was an old trick most often used by wayward husbands. But occasionally women used it, too.

"I said . . . why are you here? Why did you come by the house?"

"Oh." She toyed with the pup's leash several more seconds before answering. "I was just out for a walk with Susie here. I live a few blocks over, and sometimes I take evening walks in this direction. I saw the police cars and . . ."

"And?"

She shrugged. "And I was wondering if everything was okay, you know, with Cait."

"Hmm. I see." Savannah *did* see. She saw the seven hundred dollar, high-heeled Italian sandals on Leah Freed's meticulously pedicured feet and knew damned well that she hadn't been out for an evening stroll up and down sandy beach streets in those fancy clodhoppers. Not on your life.

"I should probably be going," Leah said, suddenly eager to disappear. She turned and headed across the dining area toward the living room, practically dragging the pup at the end of the leash.

Savannah followed right behind her, watching to see that she didn't touch or disturb anything.

At the door, Leah paused and glanced over her shoulder at Savannah. "Are you coming, too?"

"Yes," Savannah said. "I need to speak to Officer Bosco about letting anyone else inside the house before CSU clears it."

"Oh." She cleared her throat and shuffled her feet. "I wouldn't be too hard on him. Like I said, he was busy and I sort of insisted, being a close friend of the family and all."

Savannah gave her a too-sweet smile. "Still," she said. "I really should have a word with him."

Leah shrugged. "Suit yourself."

She opened the front door, bolted through it, and hurried down the sidewalk, stepping over the temporary barricade. Briefly, she tangled the dog's leash in the yellow tape, and before she could loosen it, the tall, good-looking cop in his smart blue uniform strode from his unit over to her.

"Are you okay?" he asked her as she frantically fumbled with the lead. "I'm sure sorry about your sister," he added sweetly.

"Ah, yeah. Thanks," she mumbled as she finally freed the leash. In only two or three seconds, she was scurrying off down the road, a blur of red pantsuit and clicking heels.

Savannah watched, a wry smile on her face, as the woman practically tossed the cocker puppy into a Porsche convertible that was parked half a block away and sped off.

"Evening walk, my hind end," Savannah muttered.

"I beg your pardon?" Officer Bosco asked.

"Nothing."

"Too bad about her sister."

"Yeah, too bad. But she's not her sister. She lied to ya, Mike."

Officer Michael Bosco looked like somebody had zapped him with a stun gun. "Really?"

"Yes, really." She draped one arm across his broad shoulders, briefly enjoying the closeness to youth and virility, before reminding herself that Officer Mike was about the same age as her baby brother, Macon.

So she ended the moment and slapped him on the back. "As my Granny Reid would say, Mike, don't believe nothin' you hear and only half of what you see, 'cause the rest is nothin' but bull pucky."

"Bull *pucky?*" Officer Bosco looked confused. "I thought the rest was bull*shit.*"

"Nope, Mike. It's bull *pucky.* Granny Reid lives in Georgia, and she's a fine, upstanding Southern lady." Savannah sighed and gazed out across the water at the last shimmering bit of setting sun. "Besides that . . . Gran's a Baptist."

"Oh, right."

Chapter
4

By the surreal light of the yellow halogen lamps that illuminated the beachfront streets, Savannah and Dirk watched as Dr. Liu's white coroner's wagon pulled away from the glass house, heading for the city morgue. The CSU technicians were packing up their van, and Officer Bosco was removing the yellow tape from around the perimeter of the property.

At least for the moment, the on-scene investigation into the untimely demise of super-model Cait Connor was completed.

Listening to the waves crashing on the nearby sand and smelling the salty sea air would normally have given Savannah a peaceful, mellow feeling. But for some reason she felt restless, prickled by a sense of foreboding.

She also felt sad, which she understood, but why she felt uneasy in her own skin, she wasn't sure.

"You going home?" Dirk asked her.

"Yes," she said. "You?"

"Yeah, I think I got everything I need out of the scene and the husband. I think I'll head back to the station to write it up."

"Just what you wanted on your day off. More paperwork."

"Yeah, well. What are you gonna do? When I'm done, I think I'll go get a burger. Wanna come? My treat."

As much as Savannah wanted to take advantage of the rare offer of a "Dirk treat," she wasn't really in the mood for another burger so soon after lunch. Or anything else, for that matter.

Now *that* was a scary thought! The fact that she had lost her appetite was a surefire sign that something was amiss. And, apparently, her subconscious and her stomach knew it.

"Do you think it'll be natural causes?" Savannah asked, as the taillights of the coroner's van disappeared around a far corner.

Dirk, too, stared down the now vacant street, his face screwed into a thoughtful grimace. Savannah knew Dirk all too well, and she knew the look. He had that niggling feeling, too, that all wasn't well in the world.

"Don't know," he said. "I guess it could have just been 'accidental death, due to crazy-ass, starvation dieting.' "

"That would be a shame," Savannah said.

Dirk cut her a heavy, sideways look. "It'd be better than the alternatives."

Savannah briefly considered the other choices: suicide or homicide.

"Yes . . . accidental or natural. That's what

54

we'll be hoping for." She sighed. "Sorry state of affairs when those are your best choices. . . ."

Long ago, Savannah had decided that there were few times in life when a bubble bath, a glass of wine, and a box of chocolates couldn't make a bad situation a heck of a lot better.

So it was with great expectation that she slipped into the hot tub full of glistening rose-scented bubbles. Who said you couldn't melt all your cares away? Or at least most of them.

Probably some guy who only believed in showers.

Ah, those manly men just didn't know what they were missing.

Along the countertop she had placed half a dozen votive candles, and on the wicker hamper beside the tub, comfortably within arm's reach, sat a china dessert plate covered with a delicate chintz rose pattern and four chocolate truffles: raspberry crème, lemon chiffon, mocha delight, and peach parfait. Pure heaven. And a glass of merlot to wash them down with.

Her wine connoisseur friends, Ryan Stone and John Gibson, might not approve of the combination, but it worked for her.

Usually.

But as she lay there, watching the candlelight shimmer on the bubbles, listening to them popping and feeling them tickle her skin, the typical magic wasn't working.

And when she bit into the raspberry truffle

and didn't experience the expected culinary orgasm in her mouth, she knew what was wrong: She was thinking about Cait Connor, her beautiful red hair spread out on the jade-green marble floor, her famous turquoise eyes staring up at . . . what?

What was the last thing Cait had seen before her spirit slipped out of her body and made its way into the hereafter?

Had she died alone?

A sad thought, but like Dirk had said, maybe the best of other unpleasant choices.

Savannah glanced over at the cell phone she had placed on the hamper beside the chocolates and wine. She hated having to get out of the tub to answer the phone. She hated having to get out for any reason. So she habitually brought it into the bathroom with her, just in case.

Call Dirk, she told herself. *Call him and tell him that you think. . . .*

What? the more sensible of her multipersonalities asked. *What do you think?*

That Caitlin Connor didn't just up and die all by herself. Somebody killed her.

You don't know that. There's no reason to think that.

Yes there is. She was —

Ding dong.

The sound cut through Savannah's brain waves, interrupting the domestic fight in her head. Also short-circuiting the problem-solving

56

process that had just been on the verge of figuring out . . . something. . . .

Ding dong.

"Go away," Savannah said, knowing her unwelcome visitor couldn't possibly hear her, but hoping they would somehow get the psychic message.

Ding dong, ding dong, ding dong.

"Tarnation," she muttered, rising from the sea of bubbles and stepping out of the claw-foot tub onto the plush bath rug . . . a treat she couldn't resist from the latest Pottery Barn catalog. "You'd better not be selling window cleaner or magazines at this time of night," she grumbled as she slipped on her ancient blue terry-cloth robe. " 'Cause if you are, I just might feed you some of your own products."

The bell chimed three more times before she could make it down the stairs. As she stepped off the carpet and onto the hardwood floor in the foyer, her wet feet slipped and she nearly fell.

"Hold on!" she shouted as she neared the door, the cats scurrying excitedly around her damp ankles.

"Savannah!" she heard a female voice cry from the other side of the closed door. "Savannah, it's me! Open up, girl. I ain't got all day!"

"Me? Who's me?"

Frantically, her mind searched its memory files for a female voice with a distinctly

57

Southern accent. So many choices presented themselves. So few that she wanted to believe.

As a former Georgian, the oldest of nine siblings, Savannah had plenty of female relatives who seemed to think nothing of dropping by unexpectedly — if you could consider a two thousand mile coast-to-coast trip dropping by.

Savannah flipped on the front porch lights, looked through the door's peephole and saw . . . big hair. Stiffly sprayed, meticulously styled, big, big hair.

There was only one person, north *or* south of the Mason-Dixon line, who sported a hairdo that big.

"Marietta!" she exclaimed, flinging the door open and taking her sister in her arms.

"You're wet!" Marietta cried as she pulled away. She laughed as she brushed her hands across the front of her shirt. "You'll ruin my clothes."

Savannah looked down at her sister's shirt, which was adorned with a rhinestone-bespangled tiger's face. The cat had particularly large eyes that were accented with bright green, marquise-shaped stones.

Lovely, Savannah thought. *Understated elegance . . . that's our Mari.*

"You got me out of the bathtub," she said, pulling her unexpected guest into the house. "That's why I'm wet."

She noticed a generic midsize car, which she surmised was a rental, in her driveway and a couple of oversize suitcases on the porch. Sighing inwardly, she walked out the door and picked up one case in each hand.

They were unbelievably heavy. *Must be all the rhinestones,* she thought. *Too much to hope she'd just be carrying an overnight bag.*

Not that she didn't welcome visits from her loved ones. Even impromptu visits were nice. But only for about two or three days. Experience had taught her that after a brief window of blissful familial communion, thoughts of homicide tended to dance in her head.

"Are you surprised to see me?" Marietta asked, patting her poofy updo with one hand, the other hand perched jauntily on her hip in what looked like a silver-screen pose of some sort. In Savannah's opinion, Marietta had watched far too many black-and-white movies where women with overplucked eyebrows puffed on cigarettes while leading good-hearted but hopelessly horny men astray.

"Surprised?" she said. "Yes, I guess so. I had no idea you were coming out to see me. Maybe if you'd called or . . ."

Marietta left Savannah with the suitcases in hand and walked into the living room. She looked around, evaluating with the critical eye of a Fifth Avenue decorator. "Naw, I wanted to surprise you. Besides, I was in the neighborhood."

"In the neighborhood? What . . . you took a wrong turn on your way to Wal-Mart and wound up on my doorstep?"

Marietta cut her a quick look that didn't really reveal anything, but for some reason set Savannah's nerves on edge. Miss Marietta Reid was up to something.

But then, Marietta was almost always up to something, especially when it came to the men in her life, of whom there had been plenty.

None for very long.

"No-o-o," Marietta said. Another suspicious glance. "But I was coming to West Hollywood, and since that's practically next door to you . . ."

"Actually, it's about an hour or an hour and a half, depending on the traffic."

"Like I said, nearby, and I thought maybe I could stay here with you, you know, rather than get a motel room that I can't afford."

"Sure. I've got a spare bedroom you're welcome to. I'd love to have you. If you'd called first, I'd have dusted the room and changed the sheets."

Marietta shrugged. "That's okay. You can do it later. I'm not ready to go to bed yet. I'm all revved up from my flight."

She walked around the room, checking out Savannah's knickknacks, her bookshelf, the throw pillows on her sofa. Pausing beside the desk, she scanned the paperwork that Tammy had left beside the computer.

Marietta had never truly understood the concept of respecting another person's privacy.

60

Unless, of course, it was *her* privacy that needed respecting. That was a different story altogether, Savannah had discovered over the years. On her forehead, Savannah still carried a small scar from the time she had dared to look into Marietta's "private drawer" to retrieve the sweater her younger sister had borrowed more than two months earlier.

"Boy, I sure hate to fly, don't you?" Marietta said, picking up one of Tammy's monthly reports on the agency's financial status and squinting to read the fine print. "I mean, it's exciting and all, lookin' out the window, but once you're up there, especially after it's dark, it's just so boring. I was trying to have a pleasant conversation with this good-looking guy sitting next to me, but he kept reading his stock market magazines. He practically ignored me, he did. Really just downright rude if you ask me."

Savannah grinned, imagining the horror some weary frequent flier must have experienced when Marietta had tried to engage him in "pleasant conversation." The poor guy had probably looked forward to a nice, quiet flight where he could catch up on his reading, take a nap, commune quietly with his inner spirit. And then . . .

Marietta.

Chatty, always on the prowl for a man, big-haired, sparkly-shirted . . . Marietta.

Savannah walked over, took the paper out of

her sister's hand, and stuck it in a drawer. "Are you hungry?" she said. "I think I've got some leftover fried chicken in the refrigerator and some potato salad and baked beans. I'd be glad to dish you up a plate."

Marietta thought for a moment, obviously tempted. Then she shook her head. "Naw. I think I'll pass this time. I dieted like crazy for the past two weeks to look good for this trip. No point in gaining it all back the minute I get here — before I even see him."

"See . . . *him?*"

Savannah was afraid to ask. Most of the "hims" in Marietta's life had brought her grief. And anything that brought Marietta grief soon brought everyone in the family grief. Marietta wasn't exactly a stiff-upper-lip, bear-it-all-with-quiet-dignity, keep-your-troubles-to-yourself sort of girl.

Marietta's eyes suddenly lit with the glow of passion, and she instantly halted the examination of her surroundings. She was very clearly, as Savannah liked to call it, in Marietta Loo-Loo Land.

Yep, the worst had happened . . . again. Marietta Jank Reid was in love.

Lord help us all, Savannah thought.

"So, you've met Mr. Right?" Savannah resisted the urge to add "again" as she stifled a yawn.

The two sisters sat at Savannah's dining table

62

beneath her Tiffany-style lamp and sipped their Baileys-laced decaffeinated coffees. In the middle of the table before them sat an empty carton that had — until twenty minutes ago — held Ben and Jerry's Chunky Monkey ice cream. In front of each sister sat an empty bowl that was all but licked clean.

Marietta had succumbed to dietary temptation.

Savannah had known she would; it was a Reid genetic thing.

"Oh, this guy is so-o-o-o much more than just my Mr. Right," Marietta gushed. "He's my —"

Oh, gawd, Savannah thought, *please don't tell me he's your friggin' soul mate. You've had so-o-o-o many soul mates and —*

"Soul mate. Really, he is! I've never connected with any man in my life the way I've bonded with this man. He's just so perfect for me in every way. We are just alike, really we are!"

He has big hair? He wears rhinestone tigers on his shirts? Well, you did say he's in West Hollywood, but . . .

"Oh?" Savannah buried her nose along with her opinions in her coffee cup.

Her sister had been in her house less than an hour. No point in getting her riled up this soon. Surely their first really big row could wait until tomorrow morning.

But Mari didn't take offense. Her eyes were

63

still glassy. She was still deep in Love Loo-Loo Land and the inhabitants of that bright place seldom took offense. Even when offense was intended. Insulting such a person, Savannah had learned, could be a highly frustrating experience.

"He's so handsome and smart and rich and sensitive! That's the best part, his sensitivity! I never had that with my other two husbands, you know, or with Lester, my last fiancé. Lester had all the sensitivity of a rock, but you know that. You went to our wedding. Well, not our wedding exactly because his wife broke it up with a shotgun, so . . . but you remember all of that."

Savannah flashed back on that lovely memory — of her standing between her sister and the raging woman with the shotgun, trying to talk the woman out of perforating Marietta's hide.

Yes, one seldom forgot such rich life experiences as staring down the double barrel of a shotgun, contemplating the indignity of dying in a peach-colored monstrosity of a bridesmaid's dress.

Remember?

Yes, she'd been scarred for life. She now felt nauseous every time she saw peach taffeta.

"So, where did you meet this love of your life?" she asked. "How did you get to know a guy in West Hollywood?"

Marietta's eyes darted to the right, then the

64

left. She sipped her coffee before answering.

Savannah braced herself.

"Well, we've sorta been like pen pals for a while. You get to know a person really well that way. There's something about writing instead of speaking directly to each other. You're actually able to get to know the true person that way. You open yourself and so do they and you expose your soul, raw and —"

"Oh, my God, Marietta Reid! You're here to see some asshole you met in an Internet chat room!"

Ding, ding. Okay, so much for waiting until tomorrow morning for round one.

"Asshole? Asshole! How can you even say that, Savannah Reid!" She leaped up from her chair so abruptly that it nearly overturned. Her coffee sloshed onto Savannah's white linen tablecloth.

"Okay, I'm sorry about the asshole part," Savannah said. "I shouldn't have jumped to conclusions, but —"

"That's right! You shouldn't have! He's a wonderful, deeply spiritual and soulful person and —"

"And you could tell that just from chatting with him online? You could absolutely tell that he's not . . . say . . . Ted Bundy."

Marietta's eyes narrowed, and she crossed her arms over her chest, which was as ample as Savannah's. "Ted Bundy," she said with sinister deliberation, "is *dead!* And I'll thank you not to

65

question my judgment in this matter, Savannah. Just because you're older than me doesn't mean that you can get all high and mighty and give me advice about a personal matter that has nothing to do with you!"

For a moment Savannah entertained a mental picture of herself grabbing a pot off the kitchen stove and smacking her sister on the head with it, rearranging that updo of hers. Maybe even relocating it to . . . say . . . her butt crack. But then she switched the picture to one of herself biting down on her own tongue.

Until blood began to trickle down her chin.

While she silently quivered from head to toe. The very image of self-restraint.

Yep, Savannah Self-Control Reid. That was her.

Slowly, she opened her mouth, preparing to say something kind, patient, conciliatory. "You can't fly across the country to go on a date with somebody who you've met in a chat room, Marietta! What the hell's the matter with you, girl? That's just plain dumber than dumb!"

Okay, so much for restraint.

Marietta drew herself up, hitched her nose into the air, and looked down its length with all the disdain of offended royalty.

"If you would be so good," she said, "as to get my room ready, I think I'll go to bed."

"No problem. I'd be glad to do that," Savannah said.

She sighed and rose to her feet. *After three*

days, both fish and visitors stink, she reminded herself as she walked past her sister, into the living room, and up the stairs.

But that was your average, run-of-the-mill visit. This was a Reid sister visit that was only forty-five minutes old. And there was no doubt — it was already as smelly as a week-old cat-fish.

Savannah lay in the middle of her bedroom floor, her arms outflung, staring up at the ceiling. As she watched her ceiling fan spinning above her, the thought occurred to her that she must look like the bad guy in an old Western who had just faced down the sheriff at high noon. And lost the gun battle.

That was about the way she felt, too.

The clock on her nightstand said it was well after midnight, and she wasn't even in the vicinity of "sleepy" in spite of her exhausting evening with her sister. While listening to Marietta drone on about her beloved cyberprince, she had fought to stay awake and feign interest. But once in bed, she had started thinking about Caitlin Connor, and now she was wide awake and frustrated. Not a good combination.

For the fifth time, she stood up, rearranged her flannel pajamas, patted her hair into place, and then hurled herself backward onto the floor again.

Fortunately, she had chosen an especially thick carpet when she had replaced the old one in her bedroom last summer. And she had martial arts training, so she knew how to fall without breaking or even severely straining anything vital. Plus there was that layer of Godiva/ Chunky Monkey/Nacho Doritos padding to cushion her.

On the floor again, she lifted her head, looked down at her pajamas, and frowned.

"Mmmm . . ." she said. "Still not quite right."

The bedroom door swung open, and Marietta stood there, glaring down at her. She was wearing a slinky rayon nightgown with a plunging neckline and a wild purple leopard print. Her hairdo was somehow still perfect, as was her makeup.

Marietta firmly believed in the single woman's need to be fully prepared to receive male company should it present itself . . . day *or* night. If the house had caught on fire, Marietta wanted to look gorgeous just in case some hunk fireman happened to fling her over his shoulder.

Yet another reason why Savannah sometimes wondered if her sister needed a brain transplant.

"What the hell's going on in here?" Marietta asked without preamble, her hands on her hips. "You're making so blame much racket that I can't get to sleep."

"Sorry," Savannah said as she rolled her head left and right, trying to see her hair, to check how it was lying on the carpet. But it was too short.

"What are you doing down there?" Marietta asked, nudging her with the toe of her marabou-plumed slide. "Did you roll out of bed, hit your head, and smack yourself stupid like you used to do when we were kids and sleeping four to a bed?"

"No, but thank you for your concern. It's touching. Hand me that mirror over there on the dresser, would you, please?"

"Why?"

"Because you're so sweet and because I asked you nice. I even said 'please'."

"Gran would be so proud," Marietta grumbled as she trudged over to Savannah's dresser and picked up the antique silver hand mirror that was one of Savannah's few true treasures. Tammy had given it to her several years before for Christmas, along with a matching comb and brush.

Using the set with its fine silver filigree and soft boar bristles made Savannah feel like a fine Victorian lady — like the woman who might have actually used it a hundred years ago. A nice change of persona after a day of helping Dirk wrestle down an ugly, dirty perp.

Marietta handed the mirror to Savannah, who held it over her face and studied her hair and the way it lay on the carpet. Unfortunately, she had just had it cut, and it didn't have the effect she had been hoping for.

"I asked you what you're doing down there," Marietta repeated. "Collecting dust bunnies?"

69

"Naw. I only gather those puppies up once a year when they're big enough to knit sweaters with. I'm conducting an experiment."

"What kind of experiment?" Marietta yawned, diluting the illusion of genuine curiosity.

Savannah laid the mirror on the floor beside her. "Reach down here and grab my ankles, would you?"

Marietta frowned, as though she had been asked to unload fifty bales of cotton from a Mississippi barge. "Do what?"

"Grab me by my ankles and pull me a couple of feet across the floor."

Marietta glanced up and down Savannah's length. "No. You weigh a ton, and I'll put my back out."

Savannah's nostrils flared ever so slightly as she returned the evaluating look, taking into account the amount of fabric it took to cover Marietta's fairly ample figure . . . even *with* a plunging neckline.

"You're not exactly skin and bones yourself, Miss Priss. Do it, okay? Just grab my ankles and pull me a few feet."

With the expected amount of moaning and groaning, Marietta did as she was asked. Dropping Savannah's feet back to the floor with a thud, she said, "There. Happy now?"

"I don't know. Hand me that mirror again, would you?"

Marietta scooped the mirror off the carpet and gave it to her.

70

She held it over her face, looked at her hair on one side, then the other. Holding it farther away from her, she scanned her body.

"That's what I thought," she said, rising from the carpet.

"What? What's what you thought?" Marietta was looking at her as though she had just peeled a banana and shoved it into her right ear.

"Thanks," Savannah told her, a distracted look on her face as she replaced the mirror on the dresser and walked over to the nightstand, where she picked up the phone.

"No problem. Any time you wanna be dragged around, just give me a holler and I'll come a-runnin'. Meanwhile, if you could just keep it down a bit, some of us are trying to get our beauty sleep."

When Savannah didn't reply, Marietta shook her head. "And you say that *I'm* the one who just fell out of the Dumb Tree and hit ever' limb on the way down," she mumbled as she left the bedroom, closing the door behind her.

Savannah glanced at the clock as she punched in Dirk's number. So what if it was nearly one o'clock in the morning? If the case was keeping her awake, it would be keeping him up, too. Or at least, it should be.

And if it wasn't . . . she'd change that in a hurry.

Chapter
5

"I don't like her clothes," Savannah told Dirk as she settled among the pillows on her bed, the phone cradled under her chin. "And I'm not just talking about the fashion faux pas of wearing an outfit that looks like something you'd bake a turkey in, either."

"You don't like the way her clothes were sorta scrunched up around her armpits and her crotch, right?" he said on the other end.

Savannah frowned. She hated it when he beat her to the punch. Fortunately, it didn't happen that often.

"Right. Don't tell me you noticed that at the scene."

"Nope. About an hour ago. I was looking at the Polaroids of the bathroom while I was watching the sports. The Dodgers won, by the way."

"Yeah, yeah, yeah. Dodgers-schmodgers."

"Hey!"

"Sorry." Some topics were sacred with Dirk. Baseball was one of them. Beer was another.

"Somebody dragged her around the bath-room," he said.

Savannah mulled that one over for a moment. "I think they dragged her *into* the bathroom."

"Why do you say that?"

"Well, if they didn't . . . why was she in the bathroom in the first place?"

He snorted. "Seeing that man about that horse, draining the dragon, pinching a —"

"Stop! Enough with the potty euphemisms already. She wasn't using the bowl."

"How do you know?"

"The toilet seat was up. Check your Polaroids."

He was quiet; she could hear him shuffling through his materials.

Finally he said, "You're right. I didn't even notice that."

"Of course not." She sighed, wishing she'd had a cream-filled, fudge-frosted cupcake for every time she had yelled at him for leaving her toilet seat up. What could be more refreshing than to get up in the middle of the night for a bathroom visit only to stick your unsuspecting bare bum into a bowl of cold water? It caused one to curse all of *man*kind.

"Maybe she was washing her hands," he suggested.

"The sink hadn't been used since it had been cleaned."

"How do you know?"

73

"Not a water spot in sight."

He groaned. "Something else that only a chick would notice."

"Same thing with the bathtub and shower. Hadn't been used."

Dirk thought for a moment. "Maybe she was throwing up. Her husband said she was into that when she was trying to lose weight."

"Nope."

"Why not?"

"There were pee-pee sprinkle spots around the rim of the bowl. If she'd intended to kneel there and toss her chili, she would have cleaned it first. It's part of the ritual for most bulimics. She hadn't cleaned it and didn't have anything in her hand to clean it with. Nothing lying on the floor."

"Which brings us back to . . . why was she in there?"

"I told you already. Somebody dragged her in there."

"After she was dead?"

"I guess."

"But why?"

Savannah opened her mind to the possibilities. But it had been a long day, and it seemed her brain waves were leveling out to a flat line. Nothing.

"I don't know," she told him. "*You* figure it out. I can't do *all* of your work for you."

She chuckled as she hung up on him.

The cats had snuck into the bedroom while

74

Marietta had the door open, and they were snuggling against her pajama legs, circling, arranging themselves in positions that would have been miserably uncomfortable for anyone outside of the feline species.

"Diamante, Cleopatra," she said, reaching down to stroke first one, then the other. "You two figure it out. Why would somebody drag a dead body into a bathroom and leave it there? And if they did drag it in there . . . does that mean that the dragger had anything to do with the person getting dead in the first place? Probably, huh?"

The cats blinked up at her with sleepy eyes.

"Got that?" she asked them. "Good. You girls discuss it between yourselves. I want an answer by morning."

By the time Savannah trudged downstairs in her bathrobe the next morning, she had no more information about Cait Connor's death than she had upon retiring. Not surprisingly, neither the cats nor her subconscious had formulated any more theories during the night.

She found her sister stretched out on the sofa in the living room, a sheer wrap of black chiffon over her purple leopard nightgown. She lay on her side, lounging on some throw pillows, watching an old black-and-white romance movie on the television.

As always, every hair on her head was teased on end, smoothed, and sprayed stiff. And every

75

layer of makeup had been carefully troweled on.

Marietta might have her cleavage bared for almost every occasion, including funerals, baptisms, and PTA meetings, but her naked face was only a distant memory to her friends and loved ones.

All she needs is a glass of champagne and a box of bonbons to make the picture complete, Savannah thought. She mumbled a feeble, "Good morning," in her direction as she passed through on her way to the kitchen.

"It's about time you woke up," Marietta returned. "I thought I was going to plumb starve to death before you finally showed your face. Do you always sleep this late?"

Savannah glanced up at the clock on her kitchen wall. "It's eight o'clock," she said. "Not exactly dawn-thirty, but it ain't noon either."

"Yes, but it's eleven at home, and my stomach's operating on Georgia time," came the answer from the living room.

"Too bad your butt doesn't shift into gear on Georgia time," Savannah grumbled as she poured a rich blend of chicory and French roast into the coffeemaker.

"What?"

"I said, what do you want for breakfast? Cereal? Fruit? I've got some bear claws and . . ."

"No, I want the works — eggs, sausage, biscuits. Grits, if you've got 'em. I believe that breakfast is the most important meal of the day.

76

And I've got a lot to do today so I need my energy."

Savannah shuffled over to the refrigerator and rummaged through it, gathering the eggs, sausage, butter, and peach preserves. "Just for the record," she shouted, "my home is your home and that includes the kitchen. You don't need to wait for me. Next time, don't sit around hungry. Just jump right in and help yourself to anything you want."

"Oh, I couldn't do that. That would be presumptuous."

Savannah paused, egg in hand, and considered walking into the living room and cracking it on her sister's perfectly coifed head. "No," she muttered, "we wouldn't want to be presumptuous, heaven forbid."

"What?"

"Nothing."

"Well, do you mind then? I'm trying to watch this movie, and you keep interrupting. It's at my favorite part where they kiss and make up."

"Gr-r-r-r."

By the time Savannah and Marietta had finished eating breakfast, Savannah was considering the pros and cons of skipping the country and not mentioning to her family where she had gone.

Brazil was nice this time of year, but not nearly far enough away. She had heard that the air was thin in the Himalayas, but she couldn't see any of her siblings climbing the slopes after her, and she had recently bought a red ski parka from L.L.Bean, so . . .

"I'd help you with the dishes," Marietta was saying as she sipped the last drop from her coffee cup, "but I have to get ready. I'm meeting my boyfriend at six o'clock at a fancy-dandy restaurant in Malibu, and I have to get all dolled up."

Savannah tried to erase the scowl off her face, along with any other "disapproving, judgmental" expressions. Having been severely scolded yesterday for being controlling and condescending toward her younger sister, she was determined that today she would refrain from using such words as *less than cautious, perhaps somewhat naive, or a tad too trusting.* That also left out other prime choices like *pee-pee head* and *shit-for-brains.*

Today she would be the epitome of tact, trusting that her forty-one-year-old sister actually had good instincts when it came to evaluating people's characters and intentions and used common sense in such matters.

"The restaurant is right on the water in Malibu, overlooking the ocean," Marietta was saying. "I figure we'll have a few drinks."

"That's nice."

"And then dinner."

"Hmmm . . ."

"And if he's even half as cute in real life as he is in his picture, I'll probably go ahead and

78

spend the night at his place, so don't expect me back here tonight. I'll pack a little overnight bag and —"

"Are you crazy?" Savannah groaned, covered her face with her hands, and shook her head. "Have you even got the sense that the good God gave a goose?"

"Don't you start that crap with me, Savannah Reid! Why, I oughta —"

Marietta jumped up from the table, but Savannah reached over and grabbed her arm, forcing her back down into her seat.

"Mari, I'm sorry," she said. "I shouldn't have made the goose comment. But you've gotta be smart, girl, or it could wind up costing you, big time. Really, you don't know this guy from Adam. I wasn't kidding when I said he could be a criminal. The Internet is a major hunting ground for sex offenders. This meeting of yours could be a setup."

Marietta sniffed and stuck out her chin. "My Bill is *not* a criminal. He's a Sunday school teacher for Pete's sake."

"Says who?"

"He told me so himself. And he volunteers his spare time to Big Brothers and his local Boys & Girls Club, and he even works for Toys for Tots at Christmastime."

"Well, you might be safe then," Savannah mumbled into her coffee cup. "He's probably a pedophile."

"What?"

"Nothing."

The back door opened, and Savannah was relieved to see Tammy walk in. Her sunny disposition was even more welcome than usual in the midst of a family thunderstorm.

"Hi!" Tammy said, radiating cheer and goodwill. Savannah silently blessed her.

Seeing Marietta at the table, Tammy looked confused for a moment, then beamed. "Marietta! How nice to see you again."

Marietta said nothing, just stared at her blankly.

Quickly, Tammy crossed the room, holding out her hand. "We met in Georgia, remember?" she said. "When you were going to get married and . . . Well, it didn't work out that time, but . . . Anyway, it's good to see you. I didn't know you were coming."

"Neither did I," Savannah said under her breath.

"I got in last night," Marietta said. "And my sister and I are already getting into it."

"Getting into what?" Tammy asked.

"Tammy doesn't speak Southern," Savannah explained. "She's a Yankee." Turning to Tammy, she said, "Marietta means that she and I are having a disagreement about the wisdom of flying across the country to date somebody you met in an Internet chatroom."

Savannah watched Tammy's face as her fleeting expression of alarm was displaced by a poker smile. "I see," she said evenly. "And

80

when are you meeting this . . . gentleman, Marietta?"

"At six o'clock tonight in Malibu on the Pacific Coast Highway. Isn't that romantic? We have a date for drinks and dinner and . . ." She smiled coyly. "Whatever."

"It's that 'whatever' crap that's troubling me," Savannah said.

Marietta tossed her head. "My big sister doesn't trust my judgment. She's afraid that I'm going to get myself raped."

"Or murdered, or infected or impregnated or robbed or swindled. . . ." Savannah sighed. "Gee, the possibilities just abound."

Tammy glanced from sister to sister, then nodded. "Ah. Okay."

Silence reigned for several long, long seconds.

"I have an idea," Tammy volunteered.

Savannah jumped, like reaching for a lifeline. "What? What's your idea?"

Tammy turned to Marietta. "You aren't meeting your friend until six o'clock. So you'll be here until five or so, right?"

"Yeah." Marietta looked suspicious.

"And it's only about nine," Tammy said, looking at her watch. "So that gives me eight hours to check him out for you. If you want me to, that is."

Marietta shook her head and crossed her arms over her mostly exposed chest. "No way. Love means trust. How could I face my soul mate this evening, knowing that I'd had a private investigator probing into his private affairs all day long?"

"Tammy is very good at this," Savannah said. "She's discreet. She can do most of it over the Internet. He'll never even know."

"But *I* would know," Marietta argued. "And I have to live with myself. My relationship with Bill is the real thing, and when it's real, you don't have to invade somebody's privacy like that. It's a violation, plain and simple, and I won't stand for it."

Savannah studied her sister thoughtfully across the table for a few moments, then she said, "Tammy can find out if he's really single, like he says he is, and not married with five kids."

Marietta's face registered the struggle between good and evil . . . for less than three heartbeats. She turned to Tammy and said, "William Albert Donaldson. Born 5-27-61. Check 'im out. And while you're at it, find out if he's got a pot to piss in."

Savannah met Dirk in the parking lot and walked with him up the sidewalk toward the county medical examiner's center. In keeping with the rest of the city's government structures, the M.E.'s buildings were pseudo-Spanish style with beige stucco walls and red tile roofing. Ice plants filled the flower beds along the walkway . . . drought-resistant

82

plantings only, of course. The occasional dry spell, complete with water restrictions, was just one of the unpleasant realities of Southern California living, along with earthquakes, brush fires, and Santa Ana winds.

"Thanks for inviting me along," Savannah told him, as he opened the door for her. "I needed to get away before I did Mari some serious harm."

"Yes, you sounded pretty stressed out when I called," he said with a chuckle. "I don't know why you try to keep your dingbat sisters out of trouble all the time. It's a waste of energy."

"Ain't it, though? As soon as anybody fishes them out of trouble and gets them hosed off, they find another dirty puddle to flounce around it. Sometimes I think they like the mud."

"Now you're figuring it out. What's that your grandma says about singing pigs?"

"Don't try to teach a pig to sing. It's a waste of your time, and it irritates the pig."

"Yeah, that's it."

"Easier said than done when it's your family."

"I know. That's why I don't have one. Too much trouble."

They approached the desk where they would have to sign in before proceeding to Dr. Liu's autopsy suite in the rear of the building.

As a slovenly clerk in a badly fitting, wrinkled uniform sauntered around the partition, Savannah could feel her toes curl inside her loafers. Officer Kenny Bates. Her least favorite person on the planet.

"Hey, Savannah!" His pudgy face split with a wide, lecherous grin as he hurried over to her. "Long time no see. You're lookin' good, girl!"

Savannah ignored him and reached for the sign-in pad. With the pen that was attached to the clipboard by a piece of dirty twine, she wrote the name "Wilma Flintstone" and shoved it over to Dirk. She had been using cartoon pseudonyms for years, and old Kenny had been too busy panting over her bustline to even notice.

"Back off, Bates," Dirk growled as he scribbled his name. "You're pollutin' the air over here. Cheez, use some mouthwash, would ya?"

But Kenny didn't even flinch. He leaned across the counter until his face was only inches from Savannah's. He smelled of something like egg salad and garlic, with the lingering note of eau de b.o.

"You never got back to me about when you're coming over to my place," he said in what he no doubt considered to be a deep, sexy voice.

She had received obscene phone calls with more appeal.

He glanced over at the glowering Dirk and whispered, "I just got some new black satin sheets. You oughta come check them out."

"Trust me, Bates," she said, fixing him with

blue lasers. "I ain't your type. I'm not inflatable."

As she and Dirk walked away, Bates called after them, "One of these days, girl, I'm gonna tell the captain that you come in here with Coulter. He'd take exception to that, I bet. You and him never did get along. People around here say that's why you got fired."

Dirk spun on his heel and in less than a heartbeat had reached across the divider and grabbed Bates by the front of his too-tight shirt. He yanked him halfway over the counter, where he held him until Bates's face went from red to purple.

"The day" — Dirk began with deadly emphasis on each word — "the day that you cause any trouble for Savannah or for me is the day that you suffer, Bates. You got that? And we're talking more hurt than you've ever felt in your long, miserable life. Do you understand me?"

Kenny Bates nodded, gulped, choked, and then nodded again.

Dirk dropped him so abruptly that he smacked his chin on the counter.

Savannah couldn't help giggling as they walked away from him and down the hall toward the back of the building. "That's gonna leave a mark," she said.

"Eh, numb-nuts like Bates are used to having to explain away suspicious bruises," he replied. "He had a cast on his arm and a black eye when I was in here last month. Rumor had it that he tangled with some big Samoan chick that came in here to identify her old man's body."

"Oh, yes, I heard about her. Didn't they figure out that she was the one who'd hacked him up with the machete?"

"Yep."

"So Kenny boy got off easy."

"Yeah, but his luck's bound to run out one of these days."

"I'd like to be there when it happens."

Dirk grinned his nastiest grin. "Maybe that could be arranged."

"One can always dream."

They rounded the corner and saw that the double swinging doors leading to the autopsy suite were wide open. Savannah was relieved to see that the only activity inside consisted of a janitor who was mopping the floor. The strong disinfectant smell of his cleaning fluid filled the hallway, but the odor of bleach was highly preferable to some of the other things she had smelled in there.

"County Medical Examiner" had never been high on Savannah's list of things she wanted to be when she grew up. It was one of those jobs she was infinitely thankful that *somebody* did. But being a cop and a private investigator had required her to witness more than a few autopsies.

Viewing was as close to the reality as she ever wanted to get. And she didn't even like that when she had known the person.

And while she hadn't actually known Cait Connor personally, she was happy to be spared the experience of seeing her stretched out on Dr. Liu's stainless steel table.

"She must be done with Connor," Dirk said, echoing Savannah's thoughts. "Good. Maybe she'll have some results for us."

"She's probably in her office, doing the report," Savannah replied as they turned down the hall to their right, heading toward the half dozen offices in that wing of the building.

The door was open to the last office at the end of the hall, and as predicted, they found Dr. Liu sitting at her desk, dictating into a small microphone.

She stopped what she was doing the moment she saw them and motioned them in, a smile on her face.

For years, Dr. Jennifer Liu had been one of Savannah's favorite people. Tall, slender, and outrageously sexy, she looked more like a lingerie model than a coroner. In her autopsy suite, Jennifer wore her surgical scrubs, a disposable tissue cap over her long black hair, and paper booties over her shoes.

But once she had left the suite, tossed her scrubs into the laundry and the disposables into the biohazard trash can, she looked like she was ready for the local dance club.

She stood, walked around the side of her desk, and embraced Savannah with air kisses to both cheeks.

Out of the corner of her eye, Savannah saw Dirk do a quick once-over, taking in the M.E.'s black leather miniskirt, red cashmere sweater, and mile-long shapely legs.

Savannah couldn't blame him. Dr. Liu was an eyeful.

On the other hand, Dr. Jen didn't give Dirk much more than a curt nod in the way of a greeting.

"You done with Connor?" he asked with an equal lack of social grace.

"Yes, I'm done with Connor," she replied as she motioned for them to take seats and returned to her own behind her desk. "How many times do I have to tell you that I'll call you when I'm ready to discuss my findings with you on a case, Coulter?"

"We were in the neighborhood." Dirk cleared his throat and shuffled his feet. "Savannah here asked me to drop by. She wanted to see you. Huh, Van?"

"Sure."

Savannah gave Dr. Liu her brightest smile, and Jennifer pretended to buy it. "Well, since you're here . . ."

She picked up a stack of papers on her desk. Savannah and Dirk sat to attention in their chairs.

"The bottom line is," Dr. Liu began, "she died of hyperthermia."

"Hypothermia?" Dirk shook his head in disbelief. "How could that be? It was over eighty degrees yesterday, for pete's sake. How do you die from getting too cold in your own house in Southern California on a summer day? It's not like she fell through the ice, skating in her backyard."

"Hy-*per*-thermia," Dr. Liu replied. "Heat stroke. Dehydration. Heat exhaustion."

"Oh. That's more like it."

Savannah felt her heart sink. It was true then. Cait Connor had foolishly killed herself.

What a terrible waste.

"When you spoke to the husband yesterday," Dr. Liu said, shuffling through her papers, "did he say anything about her being on some sort of crash diet and exercise program?"

Savannah and Dirk answered together, "Yes."

"That's what I figured." She slipped on a pair of designer tortoise-rim glasses and read from one of her forms. "Systemic hyperthermia with extreme generalized dilation of capillaries and cerebral edema."

"English, please," Dirk said.

"She died of cardiovascular shock and brain swelling. I suspect she hadn't eaten for days, hadn't drunk anything for hours, and was exercising like a maniac. I found damage to her dental enamel and her esophagus consistent with bulimia. Why the hell do women torture and destroy themselves like this?"

Savannah was a bit surprised to see the anger in Dr. Liu's eyes and to hear it in her voice. The M.E. was usually quite detached and clinical about her findings. Apparently the needless loss of young life affected her, too.

"She was under contract with an ad agency to lose a ridiculous amount of weight in a short time to promote a diet cereal," Savannah replied.

"And her husband said she'd had problems with bulimia for years," Dirk added.

"Well, that explains it." Dr. Liu picked up another paper and glanced over it. "Except for the highly elevated body temperature. From my calculations, she was probably up around a hundred and eight degrees when she died. Usually you only see temperatures like that when people are exercising strenuously in very hot environs. It wasn't *that* hot yesterday. Where was she doing her workout?"

"There in the house, I guess," Dirk said. "They'd turned one of the extra bedrooms upstairs into an exercise room."

"Was there any reason to think it was especially hot in there when she was working out?"

Dirk shook his head. "Not really."

"The bathroom was unusually hot," Savannah interjected. "I remember when I knelt beside her and put my hand on the tiles, they felt warm, even through my glove. Normally bathroom tiles would be cool. And the air was hot in there, too."

"That was because of the skylight," Dirk said. "Those things look good, but they let a lot of heat in, especially when the sun's coming straight through them. I wouldn't have one my-self."

Savannah chuckled. "A skylight in a trailer. I think that's called a sunroof."

He shot her a look and grunted. "Anyway."

"Yes, anyway . . ." Dr. Liu reached for a sta-pler and fastened several sheets of paper to-gether before placing them in a green folder on her desk. "Ms. Connor accidentally killed her-self with harsh dieting and strenuous exercise. Let it be a lesson to society."

Savannah and Dirk stood and headed for the door. Dirk murmured a half-hearted, "Thank you."

As they were leaving, Savannah turned back to the doctor and said, "I always wondered how you do it. Stay slim and trim, that is."

Dr. Jennifer shrugged and grinned. "I do it the healthy, all-American way," she said. "I smoke three packs a day."

Chapter
6

Savannah and Dirk were only halfway across the station house parking lot on the way to their cars when his cell phone buzzed.

"Coulter," he barked into it.

Savannah could tell by the scowl on his face as he listened that their plans for an early lunch at their favorite barbecue joint were about to be postponed. Nothing put Dirk into a foul mood and made him growl faster than to have something getting between him and his feeding dish.

"Where?" he said. He listened, then added, "Yeah," and hung up.

She had always marveled at his economy with words — especially when on the phone to a boss. And even though, after years of hard work, Dirk had risen to the rank of Detective Sergeant First Class, he wasn't and never would be one of the "suits," as he called them.

"We got another body," he told Savannah. "Up on Citrus Road."

"In the orange groves?" she asked.

"Not this time. It's layin' on the side of the road."

The county's citrus orchards had long been a favorite site for body dumpings, rapes, and other nefarious activities. *So much for strolling among the lemons and communing with nature,* Savannah had decided long ago after moving to Southern California.

Although she had spent her childhood wandering among the peach and pecan orchards of Georgia, she had abandoned the Nature Girl routine and switched her relaxing, get-in-touch-with-the-inner-spirit walks to the local three-story mall. It was safer and you could stop for a peach milkshake or a butter pecan cone at the Baskin-Robbins.

"Wanna go with me?" Dirk asked as they continued across the parking lot to their cars.

"Nope. Thanks anyway," she said. "I should get home to Marietta, listen to her rattle on about her Internet sweetie, and try not to gag or laugh at her. She takes offense easily."

"Some of those Internet romances actually work out," he said. "I saw a couple on *Oprah* who met that way and —"

"*You* watch *Oprah*?"

He grinned sheepishly. "Dr. Phil was on."

"Oh, that explains it." She considered what he'd said for a moment, entertaining the thought that this long-distance cyber-relationship might work out for her sister. She thought it over carefully. Five seconds later, she said, "Naw. It won't work. Marietta's got her good points, but she's a little whacky when it comes to the men in her life."

"Not the brightest egg in the Easter basket, huh?"

Savannah grinned. "Let's just say that her cornbread ain't quite baked in the middle."

"You sure you don't want to come with me?" he asked with his hand on the Buick's door handle.

"I really shouldn't."

"The body is a young, good-looking fat chick. And before you yell at me, those were the captain's words, not mine."

"A good-looking fat chick . . . dead on the side of the road?"

He nodded. "That's what the man said. A 'young' one."

A cold, creepy, dirty feeling rolled over Savannah, making her wish she could step into a nice warm shower with a bar of strong antiseptic soap and just wash it away.

She walked around to the passenger side of the Buick and jerked the door open. "Let's go," she said.

Even before Savannah and Dirk arrived at the scene on Citrus Road, Savannah had a feeling that she might know the name of this unfortunate as well. Months ago, she had read an article in the local paper about Cait Connor's close friend, Kameeka Wills, another plus model who had followed Cait's example and moved from Los Angeles to San Carmelita.

Kameeka hadn't been in the business as long as Cait, but she was a rising star in the fashion world. The African-American beauty with her high, sculpted cheekbones and exquisite copper skin had her own line of plus-sized lingerie fashions at one of the high-end department stores, and her face had graced the cover of *Real Woman* twice in the past year.

The news article had said that she'd bought a house in the foothills above the town. And while the paper hadn't given her address for security reasons, they had named the specific area, and it was less than half a mile from where Dirk had been told they would find the body.

All in all, Savannah wasn't holding out a lot of hope for Kameeka Wills, but she decided to keep her suspicions to herself and not share them with Dirk until they saw the body in question.

Citrus Road ran along the top edge of the town and for years had been the divider between land that had been developed and the virgin foothills. Untouched, the hills stretched into the distance above the town, providing a tawny suede backdrop for the glowing white stucco buildings and their red tile roofs.

With its sharp curves, the road presented a bit of a challenge to the locals' driving abilities, especially on a moonless night or during a storm when boulders or mud sometimes slid off the hills and down onto the pavement. And since joggers enjoyed the rural peace and the scenic views afforded by the road, the occasional accident wasn't uncommon.

They rounded a curve and were upon the scene before they knew it. Again, yellow tape signaled passersby that something was amiss in society. And if that hadn't alerted the witnesses, the bright yellow tarp spread over the body on the side of the road would have.

"Right here next to the pavement," Dirk said as he pulled in behind one of the three cruisers that were parked on the dirt shoulder. "Somebody probably got her when they came around that curve back there."

"Yes," Savannah said, but with little enthusiasm. "Maybe."

He gave her a quick, questioning look, then got out of the car. She followed him, walking along the edge of the road where the scrub brush, sage, and marguerites surrendered to asphalt.

As they approached the body, a middle-aged uniformed officer recognized them and came over to meet them.

"Hey, Howie," Dirk greeted him, "how does it look?"

"Jogger," Officer Howard Potter replied with a shrug. "They get it out here all the time. Car whizzes around the corner and 'Bam!' That's all she wrote."

Savannah winced. "Fresh?" she asked.

"Yes. Probably early this morning."

"Any I.D.?" she said.

"Nope. Nothing on her but her clothes."

"Who found her?" Dirk wanted to know.

Officer Potter nodded toward a twenty-something guy with red running shorts who was sitting in the back seat of one of the cruisers. He was talking to a policeman who was squatting beside the open door and taking notes.

"He was out here running this morning at daybreak and practically tripped over the body," Potter continued. "He's barfed a couple of times."

"Is she messy?" Dirk asked.

Savannah cringed again. She'd seen it all . . . but she didn't relish seeing it all again. The really bad scenes made her old before her time.

"Not too bad," Potter replied. "Car ran over her, though. You can see the tire tracks."

"So much for hoping it was a coyote attack," Savannah said dryly as she left them and walked on toward the body.

"Coyote?" she heard Potter say behind her. "They don't hurt anybody, 'cept maybe a miniature poodle or . . ."

"Eh, Van's got a weird sense of humor," Dirk replied. "Don't pay any attention to her. I don't."

Savannah's eyes searched the ground as she approached the area that had been cordoned off with the tape. It was a matter of habit after years of investigating crime scenes. You never knew what you were looking for . . . until you found it. And she'd rather find an unexpected clue at a scene than a pearl in a fried oyster.

But all she saw was roadside litter and none of it exceptional. The CSU would no doubt collect most of it because, even though the victim might have been hit accidentally, the motorist had left her there to die. And that turned an accident into a possible vehicular homicide.

Savannah nodded to one of the cops who were kneeling beside the body, and when he acknowledged her, she stepped over the tape.

"Mind if I take a look?" she asked. "I might be able to I.D. her for you."

"Sure." The youngest of the two reached over and pulled the tarp back from the face. "There you go. Know her?"

Even with the road dirt, the scraping, and the blood that covered a bad wound on the left side of her head, Savannah recognized her instantly.

"Her name is Kameeka Wills."

"I'm sorry," the young cop said. "A friend of yours, huh?"

"No, I never met her. But I've seen her pictures often enough. She's . . . she was a high-fashion model."

The policeman looked down at the body and pulled the tarp halfway down so that he could see her figure. She was wearing a simple tank top that had been partially torn, revealing a lacy bra, and running shorts. Across one thigh Savannah could see the distinct mark of tire treads where the vehicle had run over her.

"She's a *model?*" he said. "No way! She's a blimp."

For the tenth time in twenty-four hours, Savannah fought the urge to feed somebody their front teeth. She looked down at the dead woman's toned, muscular body . . . voluptuous, yes, but beautiful even in death.

She gave the cop a quick once-over, taking in his flabby middle, double chin, and pudgy cheeks. Funny how many men held a completely different standard for women than they did for themselves.

She turned and walked back to Dirk, who was finishing his conversation with Howard. "Her name is Kameeka Wills," she told him. "She's a model. A close friend of Caitlin Connor."

For a couple of seconds she let her information sink in and watched Dirk's brow cloud. Then she added dryly, "What do you figure the odds are of them both being accidents?"

"About the same as you and me running off to Vegas, getting married, and winning a million at the blackjack table."

"Yep. That's about right."

Chapter
7

Dirk had called the station house, requesting an address on Kameeka Wills, at the same time that Savannah had phoned Tammy and asked her to find it on the Internet. Tammy had beaten the station by more than two minutes —, a personal best record for her. Usually her lead was only a matter of seconds.

When Savannah and Dirk pulled up in front of the modest bungalow, hidden among a thicket of trees in the crook of a cul-de-sac, she couldn't help doing a mental comparison to the glass house on the beach.

The home had a woodsy charm with natural siding and a pseudo-cedar shake roof. Real shake roofs had been outlawed long ago after San Carmelita had lost an entire neighborhood to a blazing inferno, which had leaped from one wooden roof to the next, devouring the dried cedar shakes and the houses beneath them.

The new fake shakes didn't look as good, but they didn't burn either, and there was a lot to be said for that.

As Savannah and Dirk walked up the sidewalk, they passed a small but pleasant pond stocked with koi to the left of the path and an interesting sculpture on the right. Carved from some sort of exotic, gold-toned wood, the piece reminded Savannah of a Polynesian fertility goddess with enormous, pendulous breasts and a full, rounded belly that could have been carrying a baby or simply an abundance of good food.

Bees buzzed in a nearby bottlebrush plant, and the smell of wild honeysuckle hung heavy and sweet in the warm air.

She watched the windows of the house as they approached, but she saw no movement.

"I don't think anybody's home," Dirk said. "Maybe you're right; that mighta been her back there on the side of the road."

"I've been known to be right before."

"Eh, you luck out sometimes."

"I'd like to be wrong this time."

Dirk shrugged. "Well, if that body ain't this Kameeka person, it's gotta be somebody else, so either way it's bad news."

"But if it's somebody other than a second full-figured model, it's more likely that the lady on the road was killed accidentally rather than murdered. And I could still believe that maybe Cait Connor died of dehydration."

"True. Killing yourself through stupidity is better than getting murdered."

"A little better."

"Yeah, a little. But, then, dead is still dead."

Savannah sighed. *Detective Sergeant Dirk Coulter*, she thought, *a man of few words. But not few enough.*

On the front door of the cottage hung a wreath of dried grape vines sprigged with lavender and wild sage. The aroma scented the whole porch and gave the home a cozy, welcoming presence.

Dirk rang the doorbell several times, but there was no sound of movement within, and no one pulled the curtains aside to look out.

He turned the doorknob and gently pushed; the door opened an inch. Turning back to Savannah, he said, "How sure are you that was Wills back there on the road?"

"Sure," she replied.

"Sure, sure?"

"I hate to say it, but I'm sure as shootin'."

"Okay then," he said, slowing pushing the door open. He took one step inside. "Anybody here?" he called. "San Carmelita Police Department. Anyone home?"

Instinctively, Savannah's hand slipped under her sweater, and she unsnapped the holster that held her Beretta. She noticed that Dirk had reached under his leather jacket, too, for his Smith & Wesson.

She followed him into the gloom of the living room, where they waited just inside the doorway for their eyes to adjust to the dim light.

White wooden shutters were closed over the

102

windows, and only a small amount of sunshine filtered between the slats, throwing thin blades of golden light onto a cream-colored Berber carpet.

The room was sparsely but tastefully decorated with the clean lines of contemporary furnishings. In front of the window sat a tan leather sofa, and a chest with brass fittings served as a coffee table. Over a fireplace in the center of the far wall hung a large black-and-white photograph of Kameeka Wills. Draped in a sheer, hooded robe, she stood on a rugged cliff overlooking the ocean in a landscape that reminded Savannah of the Monterey area.

A wind was whipping the garment around her long, shapely limbs, and she had a look of unworldly peace and soul-deep contentment on her beautiful face as she stared out across the horizon.

Savannah's mind flashed back to the bruised and bloodied body she had just seen on the side of the road, and her heart ached.

"That her?" Dirk asked, nodding toward the picture.

"It was," Savannah replied.

"Too bad. A pretty girl," he said.

Savannah smiled in spite of her sadness. One of Dirk's most endearing qualities as a man was his complete oblivion to weight issues. The only time she had ever heard him complain about a woman's build was when he occasionally remarked upon seeing an extremely thin woman, "Boy, she looks like she could use a cheeseburger and a milkshake."

"Anybody here?" Dirk called out again, projecting his deep bass voice down the hall to their right.

As before, there was no reply.

Ahead lay a dining area with a glass-topped table and bamboo chairs with comfortable-looking seat cushions. In the middle of the spotless glass sat a crystal vase and a simple arrangement of multicolored tulips.

On the wall, stainless steel shelves that were equally free of dust or fingerprint smudges held a dozen picture frames containing photos of what must have been Kameeka's family and friends.

Loved ones — who probably didn't know yet that she was gone from their lives, Savannah thought as she studied one picture in which Kameeka was in the center, her arms around the shoulders of two younger women who looked so much like her that they had to be sisters.

For a moment Savannah allowed the thought to play through her mind of how she would feel to lose one of her own sisters in such a way. But just as quickly as the thought sprang into her mind, she pushed it firmly away. Professionals couldn't think of such things when they were "on the job." It clouded the judgment.

Later, she knew it would return. When she was in bed and trying to get to sleep, about

104

three in the morning, the thoughts would come back to haunt her the way they always did. But she would battle that problem when it presented itself. For now, one dragon to slay at a time.

She looked around the living room and dining area for anything that might appear to be out of place. But the home was impeccably kept.

"Either Kameeka's a heck of a housekeeper or she's got a great cleaning service," she remarked.

"Yeah, this is about the spiffiest place I've been in . . . ever," Dirk added as he passed the table and chairs and headed toward the kitchen.

Savannah followed and nearly bumped into his back when he stopped abruptly and sniffed the air. "What's that smell?" he asked.

She breathed deeply and grinned. "It's called floor wax. An unfamiliar scent?" she asked, nudging him. "Like furniture polish and window cleaner?"

He scowled at her. "I'll have you know I bleach my toilet and my bathroom floor every Saturday morning, rain or shine."

"Yeah, well, big whoopty-do. With an aim like yours, you'd have to."

Standing at the doorway to the kitchen, she glanced quickly around the room, taking in the shining copper pans hanging from an iron rack on one wall, the garden window above the sink that was filled with growing herbs, and the butcher block counters lined with decorative bottles of spiced cooking oils.

Again, the place looked comfortable and lived in, but perfectly maintained. The only thing that might even be considered to be out of place was a daisy-spangled mug sitting on the counter beside the coffeemaker, and next to the cup was one small packet of a sugar substitute and what appeared to be a vitamin pill.

The coffee pot was the same model Savannah had been considering buying, but hadn't because it was beyond her budget. It had a timer that you could set so that it would grind the beans and make the coffee before you got up — a lovely luxury that she intended to treat herself to the next time she actually scored a paying job.

Apparently, Kameeka had been able to afford such an extravagance because her pot was full of a dark, thick brew. The POWER light was off. Otherwise, everything appeared undisturbed by human hands.

But then Savannah looked down at the floor with its snowy white, two-inch tiles.

Reaching for Dirk, she grabbed his sleeve and prevented him from stepping from the carpet of the dining area onto the kitchen floor.

"Wait a minute," she said.

"What?" He froze, recognizing her tone as all business.

"The floor," she said, pointing down.

106

"Yeah. It's clean. Really clean. You said that's floor wax you smell, so —"

"So somebody just mopped and waxed it."

"O-kay. That's unusual at my house, but . . ."

Savannah sank to one knee on at the edge of the carpet and studied the tiles before her. "And they did a lousy job."

Dirk squatted beside her and looked from one side of the floor to the other. "Looks pretty good to me."

"That's 'cause you're a guy. You figure if there's no ketchup smears, coffee grounds, or beer puddles, it's clean."

He nodded soberly. "That's true."

"This house is perfect. Like I said, either Kameeka's a neat-nik or she's got professional help."

"But . . . ?"

"But there are streaks all over this floor where the person who was spreading the wax missed spots. Look over there by the stove." She pointed to a somewhat dull area that even looked a bit cloudy, as though it had a white film of some sort of chemical residue.

She nodded toward the refrigerator. "And over there in front of the icebox. There's a big patch that they missed."

"And your point is?"

"My point is that any woman who would make sure that her windows were spotless, that the mirrors didn't have a smudge, and that every speck of dust was off the furniture, wouldn't have done such a slap-happy job of mopping. No way."

Dirk gave her a hard, sideways look. "So, are you saying something completely sexist, like — a *man* must have mopped this floor because they did a lousy job?"

"Of course not. I'm saying it was either a guy who didn't know any better or a woman who didn't give a darn about housekeeping. Or maybe a woman who was in a big hurry."

"Like Kameeka?"

"Nope. Even in a hurry, she would have done it right or not at all."

"What do you figure that white stuff is?" He pointed to the filmy area near the stove.

"Some sort of disinfectant or detergent that wasn't meant for floors."

They both studied the tiles for several long moments, thinking, evaluating.

"Maybe we ought to get the crime scene investigators to Luminol the surface," Savannah said.

"That's just what I was thinking." Dirk's lips tightened. "You figure it'll fluoresce?"

Savannah thought back on a number of crime scenes she had investigated where the CSU had sprayed supposedly clean surfaces with Luminol. The chemical reacted with blood, causing it to give off an eerie glow. Seeing clear evidence of blood spatter, where a moment before nothing had been visible, was startling.

"Maybe we shouldn't walk on it. They might be able to find a shoe print, too," Dirk added, putting his face low to the carpet and peering across the surface.

"Might could," Savannah replied, doing the same, "although I don't see anything."

"Yeah, but you never know what those guys can find when they set their minds to it." Dirk rose, groaning a little. "Let's check the rest of the house."

Savannah stood, stifling her own small moan as her joints complained. They might be getting a bit older, but she was determined not to broadcast the fact.

It didn't take long to investigate the rest of the one bedroom/one bath cottage. And, once again, they found nothing extraordinary in the clean, neat rooms.

In the bathroom, Savannah glanced into a white wicker wastebasket next to the sink and saw only one item — a large cotton ball. Gingerly, she picked it up, sniffed it, and touched it with one fingertip.

"What is it?" Dirk asked her.

"Skin toner," she replied. "Still a little damp."

"What's skin toner? Something like after-shave?"

Savannah smiled. If all consumers were like Dirk, Procter & Gamble would be out of business. A tube of toothpaste, a bar of soap, and a spray can of deodorant were his only toiletries.

"Ladies put it on their faces first thing in the morning when they wake up. It tightens the skin, minimizes pores, refines and tones . . ."

His eyes were starting to glaze over, so she stopped. Like most members of his gender, Dirk had a low overload threshold when it came to "girl" topics. Or pretty much any other topic that didn't directly pertain to him.

But he quickly recovered and switched back into "investigator mode." Running his thumb lightly over the toothbrush in the stand beside the sink, he said, "It's dry."

"Hmmm," she said.

"Definitely a hmmm," he replied.

In the bedroom, they found the only sign of anything out of order — an unmade bed. The snowy white quilt was bunched at the foot of the bed, the pillows tossed against the head-board, and the pale blue sheets rumpled.

"Well," he said. "She was human after all. Look at that bed. I would have figured she was the type to turn around and make it the minute she got up."

Savannah lifted one eyebrow. "No way," she told him. "You're supposed to let it air at least a few minutes before you make it."

His chin dropped. "Are you kidding me? Let it 'air'? You mean, like opening the bathroom window after you take a —"

"Yeah. That's the idea."

He shook his head. "Boy, you gals have a lot of stupid rules about stuff. I never thought I needed to air out my bed before I make it."

"You actually *make* your bed?"

He grinned. "Once in a while."

She snickered. "Like maybe on a Friday morning when you've got a date that night and are hoping you'll get lucky."

Laughing, he said, "I'm glad you think I still get lucky sometimes."

"Well, don't you?"

He shrugged. "Yeah, maybe once in a blue moon. And you?"

She decided to ignore that one. Instead of answering him and admitting a depressingly long spell of celibacy, she walked over to the dresser and opened a couple of drawers, searching until she found Kameeka's stash of bras.

"That's what I figured," she said.

"What did you figure?"

"She's got a whole set of athletic bras in here. Not surprising for a woman who has her own line of lingerie."

"And your point is?"

"Kameeka's a full-figured lady." She looked at the size tag on one of the bras. "A 42DD."

His eyes lit up with predictable male appreciation. "Yep, that's a big girl, all right."

"And she was out jogging."

"So . . . ?"

"In a flimsy, lacy little Saturday night date bra. That's a good way for a full-figured lady to cause herself some major pain. A jogger with big boobs knows that you wear a substantial athletic bra when you're running."

He grinned knowingly. "Or you bounce too much and give yourself black eyes?"

She wrinkled her nose and gave him a piggy snort. "Don't be such a guy if you can help it, Coulter. Let's just say that I went horseback riding once wearing a 'come hither' bra instead of a 'granny full-support' type and I was in pain for a week."

Again, his eyes were starting to glaze over, and she realized that even female topics relating to breasts had their limitations.

"Then you don't think she was out there jogging?" he said.

"No, I don't. I think she got out of bed, went into the bathroom and slapped on some toner, walked to the kitchen where her coffee was already brewed . . ."

"And somebody got her in the kitchen."

She nodded. " 'Got her,' as you put it, badly enough that they had to clean the floor afterward."

"Then they dressed her in shorts and a T-shirt and running shoes to make it look like she was jogging . . ."

"And took her up to Citrus Road and dumped her."

"And ran over her to make it look good."

Inwardly, Savannah shuddered, remembering the tire marks on the woman's thigh. "Yeah. And ran over her like she was some sort of road kill."

They both stood there in the bedroom, looking at the rumpled bed where the beautiful model — the one who had stood on that wind-swept cliff overlooking the ocean — had spent her last night. Probably never realizing that it was to be her last night.

"We'll have to wait and see what Dr. Liu finds out," Dirk said softly, a rare note of reverence and sadness in his voice.

"Yes," Savannah replied. "And the crime scene techs need to Luminol that kitchen floor."

"So that they can tell us what we already know."

Savannah took a deep breath and suddenly felt tired and old. "Yeah . . . that we've got two plus-sized fashion models in the same town who died in less than twenty-four hours of each other under suspicious circumstances."

"In other words . . . who were deliberately croaked."

She gave him a long, hard look. "Dirk," she finally said, "sometimes I wish you were more like your hero, John Wayne. You know . . . the strong, *silent* type."

Chapter
8

When Savannah returned home late that afternoon, she nearly collided with her sister as she entered the house. Loaded down with a makeup case in one hand and an overnight bag in the other, Marietta was on her way out, a flushed look on her face.

"I don't have time to chew the fat with you," she said as she jostled Savannah out of her path and barreled through the door. "See ya later." From many years of "big-sister duty," Savannah knew a guilty look when she saw one. And nothing piqued her curiosity more than thinly veiled avoidance.

Miss Marietta Reid had "I'm up to no good" written across her forehead, and having been gifted with more than her fair share of pure nosiness, Savannah had to investigate.

"Hold on a second," she said, rushing to catch up with Marietta on the porch. "Where are you off to like a cat with its tail on fire?"

"I don't want to be late," Marietta exclaimed as she tossed the makeup bag and small suitcase into the back seat of her rental car. "I'm nervous enough about tonight without worrying about whether I'm gonna hit heavy traffic on the highway."

"If you're taking the P.C.H. at this time of day, you can be sure you're going to get caught in some clogs." She gave her younger sister a quick glance up and down, taking in the knee-high zebra print boots, the black satin miniskirt, and the sheer tiger-striped spandex top that clearly displayed every bulge, nook, and cranny of the famous Reid-girl bustline.

Yep, she thought, *Marietta's going trolling. Lord, please don't let her catch something so big and nasty that she can't throw it back if she needs to.*

"Have a good time," she said, trying to sound more enthusiastic and less judgmental than she felt. "I'll wait up for you, and when you get back we'll have a nightcap and you can tell me all about him."

Again, Marietta shot one of those suspicious looks at her, and Savannah's radar pinged.

"No, don't wait up for me." Marietta jerked the driver's side door open and tossed her purse to the passenger seat.

Savannah pointed to the suitcase in the back. "I don't mean to be nosy, but . . . you're not really figuring on spending the night with this guy, are you?" she said.

"Then don't be," Marietta snapped.

"Be what?"

"Nosy. Just mind your own business and

115

don't give me no lip about my social life. At least I've got one!" She got into the car and jammed the key into the ignition.

Savannah stepped up to the car and put her face through the open window. "And what's that supposed to mean?"

Marietta gave her a smirk that could only be classified as ugly. "Think about it, big sis. . . . I spent my day getting dolled up so that I can spend the evening in Malibu with the hunk of my dreams. You, on the other hand, spent yours looking at dead folks. Now, who do you figure's got the big end of that turkey drumstick?"

She started up the car, put it in gear, and backed up so fast that Savannah had to scramble to get out of her way. A second later Marietta had disappeared down the road on her way to Malibu . . . her Internet prince . . . and her cyberpalace in the clouds.

"Eh, bite me," Savannah mumbled as she watched the dust settle in her driveway. "The nice thing about dead people is that they don't mug you, kill you, knock you up, or give you the creeping crud. And there's a lot to be said for that."

She was still grumbling to herself when she reentered the house and found Tammy sitting at the desk, scribbling on a notepad. "Oh, there you are," she said as Savannah tossed her purse and keys onto the table in the foyer. "Did you run into your sister?"

"I sure did . . . hence the bright smile on my face."

She bared her teeth, and Tammy giggled.

No sooner had she settled into her easy chair than the two cats left their sunlit window perches and ran to claim their favorite spots — Cleopatra across her thighs and Diamante on her chest.

"You know," she told them, "just because Mom makes a lap doesn't mean you necessarily have to use it."

Diamante rubbed her cheek against Savannah's chin and purred like her Mustang's Holly carburetor right after the mechanic gave it a fine tuning.

Part of the irritation she had felt toward Marietta floated away. Ah . . . the healing qualities of unconditional kitty love.

"What did you find out about Mari's mystery man?" she asked, dreading the answer.

"Nothing much. Not anything bad anyway," Tammy said. "No criminal record that I could find. Not married. No kids. Pretty good credit rating. Owns his condo in West Hollywood."

"Sounds too good to be true. He's probably an ugly little nerd who sent her a picture of his next-door neighbor, or maybe a pervert who —"

She paused when she saw that Tammy was giving her an over-the-shoulder look she couldn't quite decipher.

"What?" she asked. "Is it something I said?"

Tammy gave her a sweet, somewhat understanding smile that, for some inexplicable reason, irritated the crap out of her.

"You think I'm being too hard on my sister and her so-called boyfriend?" she asked.

Tammy shrugged. "Maybe. I mean . . . I don't really approve of hooking up with people that you meet on the Internet, but I've heard of some cases where it actually worked out. People really *have* met their soul mates in chatrooms. Stranger things have happened."

Savannah scratched behind Cleo's ear and was rewarded with a wet, sandpapery kiss on her wrist. "I suppose," she said. "I want Marietta to be happy. And she sure appears to be smitten with this guy."

"Besides, you may be worrying over nothing. Chances are, she'll get one look at him in the flesh and decide that a drink is all she wants from him. She could be back here in an hour."

Somehow, that thought didn't offer Savannah any substantial comfort. And she felt guilty about it. She should be happy at the prospect of spending time with her own flesh and blood. And she probably would have been, had she not been plagued with thoughts of homicide every time she was around Marietta.

She hadn't always felt this way about her sister. They had once been close . . . in their preschool years.

But on the first day of kindergarten Marietta had started chasing boys, and she had been a

118

sharp, aching pain in the hind quarters ever since. The very thought of being without a man to call her own was enough to send her into a dither. And Savannah had never had a lot of patience with dither-prone women. Life was too short and too precious to spend it in a state of agitation about a man. Her motto was: As appealing and delicious as some guys might be, there were just too many men in the world to get yourself all worked up over any one of them.

Savannah sighed. "If she does come back in an hour, she'll be crying in her beer over the dirty, rotten liar who broke her heart. And if she stays the night with him —"

Fortunately, before her mind could wander too far down that dreary path, the phone rang.

Tammy grabbed it, the picture of efficiency, and in her most official voice — the one tinged with just a tad of silver-screen siren — she said, "Moonlight Magnolia Detective Agency. May I help you?"

Her eyes widened with interest, and she looked over at Savannah. "Leah Freed? Certainly. Let me see if Ms. Reid is available."

Savannah jumped up from her chair, dumping both cats unceremoniously off her lap in the process. They sauntered back to their window perch, the picture of wounded dignity.

Taking the phone from Tammy, Savannah entertained at least a dozen mental possibilities as to why Caitlin Connor's agent might be calling her. But none of them made a lot of sense.

"This is Savannah," she said into the phone, trying to keep the curiosity out of her tone.

"Yesterday you told me that you're a private detective," the voice on the other end stated without the customary greeting. Instantly, Savannah recognized the agent's no-nonsense manner.

"Yes, I am," Savannah replied.

"And that you sometimes work with that detective who was at Cait's house yesterday . . . ?"

"That's right. In an unofficial capacity, that is."

"Are you working with him on Caitlin's case and Kameeka's?"

So, she's heard about Kameeka, Savannah thought. *News travels fast.*

"Like I said, only unofficially. Detective Coulter and I were partners for years when I was on the police force. Now, as friends, we sometimes help each other with our cases. May I ask why you want to know?"

There was a long pause on the other end of the phone, and Savannah thought she heard Leah Freed sniff. Then she said, "Ms. Reid, two of my girls are dead. I want to know all I can about what happened to them."

"Your girls? You were Kameeka's agent, too?"

"Her agent and her friend, just like Cait. I can't believe that they'd both die, unexpectedly

120

like that, within twenty-four hours of each other . . . not accidentally anyway. Do you believe it?"

"That they both died accidentally? It could happen, I suppose, but —"

"You don't think so either, do you?"

Savannah made it a practice not to reveal too many cards too early in any poker game. But the woman seemed sincere and, considering her loss, deserved an honest answer.

"I have my doubts, Ms. Freed, that they died as a result of accidents. The coincidence is a bit much."

"Then I want you to find out what really happened to them."

"Well, this is Detective Coulter's case, and he's the best detective I've ever known. I'm sure that he'll —"

"No, I want to hire you. I want you actively investigating this and reporting everything you find out directly back to me."

At first, Savannah was taken aback by the job offer so blatantly stated. Then she decided that it had been too long between gigs if it took her that long to realize someone wanted to give her money for what she was doing with Dirk for free.

"Of course," she said. "I'd be happy to have you as a client." She waggled one eyebrow at Tammy, who suppressed a series of giggles with one hand over her mouth and did a little dance in her desk chair. "Let me give you back to my assistant. She'll discuss my rates with you and set up an appointment for us to meet."

"I'm sure your rates are fine," came the immediate reply. "And I don't have time to wait for an appointment. I want you to come to my office. Now. I'm on the tenth floor of the Plaza Del Oro Tower, Suite B. I'll see you in . . . ?"

"Fifteen minutes," Savannah said.

"Good."

Even the click as Leah Freed hung up sounded more decisive than most, Savannah thought as she handed Tammy the phone.

"We've got a client?" Tammy said, jumping up from her seat and following Savannah as she headed back to the hallway.

"We sure do." Savannah snatched her keys and purse off the table beside the door. "Leah Freed was both Cait's and Kameeka's agent. She wants me to find out what happened to her girls, as she calls them."

"And she's going to pay you?"

Tammy's shock seemed to be as deep as Savannah's — a realization that gave Savannah a moment's pause to consider whether maybe she should have grown up to be a flight attendant or a movie star, as she had intended to when she was an adolescent. Something that actually made money frequently enough that getting paid wasn't a novel experience.

"Yeah," she said as she hurried out the door. "She's going to pay me. And that's how I know she's up to something."

"What do you mean?" Tammy called after her.

"She's an agent . . . and she didn't even bother to dicker about the price. Something's up, for sure."

With fourteen stories, the Plaza Del Oro Tower provided the only high point in the San Carmelita skyline. As Southern California was earthquake country, high-rise buildings were the exception rather than the rule. Savannah would never forget how disappointed she had been the first time she had beheld the Los Angeles skyline. Expecting something similar to the photos she had seen of Manhattan and Chicago, she had wondered where the skyscrapers were. From a distance, L.A. looked more like a giant parking lot than a bona fide city.

But after having been jarred from her bed by several quakes, she found herself of the same opinion as most of her fellow West Coasters — skyscrapers were overrated . . . especially during a 7.1 rumbler.

So, as she approached the Plaza Del Oro financial center, she looked up at the "massive" fourteen-story building and congratulated herself for not being successful enough to warrant an office at that prestigious address.

The lobby with its sunlit atrium was cheerful enough, as was the bank of elevators with their tiled walls and floor, bright with primary colors and South American motifs.

She quickly made her way to the tenth floor, and when she stepped out of the elevator she entered a new world.

The colorful tiles and Spanish influence disappeared, replaced by a chic suite of offices that looked like an Ansel Adams photo.

The walls, the clean-lined, contemporary furniture, and the decorating accents were all shades of black, white, and gray. And on the walls hung life-size, full-length photographs similar to the one they had seen in Kameeka Wills's house.

Beautiful women of abundant proportions lined the walls, each more exquisite than the one before. Whether they were standing on a beach, sitting in a tropical garden, or posed against a blank backdrop, they commanded the camera with their presence.

Not a skinny, heroin-addicted-looking one in the bunch, Savannah thought as she walked across the dove-gray carpet to a sleek ebony desk in the corner of the room. They all looked healthy, vibrant, and fulfilled, their eyes sparkling with consciousness and confidence.

Females . . . in every sense of the word.

If this was what Leah Freed's agency was all about, Savannah decided she liked her a lot more than she had five minutes ago. There needed to be more of these photos in the world — pictures that celebrated the beauty of women in all shapes and sizes.

"Hello," she said to the receptionist, a young

124

woman who was herself a generous size. "My name is Savannah Reid. I believe Ms. Freed is expecting me."

Instantly, the receptionist jumped to attention. "Oh, yes. Leah *is* expecting you. Just one moment, please." She lifted the phone and punched a button. "Ms. Reid is here to . . . yes, I'll send her right in."

Hanging up, she rose and ushered Savannah to one of the three doors that led off the reception area, the door imprinted with the gold letters "L. J. Freed."

Opening the door, she announced, "Ms. Reid, this is Leah Freed and —"

"Yes, yes, Belinda, we've met." Leah Freed came out from behind an enormous desk piled high with papers, glossy eight-by-ten photos, and multicolored files. One glance around the untidy office told Savannah that the agency's first impression of chic and organized, given by the reception area, might be smoke and mirrors.

Today, Leah was dressed in a hot pink suit with white piping and a white neckerchief with pink polka dots. On a woman of lighter coloring, the ensemble might have been gaudy, but on a deeply tanned person with Leah's black hair, it was only mildly garish.

Leah's more attractive accessory, the cocker spaniel puppy, was nowhere in sight, and the agent seemed less personable without the softness of her canine companion.

She motioned Savannah inside with an impatient wave of her hand.

The receptionist, formerly identified as Belinda, asked Savannah, "Would you like a cup of coffee or tea or — ?"

"Nothing!" Leah snapped. "Leave us alone and hold all my calls."

With a submissive nod, Belinda turned and quickly disappeared.

"Here, sit down," Leah said as she swept an armload of papers and files off one of the chairs beside her desk.

Savannah could feel the ruff on her back rising, as it always did when she encountered gruff, controlling people. Or at least, anyone who was more gruff and controlling than she was. But she decided to give Leah Freed the benefit of the doubt and chalk it up to the fact that she was probably in shock, grieving the loss of her friends.

"What do you know so far?" Leah said as she plopped down in her own chair behind the desk and folded her arms in front of her.

"Bottom line, huh?" Savannah couldn't resist giving her a small, baiting grin.

Leah registered the challenge and, for a moment, lowered her intensity a notch. "Always the bottom line," she said, a bit more softly. "I'm not one to pussyfoot around."

"Me either."

"Good. Then we'll get along. So, what really happened to Cait?"

Before Savannah could answer, Leah added, "I figured that stupid husband of hers did her in, but now that Kameeka's gone, too . . . ?"

For a moment, the agent's lower lip trembled just a bit; then her face hardened as though she were steeling herself for Savannah's answer.

"It's a bit early to make any sort of determination about either of their deaths," Savannah told her. "According to the medical examiner, Caitlin died of heat stroke, brought on by strenuous exercise coupled with dehydration."

Leah gasped and covered her face with both hands. Savannah saw a shudder go through her as she fought to control her emotions.

When she finally moved her hands, Savannah saw tears in her eyes.

"Then Kevin was right," Leah said. "Cait *did* kill herself trying to lose weight for this stupid cereal campaign."

Savannah hesitated, wondering just how straight to aim with this self-acclaimed straight-shooter. She looked genuinely distressed, as anyone might who had lost a friend under tragic circumstances. The last thing she wanted to do was add to her grief.

"I'm just telling you what the medical examiner said," she said. "The case is still open."

Leah grabbed a tissue from a box on her desk, wiped her eyes — smearing her liner — blew her nose, and tossed the tissue into a waste can. "And what do *you* think? Do you think she died because she was dieting and exercising too much?"

"I think the *cause* of her death was heat stroke, like the coroner said. But I don't necessarily think her *manner* of death was accidental."

"You aren't saying she deliberately killed herself, are you?"

Leah's dark eyes searched hers so intensely that Savannah was tempted to glance away. But she didn't.

"No, I don't think she committed suicide," she replied evenly.

Leah thought for a moment. "Then you're saying it was homicide. That somebody murdered her."

"You asked me what I believe. And at the moment, I think that's the most likely scenario."

"Do you have any proof?"

"Nothing definitive."

Again, the agent's eyes probed hers. "Do you have any idea who might have done it?"

Savannah refused to blink. "Not yet."

"And how about Kameeka?"

An ugly picture played across Savannah's mental screen — the wound on the victim's head, the tire marks on her bronzed skin.

"What *about* Kameeka?" Savannah said, hedging.

"Do you think it was simple hit-and-run?"

It was Savannah's turn to do a visual probe, and she fixed the agent with her own blue lasers. "Probably not. How did you find out about Kameeka?"

"The modeling industry is a tight community — the legitimate sector, that is. News travels fast."

"And," Savannah repeated, unwilling to let it slide, "how did you find out?"

"Jerrod Beekman called me. He's the president of the public relations firm that handles the Wentworth Cereal account."

"How did *he* know?"

"He didn't say."

"And you didn't ask?"

"No. He called me about an hour ago and told me that Kameeka had been killed by a hit-and-run driver while she was out jogging this morning. And, of course, he had heard about Caitlin on the news this morning. Needless to say, he's quite upset."

Savannah nodded. "I see. Then he knew both women personally?"

"No, but he's based a multimillion-dollar, nationwide campaign on four plus models losing weight while eating Slenda Flakes, and now two of them are dead. He's beside himself."

"Hmmm . . . I'll bet he is." Savannah retrieved a notepad and pen from her purse and began to scribble. "And where can I reach him?"

Leah threw up her hands. "No, no, no. I don't need you poking around, acting like a detective, asking people like Jerrod Beekman questions and causing problems."

Savannah looked up from her writing. "But I thought that's what you were hiring me to do, work this case as a private detective and —"

"Heavens no. That's the last thing I want you to do. That would be a disaster!"

Savannah shook her head, confused. "Then why am I here? If you don't want an investigator, I don't think I can help you. I —"

"I don't want you to work this case as a private detective," Leah Freed said, clicking her long acrylic fingernails together in a manner that set Savannah's teeth on edge. "No, no, no. That would be far too obvious." She swept Savannah from head to toe with the experienced eye of a professional. "You're a pretty girl, so we might as well take advantage of the fact. I want you to work the case as a model."

Chapter 9

The next morning, Savannah stood at the foot of her bed and surveyed what seemed like an acre of accessories, makeup items, and foundation garments that she had spread across her satin comforter. In her right hand she held a black bag that was approximately the size of Marietta's overnight suitcase.

Leah Freed had given her the bag . . . and the endless list that she held in her left hand.

Tammy poked her head through the half-open door. "Aren't you packed yet?" she said with a sarcastic little grin on her face that made Savannah want to box her ears. "You're going to be late for your first shoot."

"Shut up and get out of here. I'm thinking."

Giggling, Tammy pushed the door open and walked into the bedroom. "Thinking? You mean it takes brains to be a model? I thought I heard you say that one of those super-models on TV ought to get a real job and stop walking around in her underwear."

"If you're going to quote me, get it right; I said, 'She should stop prancing around in her knickers there in front of God and everybody.' And I only said that because she was skinny, and I was jealous."

Savannah scanned the list once more, comparing it to the piles on the bed. "It's not all that easy, you know, being a model. It takes brains, too."

Tammy walked over to the bed and picked up a body shaper. She held it up, studied it, looked confused, then laid it back on the bed. "And when did you decide that?" she asked.

"Yesterday, when Leah Freed started telling me all the crap I'd need to know today."

"Why do you have to take all of this stuff?"

"Because Leah says a professional model carries her model's kit with her at all times, like a doctor and his black bag. And if anybody asks me for . . . say . . . some hairspray or a nail file, or a new pair of body-shaping panty hose, I'd better have them or they'll get suspicious."

"But what do you need body shapers for?" Tammy picked up a long leg girdle and frowned at the spandex panel across the front. "If Leah specializes in plus-sized models, you shouldn't have to resort to all these torture devices to squash things in. Big doesn't matter, right?"

"Wrong." Savannah laid the list aside, took the girdle from Tammy, and tossed it into the bag. "I got some depressing news yesterday. I'm too hefty to be a bona fide model. Even a plus one."

"You? No way!"

"Yep. Get this: The ideal plus model is a size *twelve*."

"What's *plus* about a *twelve*? Isn't the most common size of women in the U.S. a fourteen?"

"My point exactly. I haven't been a size twelve since I *was* twelve. And even if you're a twelve, you're still expected to be muscular and trim and super-fit. No jiggles or ripples anywhere."

"Hence the girdles and pressure-bandage panty hose?"

"Precisely."

Tammy shook her head. "Wow, I'm so disillusioned. And here I thought the plus-model industry was promoting the idea of 'beauty in all shapes and sizes.' "

"Maybe some agencies do. But Leah Freed's certainly doesn't. And unfortunately, she's the one I'm supposedly working for this afternoon."

"What sort of a shoot is it?"

Savannah tossed four pair of panty hose into the bag: suntan, black, smoke, and nude — followed by three bras: an uplifter, a minimizer, and a longline. "It's part of that cereal promotion, the stuff that was supposed to cause Cait Connor to lose weight. Apparently I'm one of the girls who *didn't* eat their cereal, being the robust, bigger-than-a-size-twelve that I am." Adding a couple of swimsuits to the mix, she said, "It's got something to do with a hot tub.

With any luck, I'll get to sit in a spa and soak all afternoon."

"Sounds like fun. Can I go along?"

"I don't think models take their personal assistants to shoots . . . at least, not the models in my category."

"Which is . . . ?"

"Just starting out. Green behind the ears."

"I thought that was wet behind the ears and green around the gills."

"Whatever."

Savannah laid the big bag aside and began to fill one of three smaller makeup bags with every bottle, tube, and compact of face goop that she had been able to gather. She had raided old purses, coat pockets, miscellaneous drawers, and the stash beneath her bathroom sink, where she threw the drugstore rejects and department store promotion giveaways.

"I don't think your heart's in this gig," Tammy said as she picked up one of the sample lipsticks and drew a line of Crimson Desire across the back of her hand. "What's wrong?"

"I don't like to go undercover, pretending to be something I'm not."

"You do it all the time."

"Do not."

"Do, too." She chuckled. "You dress up like a hooker all the time to do stings with Dirk."

Savannah gave her a dirty look. "I know hookers. Way more than I want to know, having arrested a zillion of them over the years. I don't know squat about modeling, and it's just a matter of time until somebody nails me on it."

Tammy shrugged. "Consider it incentive. You solve the murders before your cover's blown, you get out alive."

"We don't know they're murders yet."

"Yes, we do."

Savannah dropped the five bottles of foundation she'd been holding. "We do?"

"Yes. At least Kameeka's was. That's what I came up here to tell you." She smiled that little knowing grin she wore when she was holding a good hand at poker. "Dirk called a minute ago. I told him you were busy packing your girdles, and he said to tell you that he talked to Dr. Liu this morning. She says that Kameeka Wills was dead before the car ran over her."

"The tire tracks on her thigh . . . ?"

"Postmortem."

"What killed her?"

"The blow to the side of her head."

Savannah nodded as a mixture of anger and relief spilled through her system. She hated to hear that anyone's life had been deliberately extinguished by another, but in this case she had known it from the beginning. And she was relieved that now it was officially known by others, too.

"Dirk's gotta get the Crime Scene Unit over to Luminol that kitchen," she said.

Tammy grinned again. "That's where he called me from. He's over there with them now.

135

They just sprayed it and then hit it with the lights."

"And?"

"He said it lit up like Fourth of July fireworks."

Savannah had been somewhat surprised to hear that the address where the shoot was being conducted was only a few blocks south of Cait Connor's home on the beach. But this place was as traditional as hers was contemporary.

Looking like something that belonged on a rocky cliff in Maine, the house had a distinct nautical flair with its weathered gray siding, white shutters, and a turret on one corner that resembled a miniature lighthouse. Sitting directly on the beach, the property was surrounded by a heavy rope fence strung on pilings that served as posts. Driftwood had been scattered haphazardly around the house, along with some rusted, barnacle-encrusted anchors. A battered dinghy lay upside down on a sand dune near the porch. On its peeling hull a name had been painted — Timmy Tuna.

With feelings of trepidation, Savannah parked, grabbed her bag from the back seat, and got out of her car. She really hated this business of being unprepared. And she didn't like the way she had allowed Leah Freed to bulldoze her into going undercover with such a flimsy front.

In her bag she carried the hastily prepared résumé that Leah had compiled for her, along with a letter saying that although her experience was minimal, Leah considered her a "promising talent."

But Tammy was right about the incentive that lying provided. *Get in, get out, before you get caught.* That was her mantra for the day.

The sound of activity led her around to the back of the house, where a bunch of people were milling about on an elaborate, three-level deck. On the upper level was a giant spa, and that seemed to be the hub of the activity.

Half a dozen large white screens and some things that looked like oversize umbrellas were set up around the tub, which was lit with bright spotlights, some on tripods and others on poles.

Savannah's eyes scanned the crowd, looking for the photographer, Matt Slater, whom Leah had described as "tall and skinny with a long, oily ponytail." He wasn't hard to identify. The word "skinny" didn't begin to describe him. *Ichabod Crane in a Hawaiian shirt and Bermuda shorts,* Savannah thought. Not what she had expected in a fashion photographer, but . . . what did *she* know?

And that had to be Jerrod Beekman in the white slacks and purple long-sleeved silk shirt with the sunglasses on his head and the scowl on his face. Leah had described the president of Stellar, the public relations firm that was handling the Slenda account, as "pushy, antsy, and as genuine as a centerfold's bustline and front teeth."

Sitting on the whirlpool's blue-and-white tiled edge were two lovely women, one of whom Savannah recognized from a picture in Leah's lobby. A Latin beauty, she had thick black curls spilling down her back, enormous eyes, and an exotic loveliness about her that made Savannah think of every romance novel she had ever read where the heroine was a gypsy, a Polynesian goddess, or an Indian temptress. Dressed in a teal tankini, she was full-figured but well toned, and Savannah could instantly see what Leah had been referring to when she said that a model must be in top shape, no matter what size.

Next to her on the side of the spa was another equally beautiful model. Fair skinned, the brunette's short curls had golden highlights that complimented her complexion. She had a European look about her heart-shaped face, and her eyes slanted upward at the outer edges. She was speaking to Matt Slater, and Savannah could hear a distinct French accent.

Probably fifteen to twenty pounds less than the woman next to her, the French model wore a one-piece red suit with a halter strap around the back of her long neck.

Savannah couldn't have felt more awkward if she were a guppy swimming with a batch of prize koi in a pet store aquarium. And she silently cursed Leah Freed for insisting on this subterfuge.

Not that she was above subterfuge. Quite the contrary. But she preferred to spin yarns, even tell outright whopping lies, that were of her own making.

Okay, I'm here, she told herself. *Now what the heck am I supposed to do?*

Fortunately, the awkward moment was broken when a tall guy with a shaved head, wearing a tie-dyed T-shirt, came bounding over to her, a clipboard in his hand, a pen behind his ear.

"Are you" — he looked down at his clipboard — "Susan Ross?"

"Yes, I am."

He held out his hand and gave hers half a shake. "I'm Paul Loman, the art director."

"Hi."

She shifted her bag from one hand to the other, wondering what in tarnation you were supposed to say to an art director at a shoot. "Leah was supposed to call you about me," she said.

"Yeah, she did." He glanced up and down her figure with a critical eye that made her feel like a mannequin coming off an assembly line and not quite passing inspection. "Okay, you'll do." Then he focused on her face and frowned. "No foundation?"

"Oh, yes," she stammered, holding out her kit. "I have all kinds of foundation garments with me. I —"

"Foundation. Makeup. I like my girls to take care of that before they arrive for work." He snapped his fingers. "Time is money. In the future, if you're going to work for me, arrive prepared."

She gritted her teeth, then smiled. "Of course. Sorry."

"Over there," he said, motioning to a corner of the deck area where a blonde and a brunette, also dressed in swimsuits, were sitting at a picnic table, applying their own makeup. "And plenty of contour, too," he said, waving his hand vaguely in the direction of his chin while staring at hers. "You've got some, you know, too much . . ."

His voice trailed away as he left her and returned to the tub, where the photographer was positioning the two models who were apparently the "star" material here at the shoot today. A hairstylist was fussing with the Latin girl's hair while another woman dabbed the French model's forehead with powder.

Lesson Number One, she told herself. *Some models do their own hair and makeup; others have it done for them.*

And, apparently, at today's shoot, she was one of the do-it-your-own-self "others." *Oh, well,* she thought, *you can't expect to start at the top. You probably need a dozen or more shoots under your belt before they give you champagne and caviar and your own personal masseuse.*

She joined the two girls at the picnic table,

who greeted her with a subdued "Hi" and a "How's it going?"

Hauling out her makeup case, Savannah felt the way she had at her first formal dinner, when confronted with an assortment of twenty-five pieces of silverware. Granny Reid had once given her the sage advice: "When you're in a social situation, and you don't know what to do, pick out the classiest person in the room and do what they do."

While she wouldn't necessarily label either of the girls at the table as "classy," they seemed to know what they were doing, and that was — applying tons of makeup to their faces.

"Painted Jezebels," Granny would have called them. Or "Whores of Babylon," if Gran had been in a particularly foul mood.

Oh, well, when in Rome . . . or Babylon, she thought as she began to slap on an obscene amount of foundation.

"You Leah's new girl?" the blond one asked her.

"Yes. Susan's the name."

"Who'd you have before?" asked the brunette.

"Have? Before?"

"Your agent."

"Oh, ah . . ." She tried desperately to remember any of the names Leah had put on her fake résumé. ". . . just some guy in Hollywood."

There. That ought to be significantly vague.

141

And there had to be a million agents in Hollywood.

They both gave her what she considered to be suspicious looks. But she decided to chalk it up to paranoia. More than anything, they just looked bored as they continued to trowel on the goop.

She imitated them, while trying to remember all the beauty tips she had gleaned over the years by reading women's magazines and watching infomercials.

As the three of them sat there, contouring, highlighting, and accenting, Savannah couldn't help noticing that her fellow picnic table models were dressed in what she could only describe as "dowdy" swimsuits. The blonde was wearing a bright, floral-patterned suit with a silly little pleated skirt that made her rear look enormous. The brunette's one-piece had broad horizontal stripes in florescent pink, green, and yellow, a monstrosity that Savannah wouldn't have worn to a dog fight.

While she was silently congratulating herself on her own more tasteful choices that she had in her bag, the art director, Paul Loman, hurried over to their table.

"Aren't you ladies ready yet?" he said. Without waiting for anyone to answer, he turned to Savannah. "Let's see your suits."

Feeling that she at least had this one under control, she reached into her kit and pulled out a simple but tasteful navy blue tankini, an aqua

V-neck tank, and an elegant black tank with tiny red trim.

He frowned and shook his head. "Is that all you brought?"

"All?" Savannah swallowed her irritation and resisted the urge to add, "Yeah, I didn't have any ugly-ass git-ups like these gals are wearing."

"Wear the aqua one," he told her. Then, to them all, he said, "Five minutes, ladies. Then Matt wants you on your marks and ready to go."

Savannah sat there, holding the aqua suit. She had only brought it along because Leah had insisted that she bring three choices. About five years old, it had lost most of its elasticity and did precious little to flatter her figure.

"Wonder why he chose that one?" she mumbled to herself. "The black tank looks best on me."

"Don't you get it?" the blonde asked her, an unpleasant scowl on her face. "We're the 'before'." She pointed to the two beauties on the tub. "They're the 'after'."

"After?" Savannah shook her head.

"After eating Slenda Flakes. We're the blimps. We make them look good."

"Oh."

That was the moment when Savannah decided that this was one story she wouldn't tell her grandchildren someday as they sat on her lap and she reminisced about the fascinating life she'd had in the golden, olden days of yore. Nope. The little Savannah-juniorettas of the future didn't need to know that Granny Savannah had been the "before" chick at a fashion photo shoot.

"We're lucky to be working today at all," the brunette mumbled as she dusted a final powdering over her forehead, nose, and chin.

Something in her tone made Savannah's "gossip" detector beep. She pretended not to listen as she caked on a third coating of mascara.

"Yeah. One person's misfortune is another person's big break," Blondie replied with a nod toward the girls at the spa. "You'd think she'd have the decency to at least look a little upset."

"Really. I mean, two people had to die for her to move up to . . ."

The brunette seemed to sense Savannah's attention, and she let the subject drop. But Savannah had already decided which of the two girls at the whirlpool they were talking about. It had to be the one with the French accent. Unlike the Latin model, who seemed appropriately subdued, the second "star" of today's shoot conveyed a self-confidence that bordered on arrogance. With a few too many flippant tosses of her head and far too many shrill bursts of laughter that echoed across the patio, assaulting everyone's ears, Mademoiselle France would have been a bit hard to take even under less tragic circumstances.

144

"You'd better get changed," the blonde snapped, interrupting Savannah's reverie. "Matt's a real bitch if you keep him waiting."

Savannah glanced around. "Where should I get dressed?" she asked.

"Over there."

She was pointing to an area of the patio against the house. A small, thin curtain had been pulled across one side, leaving two sides — and anyone unlucky enough to be expected to strip inside it — exposed.

Apparently modesty wasn't a virtue that was held in high regard at this sort of thing.

Silently she added a bit of padding to Leah's bill — something she would privately call "The Indecency Factor," not to be confused with "The Pain in the Butt Factor," which she sometimes charged particularly difficult clients.

Grabbing her aqua suit, she headed for the semienclosure. She arrived there about the same time as the Latin beauty, who was carrying a gorgeous black suit with a series of alluring and interesting straps across the back.

"Hi," Savannah said as they stepped behind the curtain. "I'm Susan."

"Tesla Montoya," the woman said, extending her hand in a warm, firm handshake. But her smile seemed forced, and Savannah noticed that her eyes were a bit puffy, as though she had been crying.

Briefly, Savannah wondered if maybe she should step out of the so-called dressing area to give the other model some privacy, but Tesla was already peeling off her first suit.

"Isn't it awful, about Cait and Kameeka?" Savannah said. Ordinarily, she would have warmed up to the subject before plunging in, but she didn't know if she would have this rare, one-on-one opportunity to talk to her again.

Tesla shot her a pained and suspicious look before shoving her teal suit into her bag. "It's horrible," she said softly. "*Both* of them! I can't stop thinking about it."

"And now they're saying someone might have . . . you know . . . done it intentionally," Savannah said, watching the woman's face carefully as she began to slip out of her slacks and blouse.

"That's what I heard, too." Tesla already had the black suit on and was adjusting the various straps. "I can't . . ." Her voice broke. She paused and closed her eyes for a moment. "I can't stand it. Somebody has to do something. I have to —"

Savannah's ears were perked, and she held her breath as she waited for the rest of the sentence. But Tesla Montoya seemed to realize that she was talking to a complete stranger, and she ended the conversation with a dismissive wave of her hand.

A second later she was gone, leaving Savannah standing there in her underwear, frustrated, and wondering what she might have said if she'd continued. What did Tesla think someone should do about the situation? What did she feel *she* could do?

Yes, Savannah decided, *I'll definitely have to keep an eye on that one.*

And not just because Tesla seemed upset, or because she appeared to have been crying, or because she had left that sentence dangling in thin air.

But because Savannah had seen something in her eyes just before she had left to return to the shoot.

It was guilt.

In her day, Savannah had seen far more than her share of plain, old-fashioned guilt — more than enough to recognize it when she saw it.

And she intended to find out what Tesla Montoya had done, or not done, to feel guilty about.

Chapter
10

"Susan, your main light is over here. Could you keep that in mind for the rest of this shoot?"

"Are you on your mark, Susan? I hate having to tell you more than once to stay on your mark."

"Could you do something with that left hand, Susan, sweetheart? Relax, for pete's sake. That left hand looks like a claw."

"Don't tuck your chin, Susan. Believe me, you won't like the look. Did you put contour on that double chin of yours? You did? Use more next time."

From the orders being barked at her from the art director, the photographer, and even the other models, Savannah didn't need an official report card to tell her that she was flunking Modeling 101.

And she had pretty much decided that the next time Matt Slater reached out, grabbed some part of her body, and repositioned it like she was some sort of rag doll, she was going to kick him in the crotch of those ugly baggy Bermuda shorts.

Slick with the ladies, my hind end, she thought as she watched him moving among the models, handling their limbs, playing with their hair, adjusting their clothes in ways that she could only classify as slimy.

No doubt a certain amount of physical contact had to occur between professionals in these circumstances. It wasn't *what* he was doing that gave her the heebie-jeebies but the lecherous gleam in his eye when he was handling some of the ladies. Especially the gal with the French accent, whom Savannah now knew as Desiree La Port.

There was no doubt that Desiree thought a great deal more of herself than her sister models thought of her. While Savannah's partners at the makeup table simply ignored Desiree as she flounced and giggled before the camera, Tesla Montoya openly shot her hostile looks. And the lack of chemistry — or even civility — between the two women proved to be a challenge for the photographer.

"Could the two of you move a bit closer to each other?" he said. "I need some tight shots of you and the product. Tesla, your shoulder slightly behind Desiree's, and lean into her . . . more . . . more. Tilt your head a little in her direction. . . ."

Tesla was following his directions, but it was obvious that her heart wasn't in her work.

Finally, even Matt Slater acknowledged the fact: "Tesla, what's with you today? You look like crap. Your eyes are all swollen, your face puffy. Don't tell me you partied last night, the night before a shoot."

"Hardly," Tesla said, in a voice so low they could scarcely hear her.

To Savannah's surprise, Matt Slater seemed to sprout a conscience. His tone softened, and he walked over to place his hand on her shoulder. For once, there was no lusty sparkle in his eye.

"I'm sorry, honey," he said. "We're all a little down today about Cait and Kameeka. We probably should have canceled the shoot, but —"

"No way," piped up Jerrod Beekman. He had been sitting quietly in a folding chair at the perimeter of the action, leaving his seat occasionally to pace and smoke a cigarette.

He strode over to the spa, where Tesla sat on the edge, a bowl of cereal in her hand, the all-important box of Slenda Flakes prominently displayed on the tiles between her and Desiree.

"I don't know what's going on here today," he said. "But we've got a lot of ground to cover to get this campaign back on track. This thing with Cait and Kameeka couldn't have come at a worse time."

For a moment, Tesla Montoya's sad eyes flashed as she glared up at him. "I guess there's just no convenient time to get murdered," she said in a tone so smooth, yet full of bitterness, that everyone on the set held their collective breath.

"Sorry," Jerrod replied, looking anything but remorseful. "It's awful what happened to them. But life goes on."

"Not for them," Tesla shot back.

She stood and set her bowl down on the tiles so hard that they could hear it crack. Turning to Desiree, she said, "For some of us it worked out just fine. But for Cait and Kameeka . . ."

Without another word, she left the area, heading toward the makeshift dressing "room" at the rear of the deck. As she passed her, Savannah saw tears in her eyes, and her whole body was shaking.

After Tesla disappeared behind the curtain, Savannah waited for someone to go after her, perhaps to comfort her. But no one made a move until Jerrod Beekman said, "Lost ground, folks. That's what we've got to recover. Let's get going."

But Matt Slater seemed to think better of it. He shook his head and said, "No, Jerrod. I'll do some more product shots here with Desiree, but other than that, it's over for today. I was right the first time when I thought we should reschedule in a couple of days."

"A couple of days? Are you nuts?" Jerrod's face flushed and his fists clenched at his sides. "First we have a couple of models who are supposed to be losing weight, who aren't. And now we've got so-called professionals moping on the job! I don't need this! Wentworth Industries expects us to launch this campaign in six weeks and where are we? Square one!"

Matt took a couple of steps toward the ad exec, a calm but firm look on his face. "Like I said, that's it for today, Jerrod. I'm working with human beings here, not just boxes of corn flakes, okay?"

Jerrod hesitated a couple of heavy seconds, then reached into his pocket for his cigarette pack. Tapping one out, he moved back behind his chair and started to pace again.

Deciding that she probably wouldn't be missed, Savannah decided to try her luck once more with Tesla Montoya behind the dressing curtain. She might be able to glean a little something more out of her and if not, she could at least offer a bit of sympathy . . . since no one else on the set seemed interested in doing so.

But as Savannah approached the curtain, she was surprised to hear Tesla talking on the other side.

She was even more surprised when she heard her say, "Detective Coulter, yes."

Savannah stopped a few feet from the curtain and listened.

Nothing at first. Then Tesla said, "Okay, when he gets in, would you ask him to call me. Tell him it's very important. No, I want to talk to the detective who's handling the case and he's the one . . . yes . . . My name is Tesla Montoya and . . ."

She went on to leave her phone numbers, the one at home, at the agency, and her cell, insisting that he call her the minute he got her message.

Then she hung up, and Savannah could hear her making another call.

"Tesla Montoya here," she was saying. "I need to see Dr. Pappas. Now. Okay, I'll be there in ten minutes."

On the other side of the curtain, Savannah's heart was racing. Dirk had a lead, and it sounded like a hot one.

Damn, if she weren't pretending to be some sort of half-assed, wannabe model, she could just approach Tesla here and now, and identify herself. She might tell her whatever juicy info she was saving for Dirk.

It was still worth a try.

She stepped behind the curtain just in time to see Tesla slip her phone into her purse. Startled, Tesla jumped and gave her a suspicious look, one laced with fear and the still palpable element of guilt.

"Are you okay?" Savannah asked, as simply and sincerely as she could.

"No." Tesla turned her back to her and began to pull on a pair of jeans and a T-shirt over her swimsuit. "I'm not."

"Can I help?"

When Tesla finished slipping on a pair of sneakers, she picked up her purse and finally turned to Savannah. Tears were streaming

153

down her face. "No, you can't help," she said. "Nobody can help. Nobody but me."

A moment later, she was gone, leaving Savannah with a burning curiosity . . . and a desperate need to call Dirk.

"Call me, you knucklehead," was the less-than-gracious message Savannah left on Dirk's answering service. "What's the point in having a cell phone if you don't pick it up? Geez."

But by the time she'd returned to her home, she hadn't heard from him.

With anyone else she might have worried, but Dirk had been the last person she knew to get a cell phone, proclaiming that the darned things were a violation of one's privacy. Or as he had put it, "A guy can't take a drive, a leak, or a nap without everybody expecting him to be available."

He was famous for switching his off, or just ignoring the buzz when he had something more important to do besides chat — like read the morning comic strips or watch wrestling on TV.

As Savannah drove up her street, she spotted Marietta's rental car parked smack in the middle of her two-car driveway. And she realized that, once again, she'd be parking the Mustang on the street — something she was loath to do after treating the pony to a new, bright red paint job a few months ago. New paint just seemed to be a magnet for yahoos

154

with no brains in their heads and a set of keys in their hands.

But along with her irritation, Savannah couldn't help feeling a bit relieved. When she had left the house that morning, Marietta hadn't yet returned from her big date the night before. And all day Savannah had been fighting off the fear that she might find her sister in much the same sorry state as those poor, murdered girls.

At least Mari had survived her cyber-encounter, although Savannah wasn't exactly looking forward to a pity party with Marietta wearing the victim hat if it hadn't gone well.

Then there was the other possibility that wasn't pretty either — having to listen to salacious details about their lusty evening and having to smile, nod, and say, "Oh, how lovely for you, dear," in all the right places.

Not to mention fighting one's gag reflex.

Either way, she wasn't exactly looking forward to an evening spent with Mari, Mari, Sometimes Contrary and Almost Always Love-Struck.

But when she walked into the house and entered the living room, she saw a Marietta sitting on her sofa who didn't really fit either category. She looked perplexed and more than a little worried.

Tammy sat at the desk, her back to Marietta, deeply absorbed in something on the computer screen. So completely absorbed that Savannah

155

had a feeling it was an avoidance ploy to keep from having to engage in conversation with their guest.

"Hi, Marietta," Savannah said brightly as she shoved her model's kit into a space behind her easy chair. "What's shakin', sugar?"

Marietta shot a nervous look at the telephone, which was lying on the coffee table in front of her and said, "Don't know yet."

Ah, Savannah thought. *We're waiting for Prince Charming to call. Oh, joy.*

She turned to Tammy, who had suddenly become less occupied. "Heard anything from Dirk this afternoon?"

"Nope," Tammy replied. "But Leah Freed's called three times in the last hour, wanting to know if you've found out anything. How was the shoot?"

"Well, I'm shot, if that's what you mean. Dead tired. Who would have thought that getting your picture taken was such hard work? I have to tell you, I have a whole new respect for those Victoria's Secret models. Those girls work their fannies off."

As she walked past them toward the kitchen, she said, "I'm gonna have some ice tea, strong and sweet. You girls want anything?"

"I'm fine, thanks," Tammy responded.

Marietta glanced toward the kitchen, then back at the telephone in front of her. "No, I guess not."

Savannah sighed. "I'll bring it to you," she

said. "Or you can bring the phone into the kitchen. It's cordless, you know."

Marietta looked down at her watch and frowned. "Yeah, okay. Bring it to me. Lots of ice and a lemon slice, too."

A few moments later, Savannah returned with the two drinks. She gave one to her sister, then sat down in her easy chair and put her feet up.

Life was good for three seconds. Then Marietta said, "Why doesn't he call? He said he'd call me so that we could make plans for this evening, and the afternoon's near gone. Why hasn't he called?"

Savannah had heard Marietta sing this tune far too many times to be even mildly surprised. Every note was far too predictable and inevitably off-key.

"So, I guess it went okay last night?" Savannah ventured, knowing she'd be sorry she asked.

"Okay?" For a few seconds, Marietta's eyes glazed over and a sappy smile curved her lips. "It was heaven. Plain ol' heaven here on earth. That was, without a doubt, the most totally fulfilling night of lovemaking I've ever experienced. And the way we bonded . . . oh . . ."

Savannah stifled a groan and silently sent Dirk a mental message: *Call me, you nincompoop! Call me and rescue me from —*

"And oh, that guy may not look exactly like the picture he sent me, but I mean to tell you,

157

girl, he knows how to please a woman. That there guy satisfied me in ways that I never even knowed I could be . . ."

Now, Dirk! Now! Call me and I'll owe you the biggest favor. I might even have sex with you after all these years if you'll just call me. . . .

"I gotta tell you," Marietta rolled on, "that by the time he was done with my body, I was as limp as a rag doll. But no, no, no, *he* wasn't! No siree, Bob! T'weren't nothin' limp about that boy! Why he could go all night long and still . . ."

Buzz.

The phone on the coffee table was ringing, and to Savannah's ears it sounded like an angel choir.

She jumped to get it, but Marietta beat her to it.

"Hello?" Marietta breathed, in the same tone that Savannah had heard obscene callers use.

Just as quickly, Marietta's demeanor changed to that of a disgusted, pouting teenager. "It's for you," she said, thrusting the phone into Savannah's hand. "It's that Dirk guy."

"Dirk!" Savannah said, trying to conceal her glee and failing miserably. "I was hoping you'd call." She glanced at her sister, whose pout was deepening by the moment. "I mean . . . I have something to ask you."

"Ooo-kay. Shoot." Dirk sounded confused by the unexpected enthusiasm, but intrigued.

"Did you talk to a model named Tesla Montoya yet?"

"No. I got the message that she'd called. But you'd left two messages and you sounded hot and bothered so I thought I'd better return yours first."

"Call her," she said. "Call her right away. I was with her at the shoot today, and I don't know what she's got for you, but I'll bet it's good."

"Okay. I'll call her now."

Savannah glanced over at Marietta, who was obviously dying by the moment because the phone was being tied up.

"Yeah, all right," Savannah continued. "I can come over and help you out with that . . . if you really need me to, that is."

Dirk was silent for a moment. Then he said, "What?"

"My sister, Marietta, is visiting, you know, but if you really need me . . ."

Dirk chuckled. "Oh, I gotcha. I just got done talking to Kevin Connor. I'm outside his house now. But if you want to escape, I'll meet you at the park in half an hour."

"Ten minutes, you say?" She nodded vigorously. "Yes, I can be there. See you soon."

Marietta practically snatched the phone out of her hand the moment she had finished the call. "I hope he wasn't trying to call while you were gabbing there," she said.

Savannah quirked one eyebrow. "Excuse me,

but I wasn't on that long and anyway, isn't it *my* phone?"

Marietta shrugged. "Yeah, I guess, but it's really important that he get through to me if he wants to."

"I figure if he called and the line was busy, he'd call back, right? If he really wanted to get in touch, that is."

Oops.

Judging from the way that Marietta's nostrils were flaring, Savannah decided that might have been the wrong thing to say.

"I gotta go." She hurried toward the door. "Mari, hope he calls. Tammy, go on home if you want to."

Not wasting any time, Tammy caught up with her before she reached the sidewalk.

Savannah laughed. "You're running like your drawers are on fire," she told her. "Had enough of Marietta for one day?"

"Oh, please," Tammy returned, "I've been listening to that crap all day. And don't look now, Sister Savannah, but your shorts are smoking, too."

Chapter
11

Savannah found Dirk in the park, sitting at the same picnic bench where they had recently shared their lunch. It seemed like such a long time since then, she thought as she felt the weight of two lost lives bearing down on her.

Someday I've got to learn not to take this stuff personally, she thought as she passed the sandbox and swing-set area to join him at the table. *And the day I don't take it personally is the day I should quit this business and take up needle-point.*

As she approached, he put out his cigarette with a guilty smile. A week ago he had "quit." Again. Thanks to her constant nagging, he had gotten quite good at quitting. He did it at least once a month.

"Had to get away?" he said as she sat across from him on the opposite bench.

"Big time," she replied. "When you called, I was sitting there praying that I'd hear from you. I owe you one."

The smile slid off his face. "Okay, then help me with this case. I'm getting nowhere fast."

"Did you get in touch with Tesla Montoya?"

He shook his head. "Nope. I called her back, left a message at her home phone and her cell. I even drove by her house on the way over here and nobody was home."

"Where does she live?"

"Just around the corner. She's got an apartment in an old house behind City Hall."

"Hmmm . . . now that I think about it . . ." Savannah tapped her nails on the picnic table top. "She called a doctor after she called you. His name is Pappas. I think she was going to his office. Maybe she's still there."

Dirk reached into the pocket of his leather jacket and pulled out his cell phone. "I hate to bother anybody who's in the middle of a doctor's appointment," he said, "but if you think she's really got something . . ."

"She sounded pretty serious about wanting to talk to you. And she said something about nobody being able to help the situation — except for her."

Dirk punched some numbers into the phone. "Coulter here," he said. "I need an address on a Dr. Pappas." He made a face. "I don't know if he's local or not. Try for a local listing and then spread out. Sheez. Not likely to make detective anytime soon, are you, Sherlock?" Covering the phone with his hand, he said, "I don't know where the department gets these jokers. They couldn't find their butts with their hands cuffed behind 'em."

"So, next time, don't call the station house, just dial 411 for Directory Assistance like everybody else in the world."

He looked at her as though she'd suddenly sprouted another head, then grunted. "Hurrumph. Don't interrupt me when I'm talkin'."

A second later, he pulled out a small notebook and pen and started scribbling. "Okay, 452 Santa Barbara Avenue. Thanks. Now, was that so hard?"

He hung up and shoved the phone back in his pocket. "Let's go," he said. "It's over by the hospital."

As they were walking across the grass to his Buick, he suddenly stopped and gave her a funny, searching look.

Long ago, Savannah had decided that Dirk had a problem with multitasking . . . like walking and talking at the same time. It was a guy thing.

"Will they really give you an address if you call regular ol' Directory Assistance?"

"Sometimes. But you've gotta ask nice," she told him.

He thought it over, grumbled a bit, shook his head, and started walking again.

"Yeah . . ." she said, catching up to him. "You'd probably have more luck with the station."

Like many of the physicians in San

Carmelita, Dr. Pappas conducted his practice in one of the dreary, generic office buildings that surrounded Community General Hospital. The no-frills structures with their flat roofs, faded paint, and empty flower beds did little to cheer the patients who visited the obstetricians, dentists, chiropractors, podiatrists, and proctologists who practiced there.

Dr. Pappas's shingle on his dingy front door identified him as a weight-loss specialist.

"Big surprise there," Savannah remarked as she pointed out the sign to Dirk. "Do you see a recurring theme with these women?"

"Yeah, they're all nuts when it comes to their weight." He gave a contemptuous little snort. "You don't see us guys obsessing about the size of *our* butts."

She glanced down at his tummy which, over the years she had known him, had definitely expanded. It wasn't exactly lapping over his belt, but if he kept eating half a dozen doughnuts for breakfast and two Jumbo Bonanza Burgers for lunch, it soon would.

And it didn't matter one diddly-do to her.

Dirk was Dirk, no matter the size of his belly. It would never occur to her to evaluate a friend according to their weight.

And she didn't know many woman who would judge another person by size. So, why did they judge themselves so harshly?

"Girls have to get smart about weight," she muttered as they entered the office.

"Yep. And they've gotta stop worrying about what us guys think, too. A lot of us like a broad with some junk in the trunk."

"*Junk* in the *trunk?*" She didn't know whether to hit him or kiss him . . . a common dilemma with Dirk.

So, as usual, she ignored him.

They walked into a crowded waiting room and looked around. As Dirk might have predicted, they were all females, in every size and shape imaginable. But the pretty Latin model wasn't among them.

Dirk gave Savannah a questioning look, and she shook her head. He walked up to the receptionist's window and discreetly flashed his badge. "Is Tesla Montoya in with the doctor?" he asked, keeping his voice low.

The sweet-faced nurse behind the glass instantly dropped her sweet face. "No, she's not," she snapped. "She hasn't shown up, and we were expecting her over an hour ago. Didn't even call to cancel."

Savannah felt her stomach sink. One glance at Dirk's face told her that he was feeling the same.

"So, Montoya had an appointment?" he asked the nurse.

"No. She called and asked us to fit her in. Then she didn't even show. Just wait until the next time she wants to come in without an appointment."

Dirk glanced back at the crowded waiting

165

room. "Yeah, heaven knows how long she'd have to hang around, cooling her heels, if she didn't have an appointment."

Savannah reached for Dirk's arm and pulled him away from the window. "Thank you," she told the nurse. "Have a good day."

Once outside the office, standing in the courtyard with its flowerless flower boxes and cracked sidewalks, Dirk shook her hand off his arm and said, "Did that Montoya chick seem like somebody who wouldn't show up for an appointment without calling?"

"Nope."

"That's what I figured."

He took out his phone and his notebook and punched in a number. After a few rings, he said, "Ms. Montoya, this is Detective Coulter again. Call me as soon as you get this. It's very important that I talk to you right away." Then he hung up and turned to Savannah. "What now?"

Savannah's mind raced. "We've got to find her, before . . ."

She couldn't say it.

"Yeah," he said. "Before."

"Back to her house?"

He shook his head. "We're not going to find her there."

"You got any better ideas of where to look?"

This time he took *her* arm. "Let's go," he said, propelling her toward the parking lot. "She's not going to be there, but if we're lucky,

166

at least maybe the floor won't be freshly mopped."

"One can always hope."

No doubt the old house on the hill above City Hall had been lovely in its day. With its high-pitched roof, gables, and ornate gingerbread trim, the turn-of-the-century "painted lady" looked as if she needed a new coat of lipstick and rouge.

With illusions of herself as a renovator/decorator, Savannah would have loved to get her hands on something like that house, to restore it to all of its former grandeur. But not having at least a cool million socked away for such a time-consuming venture, not to mention the time and energy to spend the next ten years cleaning, scraping, and painting, she had decided to stick with her own little house.

When the burning desire to refurbish something became overwhelming — usually after watching a show on the Home & Garden TV channel — she reminded herself of the leak under her kitchen sink, and that was usually enough to stifle the urge.

But she couldn't help saying, "Beautiful old house," as they walked up the sidewalk to the front door.

"Eh, it's a dump. You couldn't give me a mess like this."

Savannah thought of his rusted house trailer and the yard that surrounded it — a bed of gravel. She opened her mouth to speak, but then closed it and swallowed the comment.

Sometimes she was just in the mood to be kind.

"She lives in the back," he said, leading Savannah to the right and along the wide veranda that wrapped all the way around the house.

At the back of the home, a quaint Dutch door bore a brass plaque with the letter B scrolled on it. The window in the upper half of the door was covered by a lace curtain. On either side of the door, the window drapes were drawn.

"Looks like it did when I was here before," Dirk said, tapping his knuckles on the window glass. "This was a waste of time."

"Probably, but you've gotta start somewhere," Savannah replied — the sunbeam forever trying to penetrate his clouds of doom and gloom. It was a thankless task, one that she couldn't seem to break herself of doing.

When no one answered his knock, he hammered his fist on the lower wooden half.

Other than a dog who started barking in the yard next door, there was no response.

"Try the door," Savannah said, nudging him with her elbow.

"Oh, yeah, right. We're gonna get lucky two times in a row. . . ."

He jiggled the knob, but it was locked.

"That's it," she said. "A no-go."

"Maybe. Maybe not."

Savannah gave him a suspicious side glance. There was no mistaking the mischievous tone in his voice. The one he always got just before he did something that would eventually land him on the police chief's carpet.

"Did you hear that?" he asked, cocking his head sideways and listening intently.

Savannah grinned. They had played this game before, but not for a while. You had to rotate games pretty frequently. Police Chief Hillquist might be a jerk, but he wasn't stupid.

"Yeah, I think I did," she said, cupping her hand behind her right ear. "Sounded like somebody calling out for help to me."

"That's what it sounded like to me, too. I think we'd better break in."

"And make it snappy."

"Chief's gonna be pissed," he said as he pulled his jacket sleeve down over his hand.

"Yeah, well . . . wouldn't be the first time. Or the last."

With hardly any force at all, Dirk gave the lower right-hand glass panel one sharp rap, and it shattered.

"What's the point of even locking your door when you've got glass three inches from the knob?" she said as he carefully reached inside and opened the door.

"Really," he said. "I wouldn't have glass in my trailer door for nothin'."

For half a second, Savannah entertained the idea of an elaborate stained-glass window in

169

the door of Dirk's humble trailer, and she nearly giggled.

But any inclination toward laughter disappeared the instant Dirk opened the door and she caught a glimpse of what was inside.

"Damn," Dirk whispered as he pushed the door all the way open.

They both drew their guns and each took a position on either side of the door, where between the two of them, they could see all of the room inside.

"Clear," Savannah said.

He nodded. "Clear."

Guns leading the way, they stepped inside the tiny studio apartment that looked as though an invading army had tramped through it.

The coffee table was overturned, its mirror top broken in several pieces. A bookshelf lay on its face, its books, pictures, and bric-a-brac scattered on the floor.

In the kitchenette area in the right rear of the room, pans, dishes, glasses, and a potted plant had been knocked to the floor. Dirt and shattered pottery lay everywhere.

Cautiously, Dirk poked his gun, then his head into the bathroom to the left. "It's clear, too," he said.

Savannah looked under the twin bed that was perfectly made, the only thing in the room that seemed to be undisturbed. All she saw was a row of shoe boxes.

"Here, too," she said, straightening up and

looking around her with a heavy, sick feeling that felt a lot like failure. "He got to her before we did," she said.

"*He?* How do you know it wasn't a *she?* Or a *they?*"

"Get real," she snapped, in no mood to argue gender-correctness with him. "It's almost always a friggin' *he.*"

But for once, Dirk didn't seem inclined to argue either. He shrugged. "True . . . but it's not exactly a given."

"How about Kevin Connor?" she asked. "It's usually a *he,* and it's usually the husband or the boyfriend."

"Connor's alibi is airtight. He was at work all day."

"You checked that?" Savannah could hear the fury in her own voice, but she didn't care.

"I checked it, Van. They say he never left the hospital. Every minute of his day is accounted for," he said softly. "Take it easy, honey."

Savannah wasn't above feeding a guy his teeth for calling her "honey" or "sweetie" or "babe." But she could tell by the soft look in Dirk's eyes that he meant it. She was busting his chops, and he was answering her with kindness.

"Sorry," she said. "I just . . ."

"I know. Me, too."

Savannah shook her head. "No, you don't know. I just spent the afternoon with Tesla. She's a doll, a real lady. I knew she was worried, and I wasn't able to draw it out of her."

"You talked to her. You did what you could. It wasn't exactly the best of circumstances to interview somebody, what with you being undercover and all."

"I should have pressed her. I should have dropped the stupid charade and taken her aside and done what it took to get her to talk to me."

"Shoulda, coulda, woulda . . . water under the bridge. We'll find her."

Savannah winced as she looked around the room and contemplated what sort of violence it would have taken to accomplish this mess. What sort of pain would be inflicted on a body that was being bounced off furniture and walls like that?

"At least there's no blood," Dirk added, kneeling down and looking at the floor. "He's getting cocky. Didn't even bother to clean up this time."

"He?"

"Yeah, he." Looking up at her, he gave her a wink. "You're right, of course. It's almost always one of us worthless dudes that done it."

"I wouldn't say you guys are worthless," she said, "just . . ."

Her voice trailed away as she knelt beside the rust-colored suede sofa and stared at a dark spot on the cushion.

"What is it?" he asked.

She pulled a latex glove out of her purse and slipped it on. Then she carefully dabbed at the

172

spot with one fingertip.

Holding up the finger, she showed him the dark red smudge on the glove. "Looks like we spoke too soon."

Chapter
12

Ordinarily, having an assortment of the people she loved most in the world around her table was Savannah's favorite pastime. She found it fun to feed almost anyone, let alone her favorite folks.

But tonight, the mood was less celebratory than usual with the meeting of the official Moonlight Magnolia Detective Agency gang. Two unsolved murders and a third missing woman could put a damper on any party.

Savannah sat at the head of the table with Dirk at the foot. To her right was Tammy, her notebook computer on the table in front of her. And to Savannah's left sat a couple of the most attractive and heartbreakingly unattainable men she knew: Ryan Stone and John Gibson.

With his stunning good looks and winning smile, the tall, dark, and handsome Ryan could have done anything from acting to shaving commercials to squiring wealthy ladies to social events for big bucks.

But both he and John, his life partner, had taken early retirements from the FBI and now spent their time doing private investigations and providing security for the rich, famous, and powerful — when they weren't summering on the French Riviera, cruising the Mediterranean, or exploring the Amazon jungle with a shaman guide.

Savannah and Tammy were both madly in love with Ryan and the older — but no less delicious — silver-haired British fox, John . . . for all the good it did them. To their dismay, no amount of feminine wiles had altered either man's sexual orientation. But Savannah had finally decided that simply being adored by these two elegant, sensitive, and charming hunks was enough. With Ryan and John, the role of "friend" didn't seem like Second Prize.

And tonight, maybe because Dirk was feeling a bit swamped by his investigations, he seemed more grateful than usual to receive whatever input the two had to offer.

"No," he was telling John, "the M.E. couldn't find anything that would indicate homicide on the Connor death. Looks like an accident, but Van and I don't think so, because of the second one. And then this other gal's gone missing."

John took a sip of his Earl Grey tea and nodded thoughtfully. "Your second young lady," he continued in his exquisitely proper British accent, "was most assuredly murdered?"

"Yeah," Dirk replied. "Dr. Liu says the body had none of the usual pedestrian versus vehicle injuries."

Tammy pointed to her computer. "That's true. I've been doing my Internet research, and when a car hits a jogger or a walker, the most common injury is to the lower legs, where the bumper first makes contact."

"And Kameeka Wills died of cerebral hemorrhage, caused by a blow to the head with a blunt object," Savannah added. "The only signs that she'd been in contact with a vehicle were the tire marks across her upper thighs."

"And," Dirk said, "Dr. Liu says those were postmortem."

"Just one blow to the head?" Ryan wanted to know.

"Yeah, but apparently it was a nasty one." Dirk grimaced and took a long drink from his coffee mug. "Fractured her skull."

"Any ideas on the weapon?" Ryan asked.

Dirk shook his head. "Not for sure, but Dr. Liu said she'd seen that sort of injury before and thought it was from a baseball bat."

"A man's weapon," Ryan said.

Tammy looked up from her computer screen where she was taking meticulous notes of the meeting. Notes no one would ever read, but she liked to feel useful. "Hey, I was pretty awesome with a bat when I was in Girls' Little League."

"Bully for you," Dirk said. "So, everybody, Tammy's a suspect, along with all the guys in the picture."

"What guys?" John asked.

Savannah got up from the table and walked

to the kitchen counter, where she began to carve up a triplelayer chocolate cake. "We've got Kevin Connor, Cait's husband," she said.

"But he has a solid alibi for the time when Cait died," Dirk added. "He was at work, and his superior vouches for him, says he wasn't out of her sight all day."

"And when Kameeka was killed?" John asked.

Dirk shook his head. "Nope. I asked him about that, and he was home alone. He said he was passed out in bed from drinking too much the night before. He's pretty upset about losing his wife."

"Most people without partners would have a hard time establishing an alibi for the early morning hours," John replied. "So you can't place much emphasis on that."

"I'll testify to the fact that he's a close friend of Jack Daniels," Savannah said, dishing monstrous slices of the cake onto her best dessert plates.

For the safety of her Royal Albert Old Country Roses china, she put Dirk's on an unbreakable Corelle plate. He'd never notice the slight . . . as long as his piece was a bit larger than the others. There was no point in feeding the bull in the china shop on your best dinnerware.

"And we've got Matt Slater," Savannah said as she set a piece of cake in front of John. "He's the main photographer on the Slenda Flakes campaign. He gave me the heebie-jeebies, the way he was looking at the girls at the shoot and the way he was handling them, way more than necessary just to pose them."

John turned his plate first one way, then the other, admiring the cake with its generous dollop of whipped cream and a drizzle of Chambord sauce. "Savannah, my dear, you certainly know how to gild the culinary lily. Do you think this photographer of yours is committing . . . shall we say . . . indiscretions with his ladies?"

Savannah thought it over for a moment, remembering how Matt had slid his hand between Desiree's thighs to reposition her leg. A gentle hand on the knee or a verbal command would have been more than sufficient. Then there had been the look that passed between them as his hand lingered a few seconds too long.

"Oh, yes," she said. "Definitely a possibility."

"Any indication that he might have been involved with either victim?" Ryan asked.

"Not yet." Dirk scowled as Savannah handed the next portion to Ryan instead of him. "But I'm working on it," he said. "If there was any hanky-panky going on, I'll be sure to find out about it."

Tammy giggled. "Yeah, Dirk's a regular bloodhound when it comes to sniffing out hanky. It's the closest thing to panky he gets."

"Shut up, bubble brain," Dirk said, swiping

the piece of cake that Savannah had given Tammy out from under her nose.

Savannah rescued the cake and, more importantly, her china from him and handed it back to Tammy. "And then," she continued, "we've got this Jerrod Beekman dude who owns Stellar, the ad agency that's handling the Slenda account for Wentworth Cereal."

"Jerrod Beekman?" Ryan turned to John. "We know him. He was seeing Michael Romano last summer. We met them at the opening of that little gallery down on San Fernando Street. Remember?"

Dirk perked up. "Oh, so, Beekman's a . . . I mean he's . . . one of you guys? Uh, no offense."

Ryan glanced over at Savannah, then gave Dirk his best "patient" smile. "None taken. Yes, I suppose you could say he's one of *us*. He's certainly not one of *you*." His eyes twinkled when he added, "No offense."

Dirk scowled. "And what's *that* supposed to mean?"

Savannah shoved his oversize cake in front of him. "Eat," she said.

"I'd keep a sharp eye on Beekman," John told her. "I've heard from more than one source that he's a wily chap when it comes to business. Not above resorting to mischief to get the upper hand."

"Thanks, John," Savannah said. "That's good to know."

"I can do some checking about, if you like," he offered. "I know this particular chap, Michael Romano, and I believe there was a bit of animosity when they ceased to keep company this past winter. He might have something to say about your fellow Beekman."

"That would be great," Dirk said with far more enthusiasm than usual for him. Savannah stifled a grin. Frequently, when stumped by a case, Dirk decided that Ryan and John were pretty good to have around.

Joining them at the table with her own dessert, she said, "And then we have the agent, Leah Freed."

"Why would you suspect her?" Tammy asked.

"I suspect everybody. That way I'm sure to think ill of the bad guy . . . or girl . . . at least once," she said. "Leah hired me to find out what happened to her girls, but she seems more interested in what Dirk has found out than what I've uncovered. She called me four times today, leaving messages for me to check in. But when I did, right before you guys came over tonight, all she did was ask me who 'the police' think it might be."

"Are you saying she hired you just to get information on me?" Dirk asked with a look of arrogance that was only slightly diluted by the whipped cream on his chin.

"Oh, yeah, Dirko," Tammy said. "It's about you. It's always about you."

"And this time it might be more than just a

figment of your inflated ego," Savannah added. "I could swear I was being pumped."

"You didn't give her anything good, did you?" Dirk asked.

She gave him a dismissive wave with her fork. "Oh, yes, I spilled everything I knew. And what I didn't know, I made up. Duh."

Dirk looked a bit wounded, but he recovered instantly when he filled his face with chocolate cake.

Tammy cleared her throat. "So . . . nobody's asked me what *I* came up with today."

"You?" Savannah washed down the bite of cake with a big swig of strong coffee, generously laced with cream. "I didn't think you'd gotten any time on the computer." She glanced toward the living room and lowered her voice to a whisper so that her sister wouldn't hear. "You know," she added, "with Marietta using it all day to chat with What's-His-Nuts."

"There was that half an hour when she was trying to track him down on the phone. I got online then for a while."

"Track him down?"

"Yeah. She called his work, his dad's house, his brother's . . ."

"How did she get their numbers?"

Tammy shrugged. "I don't know for sure. But when she finally got him on the phone, she said something that made me think maybe she wrote them down out of his address book when he was in the shower this morning."

Savannah shuddered. "Oooo, scary stuff."

"Well, what did you come up with, Nancy Drew?" Dirk asked, prodding Tammy's elbow with his finger.

"I found out about the restraining orders."

There was a long moment of silence all around the table. Then John said, "Good show, old girl! Do tell . . . who has a restraining order and against whom?"

"Yeah, cough it up, hairball!" Dirk said.

Tammy gave him her prissiest adolescent smirk. "Do you mean to tell me that *you*, Detective Sergeant Coulter, hadn't checked for that yet?"

Dirk growled and gouged her again, harder and in the ribs. "I don't wanna have to hurt you, kid. Give."

"Yeah." Savannah poked her in the other side. "Talk."

"Both Cait Connor and Kameeka Wills had restraining orders against the same person."

"And . . . ?" Savannah leaned closer, resisting the urge to throttle her.

"And so do Tesla Montoya and even Desiree La Port."

"All four ladies have restraining orders against the same individual?" John asked.

"The same person." Tammy paused, milking every drop of drama juice from the moment.

"Well, who is it?" Dirk roared.

Hitching her chin upward two notches, she proudly announced, "His name is . . . Ronald

Tumblety. Tumblety, T-U-M-B-L-E-T-Y."

Savannah looked at Dirk. John and Ryan looked at Savannah. Dirk just sat there, staring at Tammy.

Finally, Ryan asked the obvious. "Who's Ronald Tumblety?"

Savannah sighed and sank back in her chair. "The hell if I know," she said.

"Me either," Dirk said, letting out a sigh that sounded like a punctured bicycle tire oozing air.

"Well, who is he?" Savannah asked Tammy.

Tammy shrugged. "I don't know. I found out his name and the fact that the basis for the restraining order is because he was stalking them. All of them, at one time or another. Beyond that . . . it's up to you professionals." She looked at Dirk and made a face. "After all, I'm just the *amateur* sleuth around here."

But Dirk was already on his feet. The whole house shook as he left, slamming the back door behind him.

"Dirk'll find out," Savannah said as she picked up her fork and continued to eat her cake. "After all, he's got the badge and all the legal connections . . . not to mention that big check from the department every other Friday. Would you like another piece of cake, John?"

"I'd be delighted, love."

"Pass your plate."

Half an hour later, when the rest of the gang

183

had left for the evening, Savannah dished up an extra generous helping of the cake and took it into the living room. Marietta was still sitting at the computer, staring at the screen, her face illuminated by the green glow.

She didn't even appear to be blinking.

"Hey, Sis," Savannah said, walking over to her. "The troops are gone now. Why don't you take a break from that thing and chat with a live person for a while?"

Marietta's only response was a slight shake of her head. Then she began to type furiously.

"Saved you a big piece of my Death by Chocolate," Savannah said, waving the cake under her nose. "Raspberry sauce on it. Whipped cream, your favorite."

"Naw. Not now."

"But, Mari, you've been on that thing for . . ." She glanced at her watch. "Four and a half hours now. What could be so interesting?"

As though startled out of a coma, Marietta jumped and looked up at Savannah, her eyes wide and vacant. "What?"

"Come visit with me for a while." Savannah motioned toward the sofa. "I'm going to bed pretty soon, and you haven't told me the latest on your new lover boy."

Savannah heard the words coming out of her mouth and wondered — not for the first time — if she was a complete idiot. Here she was actually asking to be tortured. And why?

Just to be nice? Courteous and polite?

Where had she gotten the idea that it was a good thing, this pretending to give a hoot? Oh, yeah . . . Granny Reid. Gran had definitely overemphasized that aspect of being a Southern lady.

Sometimes "nice" sucked.

Like when Marietta looked up at her with tear-brimmed eyes, her lower lip trembling, and said, "Something's wrong. I don't think he loves me anymore."

"Who? Mr. Cyberdude?"

"Sure. Who else. The guy I spent the night with last night. I don't think he loves me anymore."

"Really? Why?"

"Because he's telling everybody in the chat room that he never did love me."

"Oh. Yeah. Well. I see your point."

Maybe it's not too late for a graceful exit, Savannah thought as she set the dish of cake on the desk beside the computer.

"I think I'll call it a night," she said. "Since you're busy there and —"

Marietta clicked off the computer. And promptly burst into tears.

Too late. The escape route is definitely closed now. Savannah sighed and reached for the box of tissues in the desk's top drawer. *And I have only myself to blame.* She handed the tissues to Marietta, turned, and walked over to her comfy chair. *Yes, Savannah, you people-pleasing idiot, you had to ask, didn't you?*

185

"I just don't understand it," Marietta was saying as she dabbed at her eyes and blew her nose. "This time last night we were layin' there in each other's arms, proclaiming our undying love and tonight . . . tonight he puts me on 'Ignore.' "

"Ignore?"

Sniff. "That's what you do when you're in a chat room and you don't even want to see what the other person's saying. So you click 'Ignore,' and they plumb disappear off the screen. That's what he did to me just now."

"Um-m-m. That's not a good sign."

Marietta left the desk and plopped down on the sofa. "How can somebody just up and turn on you like that? I don't understand it. I thought that what we had was special. A once-in-a-lifetime soul connection."

You could be soaking in a bubble bath right now, Savannah told herself as she painted a "concerned and not at all irritated as hell" look on her face. *But no-o-o-o! Yo-o-ou had to go and ask her how she was.*

"Did he really tell you that he loved you last night?" she asked.

"Sure he did."

"He actually said the L word?"

Marietta thought for a moment. "Let's see now. . . . I told him that I loved him, and he said, 'Thanks.' That's the same thing, isn't it?"

Only if you're a complete dope. "Well . . . I . . ."

"I mean, he was smiling when he said it. He

186

looked grateful and happy."

"Were you naked and in bed?"

"Yeah."

"And you hadn't actually 'done it' yet?"

"Not yet, but we were about to."

"Maybe *that* was why he was smiling, grateful, and happy."

Marietta's face screwed up in pain. "Are you telling me, Savannah Reid, that you think the only reason that man told me he loved me was so that he could have his way with me? Is that what you're saying?"

"Well, it wouldn't be the first time that a guy stretched the truth a bit to get laid, Marietta. It happens all the time. You should have figured that out by the time you were fifteen. And besides that, he didn't actually say 'love.' He said, 'Thanks.' That sounds kinda lukewarm to me."

"That just goes to show what *you* know!" Marietta cried, throwing her used tissues to the floor and jumping up off the sofa. "You don't know squat about men, Savannah! And you could put everything you know about romance into one of Gran's sewing thimbles!"

She stomped across the living room to the foot of the stairs. "And what's more," she said, pausing with her hand on the rail, "you've got a lot of nerve to sit there in your easy chair like God Almighty and tell me what's going on in *my* life! You always have been bossy, Savannah Reid. Bossy and overbearing and critical."

With that, Marietta made her stage exit,

straight up the stairs.

Savannah heard the door to her guest bedroom slam. Then renewed wailing . . . possibly even the rending of garments and the gnashing of teeth.

As though sensing Savannah's less than cheerful mood, Diamante and Cleopatra leaped down from their window perch and jumped onto their mistress's lap. Cleo began to lick her cheek.

"Why are you so sweet?" Savannah asked the cats as they cuddled warm and soft against her chest. "Is it because you're spayed? Yes, I think that's it." She glanced toward the top of the stairs. "Maybe we could get Marietta spayed . . . do the world a favor."

Diamante meowed and rubbed her face against Savannah's shoulder.

"Yes, I think you're right," she said. "Lover Chat Boy wouldn't mind if we had her fixed. In fact, we could probably get him to pay for it."

But she didn't have long to luxuriate in the unconditional love of her pets, because less than a minute later the phone rang.

She grabbed it off the end table and glanced at the Caller I.D. It was Dirk. "Yeah, who is he?" she said.

"A scumbag who's been rousted for everything from peeping to dicky waving. He's got a thing for big girls."

"Was he actually stalking them like Tammy said?"

"According to the papers he was."

Savannah laughed and resisted the urge to jump out of her chair and cut a rug right on her living room carpet. There was nothing on earth like an exciting lead on a case to take the edge off a recent sibling spat.

"When are you going to go visit him?" she asked.

"I figure now's as good a time as any to go rattle his cage."

Glancing at her watch, Savannah said, "It's nearly ten. Prime time for peeping and stalking. He's probably not home."

"Then I'll wait for him to come back. Wanna go with me?"

She looked up at the top of the stairs and listened for a moment. Marietta's wailing had settled down to plain old sobbing, but she sounded like she could go for a couple more hours at least.

"I might as well go along," she said. "It's not like anybody around here is going to get any sleep before midnight."

"I'll pick you up in fifteen minutes. And Van . . ."

"Yeah?"

"Could you bring a thermos of coffee, just in case it's a late, late night?"

"Sure."

"And some more of that cake if you've got any left?"

Savannah looked at Marietta's plate, still

189

brimming with goodies.

She knew her sister pretty well. And she knew that in a little while, grief-stricken or not, Sweet-Tooth Mari would remember the cake and hotfoot it down the stairs for a late-night snack.

She thought of how disappointed she'd be if it was gone.

"You got it, buddy," she told Dirk with a nasty grin on her face that Granny Reid definitely would not have approved of. "I'll be waiting on the porch for you in fifteen minutes — with a thermos of coffee *and* a Tupperware container full of cake."

"I love ya!" he said with the usual enthusiasm that he showed when free food was being offered.

"Yeah, I know," she replied. Then, still grinning, she added, "Thanks."

Chapter
13

Sitting on the passenger side of Dirk's old Buick, watching him lick the chocolate off his fingers, she wondered exactly what it was that she considered "charming" about him.

"Don't you have some napkins or at least paper towels in that heap back there?" she said, nodding toward the landfill in his back seat and floorboard.

"What? And waste a bite of this heavenly stuff?" He closed his eyes in ecstasy as he polished off the last bit, and for a moment she thought he might actually lick the Tupperware clean. It wouldn't be the first time. "Van," he said, "you may have your limitations, but no matter what anybody says, you're a damned good cook."

"Gee, thanks . . . I guess."

Savannah looked out the dirty window at an even dirtier neighborhood — if, indeed, this end of town could even be called a neighborhood. The object of their surveillance, Mr. Ronald Tumblety, lived in a rusty blue van parked behind an abandoned auto repair shop in San Carmelita's "industrial" area.

Though on this particular block of Potter Street, it appeared there hadn't been any bona fide industry in the past decade or more. Even the graffiti on the cement block walls was outdated, including some faded references to the Vietnam war and Watergate.

When Savannah and Dirk had arrived two hours ago, it hadn't taken long for them to realize that Tumblety wasn't living in the auto shop — the address he had given to the Department of Motor Vehicles. And a quick once-over of the property told them that his official domicile was the van with two flat tires and a broken windshield that was parked in the rear.

Apparently "Tom Peeping" didn't pay much, and neither did stalking.

"How long are we going to wait for this guy?" she asked, getting more depressed by the moment.

Dirk set the empty container on the dash, sighed, and rubbed his belly contentedly. "Why? You in a rush to get back to your sister?"

Savannah glanced at her watch. "It's after midnight. She's probably composed herself by now."

"I can't believe she'd take some Internet romance that seriously."

"Oh, you'd be surprised what Marietta, Queen of Drama, takes seriously. Especially

192

when it comes to men."

Dirk snorted. "Not me, man. I stay a million miles away from broads like her. They're way more trouble than they're worth."

"Got a lot of Marietta types after you, do you, Stud Muffin?"

"Naw. I see 'em comin' and I head the other way."

Savannah pulled the collar of her jacket up around her neck and crossed her arms over her chest. "It's chilly in here."

"Ah, stop your complaining. Since when did you turn into a pansy on a stakeout?"

"Since I stopped getting paid for it."

"So . . . bill that Leah Freed gal for your time here tonight. You're working on the case, after all."

"That's true, but she thought our killer was going to be somebody in the modeling business, not some civilian nutjob."

"Who cares who it is, as long as you catch him, right?"

"I guess. I —" Savannah caught a glimpse of movement in the Buick's side mirror. "Hey, somebody's pulling into the driveway over there."

"An old El Camino?"

"Yep. And he's getting out and walking up behind us," she said. "He fits your DMV description."

"Big, fat, and ugly?"

"Watch your terminology there, would you?

193

Big, horizontally enhanced, and attractiveness-challenged."

"Yeah, that's better."

They watched as a large, slovenly fellow in baggy sweats sauntered up the sidewalk beside the auto shop.

"I do believe that's our boy," she said.

"Yeah, let's get him before he gets into that van. God knows what he's got in there in the way of weapons."

"Knives, guns . . . bubonic plague?"

"Exactly."

They got out of the Buick, being cautious not to slam the doors and alert their mark. They caught up with him before he was even halfway to his van.

"Ronald Tumblety?" Dirk asked in his most officious cop voice.

He spun around, fists clenched at his sides. "Who wants to know?"

"The police," Dirk replied. "Detective Coulter. I need to ask you a couple of questions."

"I got nothing to say to you people." Turning his back to them, Tumblety headed for his van at double time.

Dirk caught him in three steps, grabbing a handful of his sweatshirt. Savannah pulled his right hand behind his back and held it there.

"Now why be so rude?" she said. "We're really nice people when you get to know us."

Dirk twisted his left hand behind his back

and quickly cuffed him.

"Well," Savannah added as Dirk tightened the manacles, "*I'm* nice. This guy's not all that nice — especially to perverts who flash their pee-pees at little girls. He's been known to be downright cranky with them."

"I don't flash children!" Tumblety exclaimed. And even by the dim light of a nearby streetlamp, Savannah could see his pudgy face flush with indignation.

She couldn't help chuckling. It always amused and amazed her that even society's more distasteful citizens had their standards . . . and were frequently indignant when defending them.

"No, you're a real stand-up guy," Dirk said as he turned him around to face him. "We know all about you, Ronald. That's why we're here."

"Why?" he said. "Did some woman accuse me of calling her late at night? Did she say I was hanging around outside her house? 'Cause if she did, she's lying! I went for counseling, and I don't do that stuff anymore."

Dirk glanced over at Savannah, who simply twitched one eyebrow.

"She's lying, huh?" Dirk said. "I don't think so. I think you've been calling her and following her, and we both know that's not all you did."

Tumblety's eyes widened, and he began to shiver. His teeth even started to chatter.

Savannah tried not to get excited, but this

was a better reaction than she had frequently seen in cold-blooded killers, twenty seconds before they confessed.

"I didn't . . . didn't do nothin', I . . . I told you," he said.

Dirk shoved his face closer to the guy's until they were practically nose to nose. "Well, guess what . . . we know exactly what you did to her. We've got witnesses who saw you there."

"No, you don't! There wasn't nobody th— er, that is, didn't nobody see nothing, 'cause there wasn't nothing to see. I didn't do it."

"I think you'd better come along with me, Mr. Tumblety," Dirk said, pulling him down the driveway toward the Buick. "We'll go to the station house and you can tell me in great detail all about what you didn't do that nobody saw you do."

"Huh?"

Tumblety looked genuinely confused. And Savannah silently thanked the good God above that so many criminals were basically stupid.

It made her life . . . and Dirk's . . . so much simpler.

Fifteen minutes later, Savannah and Dirk arrived at the police station with Ronald Tumblety sitting in the back seat of Dirk's Buick amid the assorted Dirk junk.

They pulled him out of the car and took him through the rear entrance. Once inside the brightly lit hallway, Savannah got her first look at their latest suspect. She shivered, thinking how unsettling it would be to have a weirdo like that fixated on you.

Long ago, she had observed that wicked living often showed on a person's face. Sicknesses of the soul frequently manifested themselves in dull eyes, muddy skin, bloated features, sluggish mannerisms, and even a rank body smell. Good old Ron had them all.

But apparently, he didn't feel the same revulsion toward her that she did for him. The moment they stepped out of the darkness and into the light, he caught a good look at her and smiled from ear to ear, in spite of his circumstances.

"Wait a minute!" he cried. "You're not a cop!"

"I never said I was," she replied.

"I've seen you before! You're a famous model!"

Savannah cut a quick look at Dirk, who was instantly alert. "Oh?" she said. "You've seen my pictures?"

Tumblety looked mildly confused for a moment. Then he said, "Uh, yeah. Some swimsuit pictures, I think. You looked really nice."

"And when did you see my pictures?" Savannah asked, forcing a dimpled smile.

"Not too long ago."

"I'll bet it was pretty darned recently," she said, giving Dirk another pointed look. "Since I just started modeling."

Tumblety's dead eyes cut back and forth between Savannah and Dirk. "Huh? What do you mean?"

"What she means," Dirk said, taking him by the arm and propelling him toward the interview room down the hall, "is that you and I have got a lot of talking to do, amigo."

Savannah watched them disappear into the tiny room that was hardly more than a cubicle. Then she hurried into the adjoining room, which was as cozy as a telephone booth with all the ambience of a broom closet. But the room's big attraction was that she could see everything going on next door through a one-way mirror. And she could eavesdrop by listening to the speaker installed there for that purpose.

"The first thing you get to do," Dirk was saying as he pushed Tumblety down onto a chair and shoved him up to the table, "is explain to me where you were and what you did yesterday. And don't leave nothing out, 'cause remember, I've got witnesses."

Dirk uncuffed Tumblety's left hand and manacled his right one to a leg of his chair.

"Talk to me," Dirk said, "and don't lie either. If you lie, I'll know, and I'll get really pissed."

"Maybe I oughta have a lawyer." Tumblety flexed his wrist against the handcuff and winced at the pain it caused him.

Dirk shrugged. "You're not under arrest. We're just havin' a little chat here. But if you've done something you shouldn't have and need

198

yourself a lawyer . . ."

"I told you before, I ain't done nothing."

"That's not what the witnesses said."

"What witnesses? There wasn't nobody watching nothing I did yesterday."

Dirk glanced over at the mirror and grinned. "They saw you gawking at those models by the hot tub. You were told to stay away from those girls. What do you think those restraining orders are for . . . for you to wipe your nose on? Huh?"

"I wasn't watching those girls. And didn't nobody see me do it neither."

Dirk leaned over him, practically breathing down the neck of his sweatshirt. "That's not what a certain husband and wife say. They told me that they looked out the second-story window of their beach house, and they saw you acting suspiciously. They called 911, and we came out there, but I guess we just missed you."

"I wasn't peeping!" Tumblety said, trying to stand. Dirk pushed him back down onto the chair. "I was just walking by that fence on my way to the beach. Since when is it against the law to walk down to the beach?"

"Don't yank my chain, dude," Dirk said, pacing behind his chair. "You were watching those models from behind that fence, watching them and playing pocket pool."

Savannah stifled a laugh from the other side of the glass. Dirk was taking stabs in the dark with this guy, but Dirk had been on the job long enough to make accurate blind jabs.

Along with her delight in watching Dirk in action, she couldn't help feeling more than a little creepy to think that this guy had been spying on her and the others . . . not to mention pulling his taffy while he was peeping.

It made her feel like she needed delousing.

"So, you followed one of the girls from her house to the shoot. And after you watched the girls, you decided to follow one of them from that location, too. Didn't you?" Dirk said.

Savannah held her breath. It was another bluff on Dirk's part, but she could easily follow his train of thought. This jerk had been watching them at the photo shot, then Tesla Montoya — who had felt threatened enough by this guy to get a restraining order against him — had disappeared within the next few hours. Not a bad bit of logic.

And from the look on Ronald Dirty-Old-Man Tumblety's face, she thought Dirk might have hit the bull's-eye.

"I didn't have nothing to do with that!" Tumblety cried. "I wasn't the one who grabbed her! It wasn't me!"

Savannah was pretty sure her heart skipped a couple of beats, then started pounding somewhere up in her throat. She took a step closer and laid her hand on the glass.

She could tell by the set of Dirk's jaw that he was holding tight reins on his own emotions.

He walked around to the other side of the table to face Tumblety. Placing both of his big hands on the table, he leaned toward his suspect.

"Then let me tell you, buddy," he said, "if you didn't grab her, you'd better tell me right now who did, 'cause you're about five seconds away from getting arrested for kidnapping, assault, and murder."

"Murder?" Tumblety looked up at Dirk with shock and genuine horror in his eyes. "She's dead? He killed her?"

"He, who?"

"The guy who grabbed her. I don't know his name. I saw . . . I saw . . ."

He gulped and wiped the sweat off his forehead with his free hand. "I was following her, okay . . . like you said. But I didn't take her. She was driving down Johnson Avenue and stopped at a coffee shop there on the corner of Johnson and Charles Street. When she got out of that little black Mitsubishi of hers, a van pulled up next to her, and its side door opened."

"And . . . ?" Dirk said.

"And I saw somebody's arm reaching out of the side door. He grabbed her and pulled her inside. Then the door slammed closed, and the van took off."

"Where did he take her?"

Tumblety shrugged, not meeting Dirk's eyes. "I dunno."

"You know. You followed them, and you know."

"Okay, I followed the van for a little ways. It went down Johnson to the freeway. Traffic was heavy and I lost them on the 101."

"Going which direction?"

"North."

"How far north did you follow them?"

"Just a mile or two. I lost them about even with the Hinze Boulevard exit."

Dirk let out a long breath, as though he, too, had been holding it. "And did you happen to get the license number of this van?"

"Huh? Naw. Didn't think of that."

Dirk muttered something, then said, "Okay. How about a description?"

"I told you, I didn't see the guy."

"I know. I mean the van. What color was it?"

"Oh. It was a an old white panel body with a rack on top."

Savannah felt her bubble deflate a little. White vans were a dime a dozen. And of course, that was assuming that Ronald Tumblety wasn't lying through his scraggly teeth. That he hadn't kidnapped poor Tesla himself.

His story didn't exactly wash, considering the trashed house and the blood on her sofa, which suggested that she had met with foul play inside her own home — not at a coffee shop on Johnson Avenue.

And apparently, the same thing had occurred to Dirk, because he was saying to his unhappy guest, "I'll tell you what, my friend. You stay here and make yourself at home for the night, while I check out your story. And you better be telling me the truth, man, or you're gonna find out what it's like to be on my bad side."

"The night? The night? You're gonna put me in jail?"

"It's more like a holding cell. Consider it a room upgrade from that van of yours."

Five minutes later, Dirk and Savannah met in the parking lot behind the station.

"Got him all tucked in snug as a bug?" she asked him as she laced her arm through his and they walked to the Buick together.

"More like a cockroach in a garbage can."

"So . . . are we off to the coffee shop on Johnson?"

"You betcha. And if there ain't a black Mitsubishi sittin' empty in that parking lot, this guy and me are gonna go a couple o' rounds."

"Yeah, yeah . . . I love it when you talk tough. But when it comes right down to it, how many perp asses do you reckon you've actually whupped?"

He gave her a sideways look and a grin. "Not enough, darlin'," he said, doing a pretty fair impression of her Southern accent. "Not even *near* enough."

Chapter
14

The intersection of Johnson Avenue and Charles Street had once been home to a couple of service stations, an empty, weed-choked lot, and a dilapidated shack that sported a sign advertising tarot and palm readings by Madame Wanda.

But in the past three years, the area had become gentrified, and the four corners were now occupied by a swimsuit boutique, an art gallery, a bookstore, and the ubiquitous coffee shop, all nicely landscaped with palm trees and flower boxes overflowing with bright-faced marigolds.

Each shop had a mini-parking lot in front of it, which provided a dozen spots per establishment. And during business hours, those spots were usually full of townsfolk, not to mention scores of Los Angeles tourists, seeking respite from the city heat and smog at the coast beaches.

But at two in the morning, the intersection was dark, deserted and silent. And the moment that Savannah and Dirk rounded the corner, they instantly spotted the black Mitsubishi, sitting alone in one of the spaces in front of the coffee shop.

"Tarnation," Savannah said.

"Yeah, no kidding," Dirk replied as he pulled into the lot and parked a few spaces away from the empty car. "I was hoping his story was a load of b.s., and I could hold him for something more than just violating an order of protection."

"Let's check this out and maybe we'll find something good."

"Naw, we're not gonna find squat. You wait and see."

"Well, aren't we just a beam of sunshine and light."

"What?"

"Nothing."

As they got out of the Buick and walked toward the Mitsubishi, Dirk reached into his jacket pocket and pulled out another pair of latex gloves. As Savannah watched him slip them on, it occurred to her that the good old days, when you could just push evidence around with a pencil or pick up it by holding one corner, were gone forever. Nowadays, the focus of defense lawyers was on the cops and whether they had "contaminated" evidence by mishandling it, breathing on it, or even being in its vicinity. Unlike the defendants, investigating officers were considered grossly incompetent until proven not guilty.

A perpetrator could murder someone in front of fifty witnesses, while a TV camera crew filmed the whole thing, and even if the killer confessed, the defense attorney would want to know if the cops had used gloves when processing the scene.

Savannah loved defense attorneys — even more than she loved root canals and Pap smears.

When she and Dirk reached the car, the first thing they noticed was that the driver's door was ajar.

Dirk squatted beside the door and studied the handle. "Looks like she left in a hurry."

"Just like ol' Tumblety Numb-Nuts said," Savannah replied.

"Yeah, yeah. He's probably the one who grabbed her, no matter what he said. Dollars to doughnuts it was his rotten old van she got pulled into, not some mysterious white one."

"That old blue van . . . the one with the two flat tires . . . the one with three-foot-high weeds growing around it . . . weeds that haven't been disturbed for —"

"Eh . . . don't interrupt me when I'm talkin'."

"Don't confuse me with the facts, is more like it."

"Whatever."

"Give me some of those gloves of yours. I'm all out," she told him as she peered through the windows of the car, trying to get a better look

206

at a bundle lying on the back seat.

He shoved a pair into her hand with a grunt and mumbled something that sounded like, "Get . . . own friggin' . . . gloves. . . ."

"Oh, please. Like you pay for these yourself. You're just being pissy because you thought you had your case solved and now —"

"Now nothing! It could still be him."

"Could be. It could have also gone down exactly like he said."

Savannah tried the handle on the rear passenger door. "Whoever got her, she wasn't exactly expecting to get nabbed. She was driving around with her doors unlocked. Not a good idea in this day and age, whether you've got a stalker or not."

"Eh, some women just don't have any —"

"Watch it, boy. Don't aggravate me."

He opened the rear door on his side and together they examined the items that lay on the back seat and the floorboard.

"What's that?" he asked as she opened a large tote and looked inside.

"It's her model's kit," Savannah said. "She was carrying it at the shoot."

"You mean like a tool kit?"

"Pretty much the same, except with mascara instead of a flathead screwdriver." She rifled through the contents. "Her address book is in here," she said, "and her cell phone."

"Here's her pocketbook," Dirk said, lifting a leather bag from the floorboard behind the driver's seat. "If that ain't a sign of kidnapping, nothing is."

"That's for sure. Women won't leave a burning plane without their purses." Savannah looked over the seat into the front of the car. "No signs of violence, though," she added.

"Yeah, famous last words. Isn't that what you said back at her apartment just before you found the blood on the sofa?"

"And speaking of . . . what did Dr. Liu say about the blood? Is it hers?"

"It's A-negative. That's as far as she got. We put a call in to that Dr. Pappas guy to see what her type is. If his office doesn't get back to us by noon, I'm gonna go over there and rattle that nurse's cage."

Savannah recalled the receptionist's less-than-warm-and-fuzzy demeanor and grinned. The thought of anybody rattling *her* cage — or any other part of her for that matter — struck Savannah as an entertaining prospect.

"If you have to do that, take me with you," she told him. "I want to watch."

Dirk stepped back from the car and closed the door. "I'll get the CSU over here to process this thing," he said. "Maybe they can find something else."

"Although," Savannah added, "if Tumblety's telling the truth and the guy just grabbed her and yanked her into his van, there probably won't be any perpetrator prints."

"That's a big if, if you ask me. It's probably

got his mitt prints all over it and who knows what else."

Savannah closed her door and walked around the back of the car to stand beside him. "You really want it to be Tumblety, don't you?"

"Sure I do. I've never liked dicky-wavers; you know that. Besides, if it's him, I've got him and he won't be hurting anybody else. Not to mention that I can sew this case up. Don't you hope it's him?"

"He's pretty mangy, all right. Society would probably be better off without his. . . ."

Her words faded as she knelt beside the driver's side of the car and squinted at something just behind the front tire. "Have you got your penlight with you?" she asked him.

He handed her the miniature flashlight, and she shined the beam at the object that had caught her eye. She started to reach for it, then withdrew her hand.

"What is it?" he asked.

"A set of keys," she replied. "We'd better leave them there. The CSU will want to mark the spot and take a picture."

"She probably dropped them when Tumblety grabbed her," Dirk said as he took the flashlight from her and looked at the keys himself.

"Or when the guy *that Tumblety saw* grabbed her."

As they left the car and walked back to Dirk's Buick, he used his cell phone to call the Crime Scene Unit. Savannah tuned him out as he gave them the specifics, her mind returning to Tesla Montoya's apartment.

When he was finished with the call, he gave her a curious, searching look. "What is it?" he asked. "What're you thinking?"

"I'm just wondering . . . if Tesla was taken from this parking lot . . . why was her place such a mess and why was there blood on the couch?"

Dirk shrugged. "I dunno. Unless they grabbed her here, then took her home."

"Exactly what I was thinking. He snatched her here, then took her back to her place. Why?"

They stared at each other for a long moment. Finally Dirk said, "When we figure that out, maybe we'll know what happened to her."

Savannah thought of the beautiful model with her large, childlike eyes and sad, sweet smile. She thought of Cait Connor's lifeless body on the bathroom floor, and Kameeka Wills lying on the side of the road. "I'm not sure I even *want* to know what's happened to Tesla," she said.

Dirk gave a heavy sigh. "I hear you."

By the time Savannah finally returned home, it was past three in the morning. She had long passed the state of just being tired and was — as Granny Reid would say — "running on raw nerves."

She crept into the hallway and, being careful

not to wake her sister upstairs, quietly put away her purse and gun. But when she glanced toward the living room, she saw a sickly green light glowing — the computer screen again.

Not foolish enough to make the same mistake twice in twenty-four hours, she decided to ignore the call of sisterly duty and sneak upstairs without asking Marietta the fatal question: "How are you?"

But she had only taken two steps up the stairs when she heard a plaintive, "Is that you, Savannah?"

The question was followed by a loud sniff that could only mean one thing — Marietta was still suffering from romantic woes.

Oh, goody, she thought as she walked back down the stairs and into the living room.

"So, you're at it again," she said, trying to keep her tone light but concerned, cheerful but compassionate, involved but objective. *What a drag.*

Sitting at the computer, no lights on in the room other than that emitted by the screen, Marietta was a sorry sight. Her eyes were swollen into tight, puffy slits, her nose bright red, and she was shivering slightly in her black lace nightgown.

"You wouldn't believe what he's saying about me in the chat room," she said, pointing to the screen. "He's turning all my roomies against me, telling lies about what happened between us last night."

Savannah walked over to the sofa and picked up a soft chenille afghan that Gran had knitted for her last winter. Draping it around her sister's shoulders, she gave her a few pats on the back.

"Go to bed, Mari," she said. "It's the middle of the night, and you've had a full last couple of days."

"Today's been the worst day of my life."

Without even trying, Savannah could remember dozens of Marietta's previous "worst days." But she decided it wasn't the time to mention that Marietta had at least one of the worst days of her life every six months or so.

"You'll feel better tomorrow, when you're rested. I'll make you a big breakfast in the morning with grits and biscuits."

"Real biscuits? Not those canned things?"

"Real ones with butter and peach preserves."

A smile replaced the forlorn look on Marietta's face, and Savannah wondered, as she had many times, at the power of good food to lift the sagging spirits of the Reid family females.

"You go upstairs, crawl into that soft feather bed of mine, and get a good, long night's sleep. Tomorrow morning, with a mug of my strong, chicory-flavored coffee in your hand, you'll be a new woman."

Marietta nodded woodenly, typed a few more words into the computer, then closed it down.

As she rose from the chair and made her way toward the foot of the stairs, she said, "You know, Savannah . . . I've learned something from this horrible experience, this degradation and humiliation."

Savannah didn't really want to know, but the laws of Southern gentility demanded that she ask. "What have you learned, Mari?"

"Men suck. Romance sucks."

Savannah could see it now: a greeting card embellished with roses, lilacs, and lace . . . with those golden words embossed across the front.

"Don't you think so, too, Savannah?" Marietta said, her foot on the first step, her eyes haunted.

"Well, I can see why you'd say that, but . . ."

"No, really. You know I'm right. There's no such thing as finding your One True Love. Don't you agree?"

Savannah shrugged. "Some men suck, Marietta. But not all — not by a long shot. A lot of them are really good people at heart. But it's true that romance hurts when it ends . . . or never really gets going in the first place."

"And there's no such thing as a soul mate."

Passing her arm around Marietta's waist, she coaxed her up the stairs. "I'm not sure about that soul mate stuff. I think if a person works hard to be a good mate — and their partner does the same — sometimes they can touch on a really deep, spiritual level. Probably not every hour of every day, but . . ."

"I *want* it every minute of every hour of every day. I want to be everything to my man." She sniffed and wiped her eyes with the back of her hand. "I want to be his whole world."

"I know you do, Marietta. But men have lives, too, you know. They have other things they like to do besides gaze into your eyes and tell you how wonderful you are. Sometimes they might want to do a guy thing that doesn't involve you — like watch sports on TV, or putter in the garage, or take a nap. You might have to settle for a deep, soulful connection once a week, say on a Friday night . . . after dinner and before sex . . . for five or ten minutes. From what I hear, that's about as good as it gets."

Half an hour later, Savannah lay in bed, staring up at the dark ceiling, listening to her sister snoring in the next room. Thankfully, even drama queens had to take a break once in a while and rest up for the next day's calamities.

On the other hand, self-employed private detectives didn't always have that luxury.

No doubt about it, she would be as grouchy as Dirk tomorrow as a result of this sleep deprivation. But every time she closed her eyes, she saw a white van pulling next to a black Mitsubishi, an arm reaching out, and Tesla Montoya being yanked inside.

And then . . .

It was the "and then" part that was keeping Savannah awake.

What did he . . . or maybe even she . . . do to Tesla then? Where did he take her and why?

Would they find her body somewhere, like the other two? Or could she still be alive?

Savannah would have felt far more hopeful if it hadn't been for that large blood spot on the sofa. Blood at a crime scene never boded well for a missing person.

But if the blood was Tesla's, and she had been attacked in her apartment, why did the assault happen there, rather than inside the van or at another location?

Why would her kidnapper take her home?

If his intention was to hurt or kill her, why did that have to happen at the apartment, rather than someplace less dangerous for the kidnapper?

Why not just take her up into the hills, where any evidence — like blood on a sofa — would be less obvious to investigators?

She lay there, studying the pattern on the ceiling cast by the streetlamp shining through her lace curtains, her mind racing on an endless loop.

It wasn't until a quarter to five that she figured it out.

She reached for the phone on her nightstand and pushed the "memory" button to dial Dirk.

When he answered, he sounded as wide awake as she was. "Yeah?"

One of the nice things about Dirk was that you didn't have to waste time with niceties like "hello" or "how are you?"

"After he grabbed her," she said, "he took her back to the apartment."

"Do you think? Duh."

"Eh, bite me." She sat up in bed and turned on her reading lamp. "And the reason he took her there was . . . ?"

"I'm workin' on that."

"To get something. She had something at the apartment that he wanted badly enough to risk being seen by somebody when he took her there."

"Something, like what?"

"Maybe something that would incriminate him in killing Caitlin and Kameeka?"

Dirk thought that one over. "Maybe. Or maybe this theory of yours is just plain stupid. You know how you get when you're thinking about a case in the middle of the night like this."

She had to admit that he had a point there. The results of these late-night mental exercises of hers ranged from truly brilliant to dumber-than-dirt dumb. And she never really knew which they were until she could re-examine them in the morning light.

"Go to sleep, Van," he said, his deep voice tinged with a sweetness that might have fulfilled even Marietta's requirements for intimacy. "Let it go for tonight. We'll work on it again tomorrow."

"It's already tomorrow."

"Then we'll tackle it after noon. Sleep tight, honey."

"You, too."

Click.

So . . . Dirk wasn't one for flowery hellos or good-byes. But once in a while, they had a soulful connection.

A once-in-a-while soul mate . . . whose boxers you didn't have to launder. . . .

As Savannah drifted off to sleep, she realized that, for her, it was enough.

Chapter
15

"Boy, I thought you were never going to get up!" was the greeting Savannah received when she trudged downstairs a few minutes before noon.

Marietta was sitting on the sofa, a cup of coffee in her hand, the telephone in the other. She didn't appear to actually be talking on it, so Savannah figured she must be waiting for a call. Still.

"Where's that great breakfast that you promised me last night?" Marietta continued. "My stomach thinks my throat's cut."

"Don't start with me, Marietta," she growled as she walked past her and into the kitchen. "Not before I've had at least one cup of coffee."

"No, really!" Marietta hopped up from the sofa and followed her. "I'm starving here, and it's almost lunchtime!"

"Well, did it occur to you to maybe make something for yourself?"

"I don't cook."

"I know. But even a bowl of cereal would

have taken the edge off that hunger. You do pour milk, don't you?"

Marietta's lower lip protruded. "Corn flakes are a bit of a letdown when you've got your taste buds set for biscuits and peach preserves."

"Mari, go back into the living room and give me a chance to work up a pulse and some brain-wave activity. Okay?" She glanced down at the phone in her hand. "Why don't you call your boys and see how they're doing? They probably miss their mom."

Marietta gave her a blank look, as though she were speaking in a foreign tongue. "What? They're teenagers. They miss their momma like they'd miss a big ol' briar on the seat of their breeches. Lord knows what kind of trouble they've gotten themselves into."

"All the more reason to check on them, don't you reckon?"

Marietta shrugged. "Yeah, I guess so. You do have call waiting, don't you? I mean, if he was to call, it would beep or something and . . ."

"It'll beep. And you can look on the Caller I.D. and see if it's him."

"Good."

As Savannah set about making a full lumber-jack breakfast for her sister, she tried not to think about her nephews, Steve and Paulie, whom Marietta had left to fend for themselves back in Georgia. With Granny Reid half a mile away, not to mention all the aunts and uncles in town, they were sure to be well cared for.

But this wasn't the first time that Marietta had demonstrated her lack of concern about them. When it came to a tug-of-war between Marietta's boys and the men in her life, the boys always ended up on their faces in the middle, having lost again.

As she rolled and cut the biscuits, she could hear Marietta's two-minute call to Georgia, and the probing questions she asked. "How's the weather? You aren't making a mess outta the house, are you?" And the advice: "Put a Band-Aid on it, for pete's sake. I don't know. Ask Gran when you drop off your laundry. Well, take it over there! I don't want to come home to a heap of dirty clothes!"

A few minutes of silence in the living room told Savannah that the call was over, and she expected Marietta to come in and complain that the food wasn't on the table yet.

But then she heard a new conversation begin: "Hello. I need to speak to a Mr. Bill Donaldson. He works there in your accounting department, right? My name? Marietta Jane Reid. Of course it's important. It's extremely important. Yes, I can hold . . . for a little while."

Savannah paused, the box of grits in her hand. Maybe she could slip just a little arsenic in there. Surely she had some arsenic somewhere in her spice cabinet.

"What do you mean, he's away from his desk? Is he really, or did he just tell you to tell me that?"

How much do you suppose it would take? Savannah asked herself. *A teaspoon, a heaping tablespoon?*

"Well, I don't believe you, not for one minute. I think he's sitting right there with his teeth in his mouth, probably listening to this call on some extension line. I know how these things work."

Hmmm, not a smidgen of arsenic in the cupboard when you need it. I've got lots of oregano. I wonder . . . is oregano toxic in large doses? How much oregano would it take to kill a stupid sister and would she notice it in the grits?

"Well, let me tell you a thing or two about that man you work with. You might think you know him, but the truth is, he ain't fit to spit and what's more . . ."

As Savannah was walking into the Plaza Del Oro Tower on her way up to Leah Freed's suite of offices, Dirk called her on her cell phone.

"I'm just leaving Montoya's apartment," he told her.

"Anything?"

"Nothing new. And if the kidnapper was looking for something — like in your latest middle-of-the-night theory — he must have found it, 'cause I couldn't find anything worth kidnapping or killing anybody over."

"I could have been wrong."

"You? Never."

She chuckled. "But say it like you mean it."

221

"Never. What are *you* up to?"

"The tenth floor in a minute or two," she said. "I'm over here in the Plaza Del Oro seeing Leah Freed. She called while I was eating breakfast and demanded to know what I had for her."

"Don't tell her anything good."

"She's paying me. Remember?"

"Just remember that she could be mixed up in this, too."

"Dirk. . . . Not being a complete moron, I won't jeopardize your case in the course of making a living for myself."

"Okay, okay. Do you wanna go with me over to that Dr. Pappas's office in a little while? Looks like I'm gonna have to lean on them to get Montoya's blood type."

"You're just afraid of that nurse, and you want backup."

"So? You want to go along or not?"

"Sure. I'll meet you over there in his parking lot in a hour."

By the time she had finished the conversation with him, she was standing in the hallway outside Leah's offices.

She dreaded this meeting, hated the thought of telling Leah Freed that she wasn't cut out to be the next shooting star on the plus-fashion horizon. If Leah wanted her to continue to investigate, fine, but this ridiculous subterfuge had to end.

Steeling herself, she entered the offices and

was quickly directed to a small room in the rear of the suite.

Leah Freed sat in front of a backlit table, peering at some photo slides with a strange-looking gadget that looked to Savannah like a cross between a magnifying glass and a jeweler's loupe.

When Savannah walked in, Leah glanced up, sighed, and said, "I hate to tell you this, Savannah, but as pretty as you are, you're not the least bit photogenic."

Okay, Savannah thought, *so much for having to break the awful news to Leah.*

"I had a difficult time at the shoot, it's true," she said.

"I can see that for myself." She pointed to the slides. "No wonder Matt was upset with me for sending you."

Savannah felt the ruff on her back bristling. "If you'll recall, when you suggested I go undercover as a model, I expressed my doubt that I could pull it off."

"And I should have listened to you."

She pushed back away from the table and stood, giving Savannah a full view of her teal pantsuit that was trimmed in bright yellow piping. Her high heels matched — eye-stabbing bright blue with yellow heels.

For one satisfying moment Savannah allowed a couple of catty thoughts to float through her head: *How many thrifts shops do you have to case to find an outfit like that? Just how far did you*

223

have to chase that bag lady to get that garb off of her? Wanna talk photogenic? Let's take some shots and see if you look like a giant peacock.

Then she remembered that, at least for the moment, Leah Freed was her employer, and she had bills to pay.

Leah walked over to a more comfortable chair in the opposite corner and sat down. Savannah waited for an invitation to sit in the chair next to hers, but Leah didn't bother.

Deciding not to be kept standing just because Leah Freed had apparently been raised among wolves, Savannah helped herself to the seat.

"Speaking of Matt Slater," Savannah said, "do tell me what you know about him and his relationships with his models."

A fleeting look crossed Leah's face, but it was long enough for Savannah to note it . . . and interpret it. Leah was jealous. Whether she was jealous because she had been one of Matt's part-time hobbies, too, or because she wanted to be, Savannah couldn't tell.

"Matt has a lot of relationships," Leah said coolly. "Some of them have been with models."

"Is he doing the grizzly bear hump with Desiree at the moment?"

"Probably."

Savannah couldn't help noticing that Leah's tone and mood seemed to be plummeting like a thermometer in a blizzard. She had gone from chilly to frosty in two questions. Might as well try for solid ice.

"And how about the other girls?"

Leah crossed her arms over her the front of her double-breasted suit. "I don't think he'd gotten very far with Kameeka or Tesla."

"I see."

Savannah flashed back on Kevin Connor's glowing account of his happy marriage and wondered . . .

"Did Cait's husband know?"

"About Cait and Matt? I suppose he did. He knew about most of the others."

"The others?" Savannah could see her sterling image of the star model tarnishing right in front of her eyes.

"Lots of others," Leah said with the nasty smile of a gossip who thoroughly enjoyed dishing the dirt. "Caitlin never did anything halfway. She binged on everything . . . not just food."

"And did Kevin seem to mind — the others, that is?"

"I'm sure he did. Who wouldn't mind? But he was crazy in love with Cait. He overlooked a lot of things where she was concerned. We all did."

Savannah searched Leah's face for signs of hate, anger, any motive for murder. But the woman was an agent; she played poker for a living, and she was good.

"Why?" Savannah asked. "Why did y'all put up with her if she was all that bad?"

Leah's expression softened so much and so quickly that Savannah was taken aback. "Because we loved her. And if you'd known her, you would have, too. Cait was the funniest, most charming, intelligent, and generous person I ever knew. She could make you feel so very special about yourself and —"

Her voice broke. She jumped up from her chair and ran to get some tissues out of a box on the table.

With her back to Savannah, she quietly sobbed, the tissues over her face.

But just as Savannah was about to rise and see if perhaps she could comfort her, Leah blew her nose hard, turned around, and returned to her seat.

"Caitlin was difficult in some ways," Leah continued, "but she was worth it. Let's change the subject."

"Okay. Do you know about a guy named Ronald Tumblety?"

"That sounds familiar, but I can't place him. Who is he?"

"A stalker who was interested in —"

"Oh, yes. *That* creep. He kept showing up at our shoots, bothering the girls."

"How did he know the locations?"

"From what I understand, he found out where Cait lived. He'd seen a picture of her beach house on the Internet, and he figured it out. Then he started hanging around outside her house, following her to the shoots. Then he

226

followed Kameeka home, and Tesla." Leah's eyes widened. "Why? Do you think he might have something to do with this?"

"We're investigating him. It's too early to tell."

Leah shook her head. "Wouldn't that be awful, if it was a stalker?"

"Maybe better that than someone close to them."

"True."

"Tell me about Jerrod Beekman."

"Like I told you before, Jerrod is a complete pain. He also owns one of the most successful ad agencies in L.A. At least, he does now. If this campaign falls on its face — which it just might, considering what's happened to the girls — his company may fold."

"That bad?"

"Oh, yes. Wentworth Industries is his largest client. And Charles Wentworth is furious about what's happened. If Jerrod doesn't pull this out of the fire . . ."

"Charles Wentworth." Savannah searched her mental files. "Let's see . . . elderly cereal tycoon, lives in Mystic Canyon?"

"That was Charles Wentworth II. This is his son, Number Three. Doesn't have a fraction of his father's business savvy, morals, or work ethic. Wentworth Industries has hit the skids, and it's just a matter of time until it goes over the cliff."

Savannah tucked that particular tidbit into

her "to be considered later indepth" file. "So, Number Three must be pretty upset that his campaign is in jeopardy," she said. "It sounds like his new cereal, this Slenda stuff, was a pretty important gamble. And with the campaign based on those two girls and both of them murdered . . ."

"Oh, Charles was upset *before* the girls died. He was already furious because they hadn't lost the required weight. He was leaning on Jerrod, who was pressuring me. Why do you think I was calling Cait every day, checking on how she was doing? I don't like coercing my girls like that. Especially Cait. I was afraid her eating disorder might kick in again under that kind of stress. And I was right."

Again, her eyes filled with tears, and she dabbed at her nose with the tissues. "Are we about done here?" she asked. "I think I've enjoyed this conversation about as much as I can stand for one day."

Savannah resisted the urge to remind her that she had requested the interview. For the first time since meeting her, Savannah actually felt a bit of warmth toward the woman. Anyone who loved a friend — warts and all — the way Leah had obviously cared about Caitlin, had to have a spark of good in her somewhere.

"Sure," she told her. "No problem." She glanced at her watch. "Actually, I have to meet someone soon. I'll write up a report for you tonight. I can drop it off with your receptionist tomorrow if you —"

"Don't bother. I don't want you wasting time writing reports." Leah stood, walked to the door, and opened it wide. "I want you to catch the bastard who killed my girls, and I want you to find Tesla . . . hopefully alive and healthy."

"Believe me," Savannah told her, "that's what I want, too."

In the rear of Dr. Pappas's parking lot, Savannah sat in her Mustang, waiting for Dirk, listening to an old tape of the Eagles. Glenn Fry still did it for her after all these years.

Someday she'd have to break down and have a CD player installed, but the paint job had been her big splurge of the decade. Besides, by the time she could afford a new CD player, they would be obsolete and there would be some other newfangled gadget that she couldn't afford either.

She was singing along to "Lyin' Eyes" when she saw a black Mercedes limo pull into the parking lot. Having lived for years in Southern California, the sight of a limousine had ceased to cause an elevation in her heart rate long ago. Every Billy Bob and his cousin's uncle's dog had one. Although, even with her jaded eye, she had to admit that this one was a beauty.

Long, sleek, and polished like an ebony grand piano, the automobile looked out of place in the dusty alley parking lot. She would have been happy to ride in such a vehicle to her own funeral, let alone to a simple doctor's visit.

The limo stopped directly behind the back door of the clinic and a driver dressed in formal livery got out. He went inside and only a few moments later returned with a gray-haired man wearing a white smock and navy slacks. He didn't have a stethoscope hanging around his neck, but he didn't need one for Savannah to know he was a doctor. He had way too much self-important swagger for a nurse or physician's assistant.

When the driver opened the rear door of the limo and directed the doctor inside, Savannah sat up to attention and turned off her tape player.

"Must be nice," she said, "having a house call in the back of your Mercedes."

The windows were darkly tinted, and she couldn't see anything going on inside, but there was something about the worried look on the doctor's face just before he entered the car that caught her attention.

She slid lower in the seat until she could just peek over the dash. Trouble — like burned coffee — had a distinctive odor to it, and she could swear that she could smell some sort of trouble brewing inside that limousine, whether she could see through the windows or not.

She waited, keeping an eye on her watch. Three minutes. Five. Seven minutes.

Seven minutes worth of any doctor's time was a precious commodity. She couldn't help wondering who rated so much personal attention — limo or no limo.

Eight minutes. Then she saw the door open and the doctor get out. This time his walk and general body language lacked its previous confidence. His head down, he trudged back to the office as though he were walking through wet cement.

No sooner had he gone back inside the building than the limo pulled away. As it left the lot, Savannah caught a good look at the rear of the car, and she quickly jotted down the license plate. It probably wouldn't amount to a hill of beans, as Gran would say, but she'd still have Dirk run the number.

As she was tucking her notebook back into her purse, he arrived. Seeing her at the rear of the lot, he drove back to her and parked beside the Mustang.

"Sorry I'm late," he said as they got out of their cars and started walking across the lot. "I decided to go by the hospital where Cait Connor's husband works and talk to him again."

"Oh, yeah? Did he tell you that his wife had been fooling around with that photographer, Matt Slater?" Savannah couldn't help grinning. She loved trumping Dirk, telling Mr. Know-It-All something he didn't know.

"No," he said. "He didn't mention it."

"I thought so."

"One of his fellow nurses told me. Said it

wasn't the first time the wife had played around either."

"Oh." She cleared her throat. "Well, what did Kevin Connor have to say?"

"He's hot to trot to sue Wentworth Industries and this Dr. Pappas, too."

They paused outside the clinic's door and lowered their voices. "Why Pappas?" she asked.

"He was the physician in charge of overseeing the models' weight loss."

"Both Caitlin and Kameeka?"

"And Tesla and Desiree. He says that his wife was threatening to sue the good doctor here a couple of weeks before she died . . . said the doc was jeopardizing her health by expecting her to lose so much so fast."

"Sounds like a possible motive to me."

"Yep, me too."

When they went inside, they found the waiting room packed again. Apparently Dr. Pappas's weight-loss practice was thriving, whether Cait Connor had approved of his methods or not.

This time, as they approached the receptionist's window, the woman on the other side of the glass didn't even bother to feign friendliness. She rose from her desk, slid the window aside, and said, "I told you not to come over here, Detective Coulter. You're wasting your time and ours."

Dirk gave her a teeth-baring smile. "I don't mind if you don't."

"I mind." She slid the window closed and turned her back on them as she began to sort files on a counter behind the desk.

Dirk's face went from pink to purple in under three seconds, and Savannah decided to avert tragedy if she could. Stepping up to the window, she moved the pane aside and stuck her head through the opening. "Excuse me," she said. "But Detective Coulter really needs that information. It's critical to his case and —"

"Get a warrant," she snapped without even turning around. "And until you've got a warrant, get out."

This time it was Savannah's face that flushed. She briefly considered jumping through the window and wringing Nurse Ratched's neck, but she decided to forego violence in favor of blackmail.

"Maybe you should scoot back there and tell Dr. Pappas that two of his patients are dead, one is missing, and at the moment, he's a prime suspect for multiple murder."

The receptionist whirled around, her mouth hanging open. A strange hush had come over the crowded waiting room. The only sound was that of a low chuckle coming from Dirk's direction.

"And while you're at it, ask the doctor if he usually treats his patients in limousines in the alley."

The receptionist disappeared so quickly that Savannah half expected to see a puff of pink smoke in her wake.

Dirk stepped up behind her. "What was that bit about the limousine?" he asked.

She turned around and saw a roomful of people staring at them, their ears practically out on stems.

"I'll tell you later," she said. "Just a hunch I had. If he's out here in less than ten seconds, I was right."

It was eight seconds before the receptionist appeared again. "The doctor will see you now in his office."

Savannah gave her a bright smile . . . the one she saved for people she didn't particularly like. "Thank you," she said sweetly. "I thought he might."

Chapter
16

Savannah wasn't at all surprised, when she and Dirk entered the doctor's office, to see that Dr. Pappas was, indeed, the fellow she had seen getting into the Mercedes limousine outside. Nor was she shocked that he wasn't particularly happy to see them.

Not only did he neglect to offer them a seat, but he didn't even speak to them. He just sat behind his desk and glowered at them from beneath bushy white eyebrows.

Up close, Dr. Pappas was even less attractive than he had appeared from across the parking lot. Looking more like a caricature of a mad scientist than a physician, with his tousled silver hair and carelessly trimmed white beard, Savannah wondered what it was about this man that inspired a waiting room full of patients.

"Dr. Pappas," Dirk said, extending his hand across the desk. "Thank you for seeing me. I'm Detective Coulter, and this is my associate, Savannah Reid."

"I know who you are," he said, tight-lipped.

"Then you probably know what I want," Dirk

said, dropping the pseudo-friendliness. "I'm afraid that one of your patients, Tesla Montoya, has been the victim of foul play . . . like Cait Connor and Kameeka Wills . . . also patients of yours."

The doctor said nothing as he leaned back in his chair and crossed his arms over the front of his white smock.

"I need to know her blood type," Dirk continued. "If you have that information in her medical files, it would help me a lot."

"I don't release personal information on my patients," he replied evenly. "No responsible physician would."

"I'm not asking you for anything all that personal," Dirk said. "I don't want to know how much she weighed or if she had AIDS, for pete's sake."

No response.

"We found a pool of blood in Tesla Montoya's apartment," Dirk added, obviously growing more impatient by the moment. "She's missing, and we have reason to think she's been kidnapped. Would you or one of your nurses just look in her file and tell me her blood type? If you'll do that I'll leave you alone."

Pappas stared at Dirk for several long, tense seconds; then he reached for a manila folder in a stack of similar ones on his desk and flipped it open. He thumbed through the papers inside, reading.

Finally, he closed the folder and tossed it

back on the heap. "She was A-negative," he said, crossing his arms again. "Is that all?"

"That's all. Thank you."

Savannah was never happier to be outside in the fresh air and sunshine than when they exited the clinic. Once in the parking lot, she paused and took a deep breath.

"I hear ya," Dirk said. "That guy smells . . . and I not talkin' about his onion breath either."

"Let's keep an eye peeled on him."

"Man, I'm running out of eyes here. I had to cut Tumblety loose, and I've got Jake McMurtry tailing him. Then there's Cait's husband and that agent gal and those other models and the photographer and that ad agency dude. Cheez. Usually you can't find a suspect in a case, and now we're drowning in them."

Savannah reached into her purse, pulled out her notebook, and flipped it open to the page where she had jotted down the limo's plate number. "Well, your life's about to take a turn for the worse," she told him, "because I have a sneaking suspicion that when you run this plate, you're going to find out that it belongs to a guy named Charles Wentworth III."

"The cereal tycoon?"

"None other."

Dirk winced as he wrote the number in his own notebook. "I hate dealing with those dudes with the numbers after their names."

Savannah laughed. "Oh, yeah? You oughta

rub noses with the guys down South like Bubba Junior and Little Billy Ray. There's just something about having to live up to the 'seniors' or numbers one, two, or three that makes a fella defensive."

Dirk glanced back at the clinic door. "Or having an M.D. after your name and something to hide."

Savannah was in the grocery store, picking up the makings of a fine pork chop and cornbread dressing dinner, when her cell phone rang. Stopping in the frozen section, she answered and was surprised to hear an unfamiliar voice on the other end.

"Yes, hi," he was saying, "I'm Officer Leo Kingston with the SCPD. I got your number from Dirk Coulter. I hope you don't mind, but I thought I should call you."

"No problem," she said, reaching for a pint of Ben and Jerry's Chunky Monkey. "What's up?"

"I mentioned to some of the guys here that I was going to have to go out and talk to somebody and one of them recognized your address."

"My address? Why are you going out to my address?" She pitched the ice cream into the cart and reached for a pint of Cherry Garcia, Marietta's favorite.

"We got a complaint about a Marietta Reid, who's staying there. Dirk says she's your sister."

Savannah froze, the ice cream in her hand. "Yes, I'm afraid she's a close blood relation of mine. What was the nature of the complaint . . . as if I have to ask."

"Apparently she's been harassing a certain William Donaldson, who lives in West Hollywood. He called us and asked us to speak to her about it, to tell her that he's considering getting a restraining order against her. It seems she showed up today at his place of employment and had to be removed from the premises by the security there."

"Lord help us," Savannah muttered. "That girl's plumb lost her mind, and she didn't have all that much to begin with."

"I beg your pardon?"

"Never mind. Thank you for calling me, Officer Kingston. I'll speak to my sister, really, and I guarantee you that she won't be bothering Mr. Donaldson again."

"Are you sure, because I really ought to follow up on this if —"

"I'm sure. Thank you, Leo."

Savannah hung up and stood there, staring at the Cherry Garcia in her hand. Then, with a determination born of fury, she shoved the ice cream back into the freezer.

"Screw you, Marietta Jane Reid," she grumbled. "No ice cream for you. No pork chop dinner. No *nothing*. You can just get your butt with your purple, tiger-striped pants on the next plane to Georgia. It's a transcontinental

239

flight. If you're lucky maybe *they* will feed you something!"

"You can't make me go home, Savannah! You can't make me do nothin' I don't wanna do!" Marietta shouted as she paced the length of the living room, waving her arms and punctuating each statement with a stomp.

In her wing-back chair, Savannah sat quietly, watching the tantrum and sipping her coffee that was liberally laced with Baileys Irish Cream. She wished it was Jack Daniels, but Baileys would have to do. She had to keep her wits about her. Assertiveness had never come easy for her when it came to her family members.

Bad guys were one thing. She had no problem threatening them with manual castration or death by slow strangulation. But when it came to her sisters . . .

Tammy had discreetly removed herself from the living room and taken refuge in the kitchen, where she sat at the table, quietly working on her computer. But she wasn't fooling Savannah. She was absorbing every detail of this drama. Having come from a relatively sane family herself, Tammy found the dynamics between the Reid sisters a never-ending source of amazement and amusement.

"Finally, I have a chance at happiness," Marietta wailed. "And you just can't stand it. I've got a man who loves me, a good man, and you're so jealous that you're throwin' a monkey wrench into the works by making me go home."

Savannah scooped Diamante up onto her lap and began to pet the cat. She'd heard that stroking an animal could lower your blood pressure. And judging from the pulse pounding in her temples, hers needed lowering.

"I'm not making you go home," she said calmly. "I'm just telling you that if you intend to stay here in California and make a blamed fool of yourself over a man who doesn't want any part of you . . . you'll have to do it someplace other than my house."

"But I can't afford a motel room! I already told you that! Why else do you think I'd stay here?"

Savannah winced, wishing there was a form of bullet-proof vest that could fend off darts from your so-called loved ones. "I don't know . . ." she said. "Maybe because you wanted to see me, to spend time with me?"

"Doing what? Listening to you put me down, tell me how stupid I am, and how I'm always messing up? Gee, that's a lot of fun."

In her peripheral vision, Savannah could see Tammy peek around the corner, a look of concern on her face. Maybe she could trade Sister Marietta in on a sister like Tammy — someone who didn't shoot poisoned verbal arrows.

"You're right, Marietta," she said as she stood and set the cat on the floor. "You're a grown woman, and your life is your own. I've taken liberties, expressing my opinions to you when you didn't ask for them. I apologize for that. Please forgive me."

Marietta looked relieved, then confused. "So . . . what does that mean?" she asked. "Can I stay here with you? At least for a few more days while I work out these little problems with Bill?"

"No. You can't stay."

"But — but you just admitted that you were wrong."

"I *was* wrong to give you advice that you didn't want. But you still have to go."

"But where? Where will I go if I can't stay here?"

"Home to your boys, maybe?"

"There you go, judging me again. That was advice . . . and a statement about me not being a good mother."

Savannah's remaining nerve snapped. "Dammit, Mari! You asked me. You asked me a specific question, and I answered it. You can go home or you can go check into a cheap hotel. Lord knows there are plenty of them in your so-called boyfriend's neighborhood. You can go fly a kite on the beach and sleep in your rented car. I don't care what you do! But if you're going to act stupider than stupid, you're not going to do it around me, 'cause I have better things to do than watch it."

At that moment, she was once again saved by

a bell; the telephone rang. As usual, it was resting on the coffee table, and both she and Marietta dove for it.

"Don't you touch that stinkin' telephone!" she shouted at her sister. "It's my dad-gummed phone, and if you so much as lay a finger on it, I swear, I'll beat you to a frazzle with it!"

Marietta must have believed her, because she backed off — all the way to the other side of the living room — and stood there sulking.

"Hello!" Savannah said into the phone with a vehemence rarely used for a simple telephone greeting unless one was expecting a telephone solicitor.

"Hi. Is everything okay?" asked a velvet voice that could only belong to Ryan Stone.

She instantly melted. "Ryan. I'm so glad to hear from you." He had no idea how glad, but someday she might tell him the sad, sad story of how she had thrown her sister out onto the cold, cold street and ruined forever any chance she had of finding her One True Love.

"I'm calling to ask you out on a date," he said, a touch of humor in his words.

"Yeah, right. Don't toy with me, boy. My heart's a fragile thing where you're concerned."

"No, really. I'm hoping you'll do me the honor of allowing me to escort you to a social function this evening. And if Tammy is free, John would like to take her. We realize it's short notice, but it shouldn't take long for you ladies to become ravishingly beautiful. It's formal, by the way."

Savannah looked over at Marietta, who was still trembling with rage and indignation. She quickly weighed the options before her: Spend the evening with two delicious men at a formal affair. Fight with her sister for another two hours and wind up committing homicide. And as fun as that might be, there was the body disposal, which could prove tricky with all the new advances in forensic investigations.

"We'll come."

"Excellent. John will be delighted. We'll pick you ladies up at half past seven."

"Where are we going?"

Again, that throaty chuckle on the other end that never failed to set her knickers atwitter. "We're going to Mystic Canyon. Specifically, to the Wentworth estate in Mystic Canyon for dinner, dancing, and a charity auction to benefit the county symphony. I believe several of the people you're investigating in these murders will be attending. It should be fun."

Savannah grinned from ear to ear. "Oh, yes. I'm sure it will be. Thanks for thinking of us."

"Always, sweetheart. Always."

Savannah had to wait a moment or two after she hung up before her legs would work again. Ryan frequently had that effect on her. Then she walked past the incensed Marietta without a word and into the kitchen where Tammy waited, an expectant look on her pretty face.

"Well, what did Ryan want?" she asked.

244

Savannah laughed. "All I can say is: Put on your dancin' shoes, darlin'. We're gonna rock the night away. And better yet, while we're there, we'll squeeze us some bad guys."

Tucked away in the hills behind San Carmelita, Mystic Canyon was a secluded and exclusive community where middle-class citizens, like Savannah, or even the upper-middle-class folk seldom ventured. This wasn't because they didn't want to venture there. It was simply because the overzealous guards at the gate made sure they didn't get the chance.

So Savannah felt more than a little pleased with herself when she sailed past the security booth with Ryan, John, and Tammy in the guys' vintage silver Bentley.

Savannah sat in the back seat of the car with Ryan, trying not to gawk and drool, as they drove past everything from stately Tudor mansions to sprawling Spanish haciendas — palatial residences that ranged from vintage Hollywood art deco to Miami Beach contemporary.

Every estate reflected the skill and taste of some renowned architect and, perhaps, that of its wealthy owner. And each property created its own fantasy land for the occupants and visitors alike, inviting them to spend a bit of time on the French Riviera, the streets of Rome, or the baronial English countryside.

"It's nice to see how the rest of the world lives," she said, thinking of her own leaky roof that needed repairs.

"A very small segment of the rest," Ryan replied, "if it's any consolation."

"A little."

She glanced down at her evening attire, a simple black dress, and felt a fleeting moment of anxiety. When she went to one of these high-society events, she always felt a bit like Cinderella — a scullery maid who knew, no matter how she dressed, she was still just a poor girl from the Georgia cotton fields.

But she dispelled her feelings of inadequacy by remembering what her grandmother had told her, "You're from fine stock, Savannah girl, so hold your head up high and look 'em all square in the eye. They've got nothin' over you, darlin', so don't let 'em think they do."

"You look fantastic this evening, Savannah," Ryan said, as though sensing her momentary lapse of confidence. "You do that dress justice," he added, glancing down at her abundant cleavage. The wrap-around silk dress revealed a tasteful but tantalizing amount of creamy curves with its low V-neck. And it fulfilled her personal standard: "Show Off The Goods, But Don't Be Trampy."

Savannah gave him a grin and a nudge. "Watch it. You'll make John jealous."

"Too late for that," John replied from the driver's seat. "I've known all along that if Ryan ever leaves me for a woman, it'll be you, Savannah. Besides, how can I be jealous when I

246

have such a lovely companion myself this evening?"

Sitting next to him, Tammy blushed nearly as red as the red satin sheath she was wearing. She did look especially lovely, Savannah thought, enjoying the look of pure pleasure on her young friend's face. Tammy's sun-bleached hair always glistened with health, as did her golden-tanned skin. But it was the kindness in her eyes that gave Tammy her greatest beauty, a warmth that enveloped and soothed everyone around her.

Savannah was glad they had invited her along this evening to share in the fun — not to mention the espionage.

"Here we are," Ryan said as they approached the end of the road and a sumptuous French château. "This is the house that cereal built."

As they pulled into the long driveway and headed toward the front of the mansion and the circular motor court, Savannah stared up at the imposing limestone façade, the slate roof with its copper gutters, the mullioned windows sparkling in the golden light of early evening. "Wow," she said. "They must have sold a heck of a lot of corn flakes."

"Not to mention puffed rice," John added. "But even more importantly, Charles Wentworth and his son, Charles Wentworth II, were brilliant businessmen. They kept their company alive through the Great Depression and two World Wars, and not only survived, but flourished."

"The only thing Wentworth Industries can't endure, it seems, is the reign of Charles III," Ryan added, revealing a bit of sarcasm that was rare for him.

"From what I hear," John said, "the family business is in deep trouble due to some appalling mismanagement on the lad's part. A dreadful shame, really."

They stopped in front of the house, where a queue consisting of a Mercedes, a BMW, a Porsche, and a Lamborghini waited while valets scrambled to greet the arriving guests and relieve them of their vehicles.

"You should have seen old Dirko," Tammy told John, sounding like a prissy five-year-old who was tattling on her older brother. "He dropped by Savannah's just before you picked us up. Boy, he was livid that we were coming to this and he wasn't."

Ryan laughed. "I can't imagine that Dirk would enjoy himself at this sort of function," he said. "It doesn't seem like his cup of tea . . . or bottle of beer, as the case might be."

"It isn't," Savannah said. "It's just that he's afraid we'll score something good on the case and he'll miss it. Believe me, that's the only reason he's jealous. He couldn't care less about the dining and dancing, let alone about fund-raising."

"Well, if we all keep sharp this evening," John said, "we might learn something that will help you catch this brute. Jealous or not, I'm sure your Dirk would welcome any help we can give him."

"Absolutely," Savannah said as a fresh-faced young valet hurried to open her door. "An evening in opulence and splendor doesn't exactly bite, but let's not forget why we're here."

As she stepped out of the Bentley and onto the granite-block motor court, she thought of Cait Connor and Kameeka Wills, who were far past helping. But Tesla Montoya was still out there somewhere and maybe it wasn't too late for her.

A shiver ran over her that had nothing to do with the cool California breeze that was sweeping through the canyon, bringing the sea fog and a damp chill with it. She wrapped her lace shawl around her shoulders, clutched her Gucci-knockoff bag, and slipped her arm through Ryan's.

Chapter
17

Along with a throng of other guests, the Moon-light Magnolia foursome moved through the château's magnificent entryway, and like all the arrivals, they took their time, soaking in the ambience. A floor of white Carrera marble and a twenty-five-foot coffered ceiling with gold-leaf molding reflected the light from two magnificent crystal chandeliers. On either side, the maple walls had niches every few feet that contained antique statuary and bronzes, which Ryan whispered to her were French, nineteenth century.

At the end of the hall, they were ushered into a great room that Savannah couldn't help noticing was bigger than her entire house. The lofty ceiling here was also coffered, and thick, colorful tapestries hung on the walls, next to oil paintings that were everything from still life to portraits to European landscapes. Savannah didn't have to ask if they had been purchased at the local poster shop, like much of her own art. Everything in the Wentworth mansion was the real thing.

Except maybe Charles Wentworth III.

Phony baloney, was Savannah's instant analysis when she saw him enter the room in his white tuxedo, his wavy blond hair slicked back in Great Gatsby style and his mannerisms just as affected.

Savannah watched from the corner of her eye as he moved among his guests. Giving air cheek kisses, occasionally even bowing and kissing hands, he cajoled and flattered his way across the room. But Savannah noted that in spite of his pseudo-charm, he didn't seem to be making much of an impression on those in his wake. Once his back was turned, more than one of his visitors rolled their eyes, gave him a derisive smile, or simply glared at him with open hostility.

"Why do they come to his party if they don't like him?" Savannah asked, knowing she sounded naive, but comfortable in the fact that Ryan wouldn't mind.

"Money," he replied, "and the power it brings."

"But you said he's practically broke."

"Yes, but they don't know that yet. At least, most of them don't. Once they figure it out, he won't be able to get anybody to come to a weenie roast."

She looked around the room and saw a number of faces that were familiar to her, mostly from the newspaper society column — members of the city council, a state senator and his wife, a popular female television news anchor from Los Angeles, and the mayor were present.

But being among the county's minor-league celebrities wasn't the attraction for Savannah. Her eyes scanned the crowd, and her spirits soared when she saw Jerrod Beekman standing in a corner, speaking to an attractive young man. And judging from their intimate body language, she assumed he was Jerrod's date.

"That fellow over there with Beekman," she said to Ryan, "is he your friend, Michael Romano?"

"Oh, not at all. John and I spoke to Michael for you yesterday like we promised, and he refuses to have anything to do with Jerrod."

"Any good dirt?"

Ryan shook his dark head. "No such luck. Just your everyday, mundane domestic quarrel that caused them to go their separate ways last summer. All he told me was that Jerrod is in financial straits . . . almost as bad as Charles Wentworth's. He was hoping the Slenda campaign would bail him out, but it appears that his boat will sink along with Wentworth's if this new product flops."

"Which it's bound to do if word gets out that a couple of top models died eating it."

"Exactly."

Savannah paused and pretended to study a nearby painting as a couple strolled by them. Once they had passed out of earshot, she told

Ryan, "Of course, that presents a problem. What motive would Beekman or Wentworth have to get rid of the models if it would only jeopardize the campaign? Having those two girls die and another one disappear would be the last thing they'd want."

"Probably. But you never know." He winked at her and caused her heart to flutter. He took her hand and said, "I've been to these shindigs before. I think the food's out by the pool. Interested?"

"Food? Food? Look who you're talking to here, sweetcakes. What do you think?"

They wove their way through the crowd and passed through a set of French doors that led them to an exquisite and meticulously maintained formal garden. A fantasy world of topiaries, marble statuary, trellis-climbing roses, and gazing pools, the grounds invited visitors to lose themselves in the enchantment. And — despite the solemn nature of her mission — Savannah allowed herself the luxury.

Squeezing Ryan's arm, she whispered, "Thank you for bringing me here tonight. This is amazing."

He patted her hand and smiled down at her. "You needn't thank me. It's my pleasure." Then he studied her face and his smile faded. "What is it, Savannah? You looked sad for a moment there."

"I was just thinking about my Granny Reid. She loves flowers. Gardening is her passion.

She's never seen anything like this, and I was just wishing that she could be here with me to enjoy this."

"Maybe she can someday. And maybe not. But either way, I know she'd be happy to know that her granddaughter is here . . . and that she's thinking of her so lovingly."

Savannah blinked back a tear and nodded.

"I didn't mean to make you cry," Ryan said softly.

"Eh, don't worry about it," she replied with a sniff. "They're good tears . . . the only kind you ever give me."

She quickly recovered when they rounded a curve in the path and saw the pool area spread before them.

Cabana suites bordered the far end of the oval pool — a vision of cool marine blue, accented with stained-glass tiles around its edge that formed a Greek key pattern of white and cobalt blue.

Small round tables, seating four, spotted the patio, and the guests were staking their claims on the most scenic locations.

An enormous buffet had been spread in the center of the patio, and Savannah and Ryan found Tammy and John there, scooping seafood delicacies onto their plates while chatting happily about their surroundings.

"Looks like they're getting along fine," Ryan remarked when Tammy reached over to plant a kiss on John's cheek.

"That was pretty predictable," Savannah replied. "Tammy's a sweetie, and John is an amazing man."

"Yes, he is. I'm fortunate to have him in my life."

"I'd say you're both pretty darned lucky. Do either you or John have any straight brothers?"

"Yes, we do. But they're married and have kids, dogs, cats, the whole domestic scene."

"Figures. Let's go tackle that buffet before Tammy snarfs up all the shrimp."

Five minutes later, the four of them were sitting at one of the poolside tables, their plates piled high with broiled lobster tails, butterfly shrimp, baked clams, and six varieties of caviar. They munched happily as they listened to a doo-wop quartet in mauve jackets with black shirts and white ties, who were strolling among the guests singing "Runaround Sue."

"Ah . . . I could get used to this," Tammy said with a sigh of satisfaction as she sipped her champagne cocktail.

"Don't," Savannah replied. "We're all turning into pumpkins at midnight. At least we girls will. And tomorrow it's back to bologna and cheese sandwiches. Or in your case, yogurt and vegetable sticks."

"Try to burst my bubble, if you want to, but this party is just too awesome." Holding up her champagne flute, Tammy watched the lines of effervescence trickle up the glass.

"It's time to discuss our plan of action for the

evening," Savannah said, lowering her voice and leaning closer to the others.

"Did you bring those two recorders?" Ryan asked.

"What plan of action? What recorders?" Suddenly, Tammy — the party animal — was all business.

"The mini-recorders I have in my purse," Savannah told her, "courtesy of our escorts."

"Hopefully, they'll work better than those stupid things Dirk loans us. Half of the time they don't even work, and when they do, you can't make out what's being said."

"Not to worry, dear," John said. "These little beauties are state of the art. Voice activated with excellent pickup. If two mosquitoes have a conversation anywhere in their vicinity, we'll be able to hear every word."

"Where are you going to put them?" Tammy asked.

Savannah reached over and snatched a shrimp off Tammy's plate. "Ryan says that Charles Wentworth frequently holds little private meetings in the library during these parties."

"Yes. He does." Ryan took a sip of his martini. "Our host can't decide which he wants to be when he grows up, Vito Corleone or Jay Gatsby."

"How old is he?" Tammy asked.

"Late forties, early fifties," Ryan replied.

"Then I'd say it's about time to nail that

down." Tammy slapped Savannah's hand away from her plate. "So we bug the library with one of the recorders. Where do we put the other one?"

"Ryan and I will take care of the library," Savannah said. "Why don't you and John carry the other one around until you find a good spot or until an opportunity presents itself?"

"John and I are going to be busy dancing," Tammy said, gazing at her companion with starry-eyed infatuation.

John laughed, slipped his hand under the table, and nudged Savannah's knee. "Give your recorder to me, Savannah," he said. "The Bureau trained me well. I can tango, plant listening devices, and juggle swords at the same time."

Savannah slipped him the recorder, and he placed it in his tuxedo jacket pocket.

Then he turned to Tammy and extended his hand. "I believe I hear the band tuning up in the great room. Shall we?"

Tammy lifted her nose a notch, flipped back her long blond hair, and delicately laid her hand atop his. "We shall."

"Oh, Lord help us," Savannah said as she and Ryan watched them walk away. "He's creating a monster there, treating her like a princess."

"It's good for her," Ryan said, smiling at the departing couple with obvious affection.

"Yeah, but it's lousy for me. Next thing you

know, she'll be expecting to get paid. She'll want medical and dental . . . weekends off . . . vacations and coffee breaks. Where will it all end?"

"Every house should have a library like this one," Savannah said as she and Ryan slipped into the dark room and closed the door behind them. He found the light switch and flipped it, bathing the room in a cozy golden light.

Mahogany-paneled walls and shelves filled with leather-bound classics set the mood in the room, one of quiet repose and thoughtful serenity. Overstuffed chairs and a banquette sofa in burgundy velvet beckoned readers to lose themselves in other, more graceful, ages and places.

"I think I'll redecorate the living room," she said, "just like this. Persian rugs, oil paintings, and all."

"We'd all like that," Ryan replied as he walked over to an ebony-and-ivory inlaid desk in the far corner of the room.

"What are you talking about? Your living room is just like this."

"Not exactly. My 'Persian' rugs aren't actually from Persia, any 'ivory' inlay I have is mother-of-pearl, and not only do I have non-leather books in my shelves, I even have some paperbacks in my collection."

"How revolting! I'm appalled."

He dropped to one knee behind the desk and

looked under it. "I was walking down the hall once, and the door to this room was open. Wentworth was sitting here at the desk with a batch of his cronies around him. They were doing some major kissing up. One of the other guests told me that was his favorite party pastime. If we put it right there, between the desk leg and the wall, we might get something."

She handed him the recorder. He turned it on and tucked it into the dark space.

No sooner had he stood and brushed off his trouser knees than they heard someone turning the doorknob.

"Damnation," Savannah said.

Before she even had time to think about how to handle the sticky situation of getting caught planting an illegal bug, Ryan had swept her into his arms and was bending her backward over the desk. As the door opened, he smothered her with the most passionate kiss she had ever had the pleasure of receiving.

And while she had fantasized about this moment at least a thousand times since meeting him, the kiss was immeasurably better than she could have imagined.

Ryan Stone wasn't just gorgeous. He was the world's best kisser, hands down. In the first three seconds, he had broken the record previously set by her high school boyfriend, Tommy Stafford, in the back seat of his Chevy Bel Air . . . a record that had stood until that moment in the Wentworth library.

As if through a haze, she felt his mouth, firm and insistent on hers, his hands, large and warm on her back, pressing her body to his, the taste and the smell of him as intoxicating as —

"Ah . . . excuse me." A harsh, unpleasant voice pierced the pretty pink fog that had so quickly enveloped her. "I thought I might use my own library, but I see it's occupied."

Ryan released her, and she nearly fell backward onto the desk. "Sorry," he said. "We were just . . ."

"Yeah, well, take it upstairs, would you? I've got some work to do in here."

Savannah shook her head, recovered her senses, and decided that she would hate Charles Wentworth III for the rest of her life. *Curse him for ending the kiss of the century!* she thought. *May his teeth rot, his hair fall out, and — unlike the mighty South — may his Wiener schnitzel never rise again!*

With some more murmured apologies that were definitely lacking in sincerity, Ryan pulled her across the library and out into the hall. He closed the door behind them, blocking out the picture of a scowling Charles Wentworth, his white tuxedo, and his slick blond hair.

When they were several yards down the hall, Savannah started to giggle. "That was close," she said. "Fast thinking."

He laughed and put his arm around her waist. "It worked, and that's what counts." He gave her a squeeze and added, "I'll have to tell

John that we were right about you; you *are* a good kisser."

Savannah stopped in the middle of the hall and stared up at him, her mouth hanging open. "Do you mean to tell me that you and John have speculated on what kind of a kisser I am?"

He grinned down at her. "Of course we have."

"But . . . but you're *gay!*"

He shrugged. "So? Gay people are curious, too. Are you going to tell me that you and Tammy haven't speculated about us?"

An instant replay of several fairly bawdy conversations between herself and her assistant flickered across Savannah's mental screen. Feeling a blush warming her cheeks, she chose not to answer him, but continued on down the hall.

"What are you doing?" he asked, as he watched her counting the fingers of her left hand, then some on her right.

"Figuring out how many months it is until Christmas," she replied.

"Christmas? Why?"

"Because that's the soonest that I can legitimately get another kiss from you, boy. You know . . . mistletoe and all that."

They walked a few more yards.

"So . . . how many months is it?" he finally asked.

"Ten . . . and a half."

"That's a long time."

She sighed. "Tell me about it."

Chapter
18

At one in the morning, when Ryan and John brought Savannah and Tammy back to Savannah's house, they found Dirk sitting in his Buick out front. Savannah wasn't surprised, since he had called her three times during the party on her cell phone, wanting to know what was going on.

She told him about the amazing house. She told him about the food. She told him they had planted the recorder.

She didn't mention the fact that she had kissed Ryan.

What Dirk didn't know wouldn't hurt him — and he couldn't bug the daylights out of her as long as she didn't tell him.

Having listened to their tape on the way home in the car, they were brimming with excitement when they hurried into the house, a disgruntled Dirk in their wake.

Savannah was surprised, though not exactly shocked, to find Marietta planted on her sofa, the telephone in her hand. Marietta had always been a person who required more than a nudge. Strong-armed force had usually been needed to get her to do anything that she didn't choose to do on her own.

"Could I speak to you, alone, for a moment?" Savannah said to her. Then she turned to her compatriots. "Go ahead and make yourselves at home there in the kitchen," she told them, "and I'll join you in a couple of minutes."

A petulant and reluctant Marietta followed Savannah upstairs. She led her into the guest bedroom and closed the door behind them.

"I thought we had an understanding," Savannah told her. "I thought you might have respected my wishes and been gone by the time I got home."

Marietta lifted her chin and placed both hands on her hips. "I thought you were surely joking about throwing me out. After all, I'm your kin."

"Yes, you are. And has it occurred to you that, because you are, it wasn't easy for me to ask you to leave?"

"Nobody made you. You're just doing it out of meanness."

Savannah suddenly felt tired. Her high heels were pinching her toes, and her head ached from the unaccustomed quantity of champagne she had consumed. "Listen to me, Marietta. I promised a policeman today that I would make sure you wouldn't harass that Donaldson guy anymore. The cop was going to come here and give you a talkin' to, but I convinced him it wasn't necessary. I swore to him that you'd behave. Now you're making a liar out of me."

"I am not!"

"So, you weren't talking to your cyberguy when I walked in just now?"

"No."

"Then who were you talking to?"

"It's none of your business."

"Who's paying for the call, Marietta? Whose phone were you using? Whose door is going to get knocked on at four in the morning because you aren't acting like a lady?"

"I wasn't talking to Bill. If you must know, I was talking to his brother, James."

"And how did you get hold of his brother's number? The same way you got his work number and his father's? Did you get that information out of his address book when you were at his house?"

Marietta's eyes blazed. "You're somebody to be criticizing somebody else for doing something underhanded. You, who sneaks around and spies on folks for a living!"

Savannah noticed that her sister was still holding the phone in her right hand. She reached for it. "Give me that telephone."

"No, I will not!"

"It's my telephone, dammit."

"But I have one more call to make before I go to bed."

"To your boys or to Gran?"

"Well . . ."

"That's what I thought. Hand it over before you're a minute older."

"No. I told you, I have to settle this here problem with my boyfriend before I'll be able to go to sleep tonight, and I just need somebody to talk a little bit of sense into Bill before he throws this all away and —"

Savannah reached out and snatched the phone from her sister's hand. "If you're going to make any more phone calls tonight . . . or tomorrow . . . or the next day for that matter, you're going to have to walk about half a mile to the nearest phone booth. But before you do, you'd better think twice, because the minute you go out that door, I'm going to deadbolt it, and you ain't getting back in! I mean it, Marietta Reid!"

"You're just being hateful!"

"And you're being a ignoramus! I swear, girl, you're a romance junkie, and you need serious help! But for tonight, I'm going to take my telephones, all three of them, into my bedroom, and I'm going to lock the door. While I'm at it, I'm going to take the cord off the back of the computer, too. So you might just as well go to bed and get a good night's sleep."

"I can't go back. I don't have the money!" Marietta wailed. "I just bought a one-way ticket! I figured it would work out between me and Bill, and he'd want me to stay, and eventually I'd send for the boys and —"

"Then you'd better sure as shootin' get that

rest," Savannah said as she stomped to the door, "because you're gonna need it. It's a damned far piece to Georgia, and that thumb of yours is gonna get mighty tired with you hitchhiking all the way."

When Savannah rejoined the gang in the kitchen, she found them comfortably seated around her table, an assortment of snacks and beverages in front of them — mostly in front of Dirk — and the recorder on the table.

"We waited for you," Tammy said as Savannah poured some French dark roast and water into the coffeemaker. It was bound to be a long night and a shot of energy from Mr. Coffee would help.

A shot from Miss Godiva might be needed, too.

"Yeah, they won't even tell me what they've got here until you sit down," Dirk grumped. "So, come sit."

"You'd better say that smilin', boy," she said as she took her seat at the head of the table. "I just went ten rounds with Marietta, and I've got energy to spare."

"How did it go?" Tammy asked.

"Who cares?" Dirk reached for the recorder, but Tammy snatched it away from him. "What's on the tape?"

"It isn't anything as good as a confession," Ryan said. "And of course, it isn't anything that can be used in court. But it *is* interesting."

266

Dirk settled back in his chair. "So, let's hear it."

Savannah gave Tammy a nod and she punched the PLAY button.

The first thing they heard was Savannah's voice, a loud "Damnation!" then some shuffling sounds and then the soft, liquid sounds of —

Savannah grabbed the recorder and pushed stop. "We . . . ah . . . we had a little trouble getting it going there at first," she said, feeling her cheeks turn the color of vine-ripened tomatoes. "Where's the good stuff?" she asked Tammy.

"Sorry, I thought I had it on the spot. I think it's around twenty-five or twenty-six on the little meter there."

Savannah could feel Dirk's eyes burning into her as she punched the buttons with a finger that shook slightly. She could also practically hear Ryan snickering at the other end of the table.

Men! They could complicate a girl's life if she didn't watch out. Sometimes even if she *did* look out.

After what seemed like a couple of years, she found the spot and started the tape.

Thankfully, it was a man's voice that spoke this time. "It could have been a lot worse," he was saying, "if they'd sued you like they said . . . think how that would have played when it hit the news. If you ask me, we dodged a bullet."

"That's why I don't ask you for your opinion on things that matter," said another, deeper voice. "You're shortsighted, Jerrod. You're a chess player who only sees one move at a time, and that's why we're in this situation. You didn't look ahead."

"I don't think I've handled it all that badly so far. We're in a pretty good place now what with the girls gone and —"

"I heard from Martin Jacobs today. He's representing Kevin Connor."

"Connor?"

"Yeah, Connor. He's suing me for his wife's untimely death. And how long do you suppose it'll be before the other ones' families figure it out and come after me, too?

"I . . . I don't . . ."

"No, you don't, because you don't think ahead."

There was a long, heavy silence. So long that the voice-activated tape stopped, then started again when Beekman said, "I'll do something. I'll take care of it."

"Bodies can't keep dropping, Jerrod," said the deep voice. "People can't keep disappearing."

"I know. I know. I'll think of something. Really."

Another long silence. Then, "Make sure that you do. I don't have to tell you that if I go down . . . so will you."

A door slammed, followed by the sound of

glass clinking and a fluid pouring. Then the recorder switched off.

"Sounds like Wentworth needed a shot of courage," Ryan said as they sat and digested what they had just heard.

"How do you know for sure that was Wentworth?" Dirk asked.

"We took turns hanging out at the end of the hallway," Savannah told him, "watching everybody who went in and out of that office. And we kept track, writing down their names if we knew who they were and their physical descriptions if we didn't."

"We listened to the rest of the conversations on the way over here after the party," Ryan said. "Most of them were Wentworth trying to squeeze people who owe him money."

"And some of those debts are ten years old," Savannah said. "Apparently, he's desperate for cash."

John reached over and patted Tammy's shoulder. "This young lady and I were watching when Jerrod Beekman went into the library and when he came out. What we just heard was the gist of their conversation."

Dirk sighed and sank a few inches lower in his chair. "It's interesting, that business about the dead girls threatening to sue Wentworth before they died. But there's not really a hook in there that I can hang either Wentworth or Beekman on."

"No," Savannah said, "but I think they both

need a closer look."

"A closer look?" Dirk shook his head. "I'm already looking at everybody as close as I can. And so far, I haven't seen nothin' that counts for closing this case."

From past experience, Savannah knew that Dirk almost always hit a wall with his cases. Fortunately, although he was grumpy and difficult when he had his nose pressed against that wall, he always rallied. And after a period of wallowing in depression, ranting and raving, he would solve it.

"That's why we're trying to help, Dirko," Tammy said, as though explaining rocket combustion ratios to a kindergartner. "Why else do you think we'd all be here at two in the morning?"

As usual, Tammy's approach didn't work with Dirk. He bristled and opened his mouth to reply, but Savannah stood, walked behind him, and put her hands on his shoulders.

"Tell us what you want us to do, buddy," she said, massaging the knotted muscles at the base of his neck.

"I want to find this girl, Tesla," he said, closing his eyes and running his hand through his hair. "Until we find her body, we've still got a chance of getting her back alive. And from what I can see, that's the only good thing that could possibly come out of this mess."

Savannah smoothed his mussed hair, much as she would have petted her grandmother's old bloodhound back in Georgia. Then she sat down in her chair and took a notebook and pen in hand. "Okay, we've got suspects galore," she said. "And we have to keep an eye on them all. Let's divide 'em up. Who's gonna baby-sit whom?"

Having drawn Kevin Connor from the figurative hatful of suspects, Savannah pulled up to the house on the beach at 7:30 in the morning, only five hours after she had said good-bye to the team at her house. She had been hoping for Beekman or Wentworth, but Dirk was hogging them both for himself. And since he was in his "Deep-Dark-Depression-Excessive-Misery" mode, she had decided not to fight him about it.

She had a couple of things to ask Kevin Connor anyway, so she didn't really mind . . . except for the getting there at 7:30 business. Having called the hospital, she had found out that he came on duty at 8:30, so she figured he would be up and about at this hour and might give her a few minutes of his time.

When she rang the doorbell, it took him so long to answer that she reconsidered her theory. Maybe Connor was one of those guys who rolled out of bed at the last possible moment, gulped a cup of coffee, and arrived at work with bed hair and sheet face.

When he answered, barefoot, wearing pajama pants and a T-shirt, his eyes half open, she realized she had blown it.

"I'm sorry, Mr. Connor," she said. "I thought that since you're on at the hospital at eight-thirty, you'd be up by now."

"I just called in sick," he replied, rubbing his eyes with his fingers.

"Oh, I really am sorry. I —"

"I'm not sick. I'm just tired. It's been a really tough last few days. We had Cait's funeral yesterday."

"Yes. I know. I'm sure the hospital understands."

"No, they don't understand. But to hell with them. I'm not going to be there much longer, so . . ."

"Oh?"

He seemed to wake up a bit. He shook his head and said, "No, I'm not, but that's not important. What can I do for you?"

"I just wanted to talk to you a few minutes, ask you a couple of questions, fill you in on what's going on with the investigation."

He looked confused, then irritated. "What's going on? What investigation? I thought it was over and done with. The coroner said she died accidentally of heat stroke."

"Well, yes, that's true. But would you mind terribly if I came in? Since you're already up . . ."

He looked back over his shoulder and hesitated. "Uh, I guess so. But just for a little while. Then I'm going back to bed."

"I won't take long, really."

Stepping back, he opened the door for her, and she entered the house. As before, it had the empty feeling of a home where the owner was absent, as though the heart and spirit of the house were gone.

Since she had been there last, the place had become badly cluttered. Dirty clothes, dishes, beer bottles, and newspapers littered every surface, and the air carried the smell of stale cigarette smoke and booze.

But among all the trash, Savannah's eye caught a couple of things in particular. On the sofa, draped across the bright tropical print cushions, was a pair of jeans And while that might not have been unusual in itself, she noted that they were a woman's cut and the size was much too small for Kevin or Caitlin.

And on the floor in front of the sofa were a pair of bright red clogs . . . also far too small for Kevin Connor's large feet.

He followed her line of vision, saw what she was looking at, and reached for her arm. With no great gentleness, he led her into the dining area and out the doors to the patio where they had sat and talked the day Caitlin died.

She had the distinct feeling he wanted her out of the house, and, considering the lady's apparel in the living room, she wasn't surprised. She would have bet a box of chocolate-iced, custard-filled doughnuts that Kevin had a honey upstairs.

And with his wife freshly buried.

That was something to think about.

He sat down at the table and motioned for her to sit across from him. "What are you talking about — an investigation?" he asked. "I thought it was all sewn up. I mean, the M.E. released Cait's body to us for the funeral. They must have been finished with it."

"I know. Dr. Liu did rule that the cause of death was hyperthermia and its heart-related complications. But there are still some questions about the manner of death."

"It was an accident."

"That's what we thought at first, too. But . . ."

"But what?"

"But now, with Kameeka dying so soon afterward, and with Tesla Montoya missing . . . I'm sure you've been following the news and realize how suspicious that is."

"Are you telling me that you believe somebody deliberately murdered my Caitlin?"

Savannah shrugged and said softly, "What do *you* think, Kevin?"

He propped his elbows on the table and covered his face with his hands. He was silent for a long time. Then he dropped his hands and said, "As much as I hate the thought, I have to admit that once I heard about Kameeka, it occurred to me that someone might have done something to Cait."

"You have medical knowledge," Savannah

said. "What do you think they might have done?"

"Who knows? It's pretty obvious how she died. She starved herself and then got over-heated, just like the coroner said."

"Kevin, when was the last time you saw Cait that day?"

"It was that morning, when I left for work. I kissed her good-bye and told her to eat some breakfast. She promised me she would."

"And that was the last time you spoke?"

"No. I talked to her on the phone, later that morning."

"What time?"

"Oh, I don't know. She called me at the hospital about ten or eleven."

"What did she want?'

A look of sadness washed over his face, and he clenched his hands together on the table in front of him. "She said she had been working out and she wasn't feeling so good. Said she was light-headed. I told her to drink a big glass of water and to lie down for a while. She said she would."

"And that was the last time you heard from her?"

"Yes. And I keep asking myself what might have happened if I'd just come home then. She said she was sick, and I should have listened."

"You didn't know," she said. "You can't blame yourself."

Savannah thought of the clothes in the living

room and decided to broach a touchy subject. "Kevin, I hate to ask, but . . . was your marriage a happy one?"

"Yes. Why?"

He didn't sound all that convincing, but considering what she had recently seen and heard, she wasn't surprised.

"Were either of you seeing someone else, outside the marriage?"

He looked her straight in the eye and replied evenly, "Caitlin and I had an open marriage."

"I see," she said just as evenly, without breaking the gaze. "So that's a yes?"

"Caitlin had many lovers. I believe she was having a fling with her photographer at the time. A guy named Matt Slater."

"Yes, I know Mr. Slater. Had that been going on for a while?"

"Not long. Cait had a pretty short attention span when it came to that sort of thing."

"Was it . . . going well? To the best of your knowledge were the two of them on good terms at the time she died?"

"I doubt that the affair mattered much to either one of them," he said. "I suppose they were still friendly, if that's what you mean."

"Yes, that's what I meant." Savannah paused, weighing her next words before speaking. "Forgive my candor, Mr. Connor, but have *you* been seeing someone recently?"

She wondered if he would blatantly lie to her, considering that they both knew she had seen the women's clothing in the living room. It certainly wouldn't be the first time somebody had looked her square in the eye and told her a whopper.

"Yes. I'm seeing someone," he said.

Savannah instantly gave him Brownie points for honesty. But she questioned whether he would have been so truthful if his sweetie hadn't left her breeches on the couch in plain view. It was one thing to be forthright about your spouse's liaisons, and quite another when it came to your own.

"May I ask who she is?" Savannah said.

"You can ask, but I won't say."

"I wish you would tell me. It could be important."

"No. The lady I'm involved with is married and has children. Her marriage isn't open. Not every couple can handle that sort of arrangement in a mature manner."

Savannah entertained a momentary mental image of how "mature" she would be if her husband decided to "open" their marriage. It involved a flurry of activity that included multiple whacks to the head with a skillet, digging a deep hole in the backyard under the magnolia tree, and that same magnolia tree blooming profusely the next spring, thanks to all that additional unfaithful-hubby fertilizer.

"That's true," she said. "Not a lot of people go for that anymore."

"Besides" — he glanced over his shoulder toward the sliding doors — "her identity isn't important. She's a very kind, gentle person. She'd never hurt anyone."

Except maybe her husband and children, her family and friends, if they found out about you, Savannah thought.

She could tell she had taken Kevin about as far down that road as he would be willing to go. She decided to try another tactic.

"I understand that you're taking legal action against Charles Wentworth III."

His face flushed dark with anger. "I sure am. I'm suing him and Beekman and Dr. Pappas. They were all complicit in her death — pushing her to jeopardize her health so that they could make a buck. They didn't give a damn about Caitlin, as long as they made money off her."

"Do you think they were involved in Kameeka's death or Tesla's disappearance?"

"I don't know. That's for you and the cops to figure out."

Savannah glanced at her watch. It was already past eight, and she had a lot of ground to cover before the day was over. "One last thing, Kevin," she said. "If you were me, where would you concentrate your efforts on this case? If someone did deliberately murder your wife, who would you put your money on?"

"Leah Freed."

That one took Savannah by surprise. "Oh?"

"Yes. Wentworth and Beekman and Pappas might have contributed to her accidentally

278

killing herself, but if she was outright murdered, I'd bet on Leah."

"Why?"

"Caitlin was furious at Leah for getting her into that contract, and the day before she died, she told Leah that she was looking for another agent."

"And how did Leah take it?"

"Like she was a spurned lover. She figures she made Caitlin everything she was, that she owned her. And Cait was talking to the other girls about leaving Leah, too. Kameeka and Tesla were seriously considering going with Cait to another agency — one in L.A."

"Hmmm." Savannah mulled that over for a minute. "Are you aware that Leah has hired me to investigate this case?"

"No, but it doesn't surprise me. Leah likes to know what's going on, and she knows you're friends with the police detective who's in charge of the case. Knowing her, she's probably been pumping you to find out everything you know, right?"

Savannah didn't reply. She wasn't going to tell him about all the persistent, insistent phone calls from Leah, night and day. She certainly wasn't going to tell him that she had been thinking along the same lines as Leah squeezed her for information.

She rose from the table. "Thanks, Kevin. I appreciate your time and your input."

"No problem," he said. "I'm glad you came

by. If there's anything else you need, give me a call."

"I will."

He escorted her through the house to the front door. Shaking his hand, she said, "Just for the record, Kevin . . . I'm with you on that lawsuit. If you can prove that those guys pushed Caitlin into ruining her health, all for the sake of an ad campaign, I hope you win a bundle. And I hope it makes the lead story on the eleven o'clock news."

He grinned broadly, and it occurred to Savannah — not for the first time — that Caitlin Connor had been married to a very handsome man.

An open marriage, huh? She chuckled as she left the house and walked to her car, thinking of that magnolia tree in her backyard bursting with buds. *Nope. Not this girl. No way in hell.*

Chapter
19

After Savannah left Kevin Connor's house, she drove to her favorite doughnut shop on Main Street and ordered a large coffee and a couple of maple bars. Sitting in her car, raising her blood sugar and her serum caffeine, she phoned Tammy to see what was happening at home. Tammy informed her that Leah Freed had called twice already, insisting on the latest update.

"And it's not even nine o'clock yet," Tammy complained. "That woman is the most irritating client we've ever had."

"How quickly you forget," Savannah reminded her. "We've had some extremely difficult clients in the past. Remember the one who turned out to be the killer?"

"Yeah, but at least he didn't call constantly," Tammy replied. "And he behaved like a gentleman . . . except for that killing part."

"Is Marietta up yet?"

"She just ran out the door. She's headed for the mall. Said she's going to buy herself a cell phone so that she can call What's-His-Face."

Savannah took a long, stiff drink of the coffee and closed her eyes for a moment, feeling it hit her bloodstream like a shot of much-needed adrenaline. "I'm surprised," she said, "that she didn't try to talk you into giving her one of the phones."

"Oh, she did! Big time! In fact, I had to lock the two extra ones in my car trunk, and I kept this one beside me all the time. Even took it to the bathroom with me."

"Good girl. You get a raise."

"A raise, huh? Yeah, right. If I had a raise for every time you gave me a raise . . ."

"You'd probably be all the way up to minimum wage by now."

"Exactly. Listen, I've got to go now. Dirk gave me an assignment."

Savannah smiled. The kid sounded so proud that it touched her heart.

"Doing what?" she asked.

"He wants me to tail Tumblety today. Isn't that cool?"

Savannah felt a twinge of misgiving, like a mother hen who worried that her chicken-little might be pecking off more than she could chew. "Yeah, it's cool. Be careful, huh? That guy's creepy. And you're not exactly inconspicuous in that hot-pink VW Beetle of yours."

"Yeah, yeah, yeah. Don't worry, Mama Savannah. I've learned from the best."

"Who? Dirk? He's not the best. He just thinks he is."

"I meant *you*."

"Oh, all right. Take care of yourself."

"Bye." Click.

End of conversation, Savannah thought. *Simple as that.*

She laid the cell phone on the passenger seat beside her and picked up the maple bar. She took a bite, sipped some coffee, and sent a silent prayer heavenward.

Lord, I'd consider it a personal favor if you'd keep an eye on the kid today for me. She means well, and she's plenty smart, but sometimes she trusts people a little too much. And you can't trust people any further than you can throw 'em. But then, I guess You know all about that.

Her phone rang. She put down the maple bar, wiped her fingers on a paper napkin, and answered it. "Hello."

"I just got done talking to Wentworth," was Dirk's opener. "He stinks, but I don't know if he's killed anybody lately."

"Yeah, well, I just left Kevin Connor. I'm pretty sure he had a girlfriend upstairs."

"Oh? Already?"

"More like *still*. According to him, he and Cait had an open marriage."

"Open? Like they both fooled around whenever they wanted to?"

"That's it."

"Sounds like good work if you can get it. Most women I know wouldn't go for it, though."

"You think?" She sighed. "I'm going to go over to Desiree La Port's house now. See if I can find her at home."

"That's a heck of a drive all the way to Arroyo Verde. What if she's not home? Maybe you should call her first."

"She's not exactly the friendly type. I have a feeling that if I called first, she'd make herself scarce. I'll do better if I just show up. Besides" — Savannah grinned — "if she's not at home, maybe I'll just make *myself* at home and look around a little. Wouldn't be the first time."

"I didn't hear that." Click.

Savannah shook her head. *One of these days I'll have to teach these Yankee heathens some manners,* she thought as she licked a blotch of maple frosting off her wrist. *At least how to properly begin and end a telephone conversation. Now . . . where did I put that other maple bar?*

Savannah should have been able to make the thirty-mile drive to Arroyo Verde in half an hour, but a traffic backup on the Ventura Freeway turned the simple jaunt into a two-hour ordeal. Whizzing along at a breakneck speed of zero to ten and back to zero, she cursed the California Tourism Board for making Southern California seem so darned attractive to the rest of the country.

Every other license plate was from out of state, and half of the bumpers sported cutesy stickers declaring that the family inside had recently visited Disneyland, Knott's Berry Farm, Magic Mountain, or Universal Studios.

Not that she minded seeing children wearing Mickey Mouse ears or even adults with Donald Duck caps, but did they all have to drive on the same roads as she did?

When she finally reached the small, affluent town of Arroyo Verde, her doughnuts had long worn off, and her stomach was telling her it was time for lunch.

That's the problem with eating carbohydrates, she thought. *In a little while your blood-sugar level plummets and then you just have to eat more to get it back up there again where it belongs. Yep,* she decided, *I should have bought half a dozen of those maple bars while I had the chance instead of a measly two. What was I thinking?*

And she was getting downright shaky by the time she finally located the tiny house that was barely more than a shack far off the paved road on the outskirts of town. Whatever sort of home she had expected a successful model named Desiree La Port to live in . . . this wasn't it.

She hadn't anticipated that Desiree's place would be as impressive as Caitlin Connor's, or necessarily as tidy and inviting as Kameeka's. But she hadn't imagined the snooty Desiree living in a dump.

The little cracker box of a structure was in desperate need of some paint, having once been white but now a dingy, peeling gray. The yard

285

didn't have a single blade of grass, just weeds that had never seen a mower blade.

Apparently, Desiree didn't feel the need to haul her garbage all the way out to the main road for pickup, but left it in fly-infested piles only a few yards from the house.

The only sign of prosperity on the property was the new Lexus parked in front. Savannah had seen Desiree leave the shoot the other day in that car and had assumed she was a woman of means. But if this was her address, as the Department of Motor Vehicles said it was, her vehicle was part of a façade . . . along with her upturned nose.

Savannah parked near the Lexus, got out, and walked up to the house. On the warped, tilting front porch sat a half-rotten sofa, whose cushions were sprouting tufts of yellowed stuffing. And long before she got to the door, the smell of stale alcohol caused Savannah to breathe shallowly.

Rapping on the rusty screen door, she called out, "Desiree? Yoo-hoo, Desiree?"

The wooden door was open, but the inside of the house was so dark and the screen so dirty that she couldn't see in. At first, she thought no one was home, but then she heard a shuffling and some mumbled objections as someone came toward her.

"What? Who is it?" asked a grumpy voice that Savannah recognized, even though it wasn't laced with the heavy French accent.

286

When the door finally opened and the woman stuck her head outside, Savannah couldn't quite believe what she was seeing. If she had passed this person on a city street, she never would have recognized her as the attractive woman who had been the star of the photo shoot.

The short, sassy curls had disappeared, and her hair fell in lank, oily strands. Her complexion looked more sallow than fair, and dark smudges of mascara ringed her eyes. The shapeless gray sweatsuit she wore hung on her body, making her look much heavier than she was, and the front of the shirt was stained with coffee spills.

She squinted against the sunlight as she peered at Savannah. At first she looked confused, but upon recognizing Savannah, her expression quickly changed to one of annoyance.

"What do *you* want?" she said. "I don't have time for visitors right now. I'm busy."

"So am I," Savannah replied smoothly. "I'm working. And right now my job is talking to you."

Desiree shook her head. "What?"

"Actually, my name is Savannah, not Susan, and I'm not a model. . . ." Savannah began.

"Oh, really?" She gave an unpleasant snort. "Gee, I never would've guessed."

Savannah continued, undeterred. "I'm a private investigator, and I'm looking into these unfortunate deaths . . . and, of course, Tesla's disappearance."

"Have they found her yet?"

"Not yet."

"They probably won't either. Not alive, anyway."

"Why do you say that?"

Desiree went from "barely even concerned" to "acutely alert" in two seconds. "No reason," she said defensively. "I just figure she's probably dead, considering that she's missing and because of what happened to Cait and Kameeka."

She might be a slob when she's off duty, Savannah thought, *but she's no mental slouch.* Desiree La Port was cunning and clever in a street-smart sort of way. There was an animal wariness in her eyes that Savannah had seen many times in hardened criminals.

Desiree stepped outside, letting the door slam behind her, then walked over and sat down on the old, dirty sofa. Curling one foot under her, she reached into her pants pocket and pulled out a pack of cigarettes.

"Can you think of anyone who would want to see those girls dead?" Savannah asked, glad that — at least for the moment — Desiree seemed willing to talk.

Lighting her cigarette and taking a long drag, she said, "Yeah, I guess a lot of people would want to see them gone."

"Why?"

288

"They're at the top of their game. Being at the top is dangerous. Isn't it?"

Savannah studied her carefully to see if she was serious. She was. "I suppose it might be dangerous, careerwise," Savannah said. "But it shouldn't be life-threatening."

"You just never know." She released twin streams of smoke from her nostrils. "And then there's Leah and Kevin."

"What about Leah and Kevin?"

"They were both about to get dumped. Nobody likes to get dumped."

"Dumped? How?"

"All three of those girls were going to leave Leah and go to another agency. They told her so a couple of days before Cait died."

Okay, Savannah thought, *that validates what Kevin said. And speaking of Kevin . . .*

"How was Kevin about to get dumped?"

"Cait found out about his new girlfriend, and she told him it was over unless he ended the affair, once and for all."

"But wasn't she seeing someone on the side, too? I thought they had an open marriage."

Desiree gave a derisive sniff. "Yeah, right. Kevin liked to call it that so he could justify his messing around. Cait had a couple of affairs over the years, but that was water under the bridge. They'd both done the forgive-and-forget business and agreed to be faithful from then on. So when Cait found out about his honey there at work, she was hurt and mad.

Told him that she was going to divorce him."

"You know this for sure?"

"Yes. She said so herself. She told me and Kameeka and Tesla at a shoot about a week and a half ago. Those two told her she was doing the right thing, kicking him out, that it was high time she gave him his walking papers."

"Did you agree with them?"

She shrugged and gave a dismissive wave with her hand and her cigarette. "I don't know. I don't get involved in crap like that. It's none of my business."

Savannah stood, watching Desiree La Port — if, indeed, her name was Desiree La Port and not something like Debbie or Linda Smith — and she wondered how much Desiree had benefited from the disappearance and deaths of her three major competitors.

"Cait's problems with her husband might not have been your business," Savannah said, "but I'd say that your career has made a jump forward this past week."

Desiree dropped her spent cigarette onto the porch and stubbed it out with the toe of her house slipper. She smiled brightly, and for a moment she looked a bit like that model who had been giggling and mincing for the camera by the pool the other day.

"Oh, well." She lit up another cigarette and took a long, long drag. She released the smoke into the air and watched it disappear on the af-

290

ternoon breeze. She looked content, totally at peace with the world — almost pretty. "What can you say?" she added. "Sometimes you just get lucky."

By the time Savannah arrived home again, it was well past her dinnertime, and she hadn't even had lunch yet. Missing one meal could make her cranky. But doing without two in a row could plunge her into a simmering, homicidal rage.

Her mood hadn't been improved by a quick visit to the police station to see Dirk. His disposition was as dismal as her own. He had spent hours interviewing the families of the dead and missing girls . . . always a depressing job.

And other than expressing their sorrow and anger, the friends and relatives had given him absolutely nothing new to aid in the investigation.

Since Dirk was a generous sort of guy, he had been kind enough to share his depression, pessimism, and ill temper with her. So by the time she pulled up to her house and saw her sister's rental car still occupying both parking spaces in her driveway, she was solidly in a murderous state of mind.

As she walked up the sidewalk to her front door, she could hear her grandmother's kindly voice whispering in the back of her mind. *Don't kill your sister, Savannah girl, just because you've had a bad day. Strangling Marietta might seem like the thing to do, but it's wicked.*

But Gran, she silently argued with the voice of reason, *it wasn't just a bad day. I hardly got any sleep last night, next to no food today, and Marietta's whining about men is driving me nuts. You know how she can be sometimes.*

That's true. Marietta's a royal pain in the ass. Go ahead and kill her. Savannah stopped cold in the middle of her porch and shook her head. That wasn't Gran's voice. Gran didn't say "ass." She probably didn't even think it.

No doubt about it, Savannah thought, *I'm hearing strange voices . . . and they don't like Marietta either.*

She decided she'd better get some food and some sleep in that order before barking dogs started telling her that she should dance the hootchie-kootchie naked on the courthouse steps.

But when she walked into her house, it wasn't a whining, sniveling Marietta who was sitting on her sofa, happily chatting on the phone. It was a bright-eyed, bushy-tailed, sunny-faced alien who had taken over her sister's body.

"Okay, darlin'," she was saying. "Yes, I miss you, too. Can't wait to see you again and . . . well . . . I can't talk now 'cause Savannah just came in. Yeah, she's the same as ever." She cut a sideways look at Savannah and said, "That's about right."

Savannah scowled. She trusted this cheerful

292

version of Marietta less than she had the whinin'-and-moanin' one. At least the old one had been familiar, and as Gran said, "Better the devil you know than the devil you don't."

Marietta was making obscene kissy sounds into the phone. Savannah walked into the kitchen, vowing to spritz it with Lysol before she used it again. She had to eat something; she couldn't take this . . . whatever it was . . . on an empty stomach.

"Did you eat yet?" she called back into the living room.

"No, I was waiting for you," came the predictable answer.

"Waiting for me to cook it and serve you, is more like it," she mumbled as she pulled a package of pork chops out of the refrigerator, along with a head of lettuce, some tomatoes, and a Bermuda onion.

Cleopatra and Diamante ran into the kitchen, tails up and waving, anticipating their evening ration of Kitten Kittles.

"Sometimes I just feel plain used," Savannah said as they wrapped themselves around her ankles. "Sometimes I feel like I've got WELCOME printed across my forehead."

No sooner had she scooped the fishy-smelling concoction into their bowls than she heard a purring sound, and it wasn't coming from the cats. It was the sound of her cell phone buzzing in her purse on the kitchen table.

"Go away," she told it. "Let me get a mess of pork chops and mashed potatoes in my stomach and a nap and then you can wipe your feet on the old Savannah doormat."

She pulled her cast-iron skillet out of the oven, set it on the stove, and lit the flame under it. But as she was reaching into the cupboard for the can of shortening, the phone started to buzz again.

"Lord Almighty, there's no rest for the weary . . . and apparently no dinner either," she said as she turned off the stove, walked over to the table, and fished her phone out of her purse.

"What do you want?" she barked, expecting it to be Dirk.

Instead it was Tammy on the other end, and she sounded excited. "Oh, I'm so glad you picked up this time," she said. "You're not going to believe where I am."

"Well, let me tell you where *I* am," she said. "I'm in my kitchen, trying to make myself a bite to eat and —"

"I know."

"You know? How do you know?"

"I didn't know that you were cooking, but I know you're home because I'm parked about a block and a half from your house."

"What are you doing there?"

"Surveillance."

"You're doing surveillance on me? Tammy, I'm not someone who needs to be —"

"I know, I know. I've been tailing Tumblety

294

all day long. I followed him all over town early this morning and then I tailed him all the way out to Arroyo Verde and back. . . ."

Savannah completely forgot about food or sleep as her brain began to spin. "Arroyo Verde? Today?"

"Yeah, and then he came back here to San Carmelita, and guess where he is right now?"

The hair on the back of Savannah's neck started to prickle. "Don't tell me. . . ."

"Yes. I'm sitting in my car, watching him with my binoculars. And right this very minute, that creep is peeping in your kitchen window."

Chapter 20

It took every smidgen of Savannah's self-control not to rush over to her window and confront Tumblety. But if she did that, he would simply run, and she wasn't in the mood to let anybody get away with anything today. And especially not violating her privacy!

Calmly, she turned her back to the window and said, "Really? Now isn't that just so-o-o-o interesting. Let's keep talking about this."

She strolled back to the table and picked up her purse. "I'm going to go into the living room now," she said, "and I want you to tell me everything he does. Okay?"

Tammy assured her she would.

Her purse in one hand, the phone in the other, Savannah walked into the living room where Marietta was still chatting happily on the phone.

"Mari," she said, keeping her voice low. "Listen close. Do exactly what I say. Okay?"

Marietta looked up at her and screwed up her face in annoyance. "Can't you see? I'm on the phone."

"Hang up right now, and call 911."

"Why?"

"Just do it." Then, into the phone, she said, "What's he doing now?"

"He's left the kitchen window and is working his way around to the living room. Your shrubs are in his way."

"If he smashes my new lilac bush, I'll kill him for sure," Savannah muttered. Turning back to Marietta, she plastered a fake smile on her face and said, "Did you dial 911 like I said?"

"No! You're acting weird, Savannah, and you're getting me spooked. Cut it out."

"Marietta. Do what I'm telling you, girl. Hang up that phone and call 911. Tell them that we have a prowler at 217 Rosebriar Lane. Tell them to send a patrol car, to get in touch with Sergeant Dirk Coulter and get him over here, too. And I want you to go upstairs to the guest room, go inside, and lock the door. And you don't come out till I come and get you. You got all that?"

Marietta's mouth fell open; then she seemed to recover herself and began to punch buttons furiously on the phone. "Yeah, okay. What're you gonna do?"

"Don't worry about it. Just make that call and walk upstairs like nothing's going on, okay?"

For once, Marietta actually did as she was told and with remarkable efficiency. Once she was upstairs and locked into the guest room,

297

Savannah tucked her purse under her left arm and walked around the living room, straightening a cushion, rearranging the magazines.

"What's he doing now?" she asked Tammy.

"Watching you. Taking your picture."

"Taking my picture?"

"Yes, he's got some sort of a little camera with him."

"Now isn't that lovely," she said through gritted teeth. "I think I'll take that camera away from him and use it to perform a colonoscopy on him."

She left the living room and walked into the windowless foyer, where she would be out of his sight for a moment. Placing her purse on the entry table, she reached inside and pulled out her Beretta.

Before walking back into the living room, she slid the gun into the waistband of her slacks and covered it with the tail of her shirt.

"He's still looking in the living room window," Tammy said.

"Okay, here's what I'm going to do," Savannah told her. "I'm going to act like I'm going into the kitchen again, but I'm going to slip out the back door and through the garage before he can figure it out."

"Gotcha. Go. And good luck."

Less than two minutes later, Savannah pressed the barrel of her Beretta against the back of Ronald Peeping-Tom Tumblety's neck and said, "If you move, I'll blow your head off. And I'd hate to have to do that; I just cleaned the outside of my windows."

He jumped and started to turn around, so she jabbed the gun even harder against his neck.

"I'm not kidding," she said. "I'll kill you. Drop that camera on the ground and put your hands on top of your head."

After a couple of seconds, he complied.

"Lace your fingers together."

Savannah was still holding the phone in her left hand. "Tammy, you still there?" she asked.

"I'm listening."

"Get up here and bring those handcuffs I gave you for your birthday."

She tossed the phone onto the grass, reached up, and grabbed the little finger of his right hand. She pulled it back just enough to cause him some minor discomfort — and enough to remind him that it could become major pain very quickly.

Lifting her leg, she shoved her knee into the small of his back while pulling on his hands. He leaned backward, off balance — just the way she wanted him.

"Don't you even twitch, you peeping perv," she said, lowering her leg but keeping him in his uncomfortable position. "Look in *my* window, will you? I oughta shoot you just for trompin' down my flower beds."

"You don't understand," he said, his voice

quivering. "I wasn't going to hurt you. I saw you at the shoot the other day, and I really like you."

"Gee, why don't I find that flattering?"

"I think you and me could get along really good if you just knew me. If we went out a few times and spent some quality time together . . ."

"Oh, we're *going* to spend some time together. But we're not going to be watching a movie and sharing a popcorn."

Tammy came running up, holding a pair of handcuffs out in front of her. "Here they are!" she said.

Savannah gave Tumblety's pinkie a tug. "Put your right hand behind your back," she told him. "Do it!"

She told Tammy. "Cuff him."

Tammy stared at Savannah, mouth open. "Me?" she asked.

"You're the one with the cuffs."

"Oh . . . okay." Her hands were trembling, but Tammy quickly snapped the first cuff around his right wrist and held it tightly.

Savannah tugged on his left hand. "Now this one. Bring it down."

In seconds, Tammy had that one secured as well, and Ronald Tumblety was in the unofficial custody of the Moonlight Magnolia Detective Agency.

As though on cue, a radio car came around the corner and stopped in front of her house, lights flashing. A uniformed patrolman got out and came running up to them.

"You want to pat this guy down and stick him in the back of your unit?" Savannah said. "He's a suspect in several murders, and I just caught him looking in my windows. Detective Coulter will be along in few minutes. And I'm sure he'll have some questions for Ronny Boy here."

When Dirk arrived, Savannah and Tammy quickly filled him in on the situation. He talked to Tumblety a few minutes, then instructed the patrolman to take him to the station and put him in a holding cell.

"You tailed him all day?" Dirk asked Tammy as they watched the radio car pull away with the unhappy Tumblety in the rear seat.

"Sure, just like you told me to," she replied proudly.

"Exactly what did he do from the time he left his house . . . er, van?"

"He went to a liquor store, then to that porn shop down on Chaparral Street. Next he went to a photo lab — the one on the east side of town between the McDonald's and the Taco Bell. Then he drove out to Arroyo Verde and sat in his car in front of a house there for over an hour."

"It was Desiree La Port's place," Savannah said. "I went out there myself and talked to her. He must have been watching her place and saw me when I arrived."

"Yeah, and when Savannah left the house," Tammy added, "he followed her all the way home. He parked over there." She pointed to his car, parked half a block down the street. "Then he got out, snuck up to her house, and peeked in the windows. He had a camera and was taking pictures, too."

"The camera's lying over there, in my flower bed," Savannah said. "And my cell phone, too."

They walked over to the window and retrieved both items from the dew-damp lawn.

"You say he went to a photo lab?" Savannah asked as she wiped her wet phone on her shirt.

"Yes." Tammy nodded eagerly.

"Could you tell if he was dropping off or picking up?"

"I didn't see anything in his hands when he went in, but he was carrying a little plastic bag when he came out."

Savannah and Dirk gave each other a knowing look.

Dirk turned and headed across the grass toward Tumblety's car. Savannah and Tammy followed close behind him.

"If he didn't go home, the pictures are probably still in the car, right?" Savannah asked Tammy.

"Yes, I guess so. Why? Do you think there would be anything good in them?"

Savannah sniffed. "Anything good? With any luck at all, it'll be something bad."

★ ★ ★

"I thought you said you aren't photogenic," Dirk said. He picked up one of Tumblety's pictures and studied it closely. Too closely, as far as Savannah was concerned.

She snatched it out of his hand and placed it back on her kitchen table, along with the other twenty-three shots they were perusing.

"I'm just saying you look pretty yummy in that blue swimsuit," he added, reaching for it again. "Can I have a copy of this one? I want to tape it to the inside of my locker at the station."

"Oink, oink," Tammy said with a snort.

"Business," Savannah told him. "Keep your mind on business, boy. And stop gawking at my hooters." She reached for another picture that showed off her curves even more than the first. "Here. If you're gonna decorate your locker, do it right."

Meanwhile, Tammy was shuffling the photos around on the table, grouping them in some manner that only she understood.

"What are you doing there?" Savannah asked her.

"Trying to decide who old Ronald liked best, you or Tesla." She pointed to a row of pictures that she had arranged in a column. "Out of the twenty-four shots, four of them are of the whole group of models. Eight of them feature you in the center and up close. And twelve of them have Tesla as the main focus."

Savannah suppressed a shudder. "Good.

That's one beauty contest I'd prefer *not* to win."

Dirk dragged several of the pictures across the table and lined them up in front of him. "These are the ones I'm interested in," he said. "The ones he took as you girls were leaving."

"Why those in particular?" Tammy asked.

"Good point," Savannah said.

"What?" Tammy looked from Savannah to Dirk. "What are you looking for?"

"To see who he's fixated on at that point," Savannah said. "Right, Dirk?"

Dirk nodded. "And just as I figured — it's Tesla. Look at this. . . ."

He pointed to the central figure of the four photos that were taken of the driveway area as the women were getting into their assorted vehicles to leave the shoot.

Tesla was the star of each picture. Front and center.

Savannah felt a tug at her heart when she saw Tesla stepping into her car, the same black Mitsubishi that they had found abandoned in the coffee shop parking lot.

Studying Tesla's expression, captured in the photo, Savannah could see that she was troubled, as she had been during the shoot. But Savannah couldn't help wondering if Tesla had any inkling that within a very short time, her life would be threatened . . . or worse.

"That's what I thought," Dirk said with a smug look on his face. "Tumblety was after her

304

even then. I'm telling you, *he's* the one who nabbed her in that parking lot. Not some guy in a white van."

Tammy picked up one of the photos off the table and held it only a few inches from her nose as she peered at it. "A white van?" she said.

"Yeah," Dirk replied. "Tumblety's mysterious, disappearing dude in an old white van."

She plunked the photo down in the center of the table and placed her fingertip on an object in the background. "You mean an old white van like this one? With a rack on the top?"

Savannah felt a shot of adrenaline hit her bloodstream, more potent than any caffeine or sugar hit, as she looked down at the picture. Tammy was right. There in the background, parked about a block away from the beach house, was an old panel body van — white with a rack, just as Tumblety had described.

She pointed to another vehicle in the background, even farther away than the van. Only the fender was showing, but it was enough for a tentative identification. "And isn't that Tumblety's El Camino?" she asked Dirk.

He frowned and nodded. "Yep, I'm afraid so."

"He drove to the shoot location in his own car," Savannah said, thinking aloud. "Maybe it's a coincidence that there's a van like he described in this picture."

Tammy tapped on the photo again. "Looks to

me like somebody's sitting in the driver's seat, too," she said, "but you can't see any more than just a dark outline."

"And the license plate number is there," Savannah noted, "but it's too blurry to do us any good."

"How could you tell?" Tammy said, picking up the photo and grinning at them. "You both need glasses and are just too proud to admit it and buy some. Let *me* take a look."

"I do *not* need glasses!" Dirk snapped.

"Me either." Savannah reached over and thumped the side of Tammy's head.

"Naw, I can't see it either." Tammy sighed and laid the photo back down on the table.

Savannah jumped up and ran over to the counter in the kitchen where the telephone sat. Opening the drawer beneath the phone, she pulled out a glasses case.

"Here," she said as she returned to the table, pulled out the glasses, and put them on. "Let me take another look at that picture."

"Don't need glasses, huh?" Tammy muttered. "Then what are those things on your face?"

"They're magnifying aids, which I use to read the phone book these days. They're printing the names in those things smaller every year. I tell you, it's a Communist conspiracy."

"Medicine bottle directions and maps, too," Dirk grumbled.

"I'm telling you, it's a plot against baby boomers." Savannah squinted, staring at the photo for ages. Finally, she tossed it back onto the table. "Nope," she said, "nothing but fuzz."

"That's too bad," Tammy replied. "It could be exactly what we need to break the case."

"Too bad we don't have the kind of fancy equipment that the feds have," Dirk said. "You know, the kind you see on TV that can take pictures and . . . do whatever they do to them."

"Enhance them digitally," Tammy supplied. "Yes, it's too bad we don't have access to —"

She looked across the table at Savannah, who was already smiling from ear to ear.

"Ryan," Tammy said.

"And John," Savannah added. "They've still got plenty of connections at the Bureau."

"Eh," Dirk said, "you broads just look for excuses to call those guys."

"Don't knock it," Savannah told him. Then, in her best impression of Mae West, she added, "In this case, they've got the equipment we need."

"Yeah, right . . ." He sniffed. "For all the good it'll ever do ya."

Chapter
21

Savannah and Dirk were in his car on their way to interview Kameeka Wills's parents and sisters the next day, when Savannah received the much-anticipated call from Ryan and John.

"The digital enhancement worked," were Ryan's opening words. "And we have a plate number for you."

"Hallelujah!" Savannah exclaimed, reaching over and slapping Dirk on the thigh. "Spit it out, my friend."

She jotted down the numbers and letters in her notebook, then thanked him profusely before saying good-bye.

"We've got it!" she told Dirk. "Phone it in to the station and have them run it. And this time . . . use some of that scintillating charm of yours so that we'll get it sometime this month, huh?"

Having postponed their visit to the Wills household, they went instead to the address given to them by the Department of Motor Vehicles. The house on the corner of Meadowbrook Road and Bellmore Avenue was easy enough to find. It was the owner, a fellow named James Lee Oates, who was difficult to locate.

"Jim's gone," a neighbor told Savannah. She and Dirk had split up and were canvassing both sides of the street. This was the first person she had found at home.

"Gone? Gone where?"

"Las Vegas," the elderly woman said, a bright, excited look on her face. "I gave him ten dollars' worth of quarters to play the slots for me. We're gonna split whatever he wins. I can't wait for him to get back in town, so I can find out how much we won. I need a new recliner and maybe even a new car if he did good enough."

"I see," Savannah replied. What she could see was a sweet lady who needed a realistic plan for replacing that aged recliner. "How long has Jim been out of town?"

"Nine days. He stopped in along the way to visit some girl that he's sweet on, and he's been in Vegas for the past three days. I haven't heard a word from him. I'm hoping that's not bad news. Do you think he would have called me if we'd hit a big one?"

Savannah shrugged and stifled a grin. "I have no idea, ma'am." She glanced across the street at Oates's house with its empty driveway. "Does Jim drive a white van with a rack on top?" she asked.

"Oh, that monstrosity of his. It's an eyesore, I tell you. That's another reason why I hope he wins a big jackpot in Vegas. He needs a new van worse than I need another car. That thing's going to break down someday and leave him on the side of the road."

"So, he drove the van to Las Vegas?" Savannah asked, her mental wheels whirring as she evaluated the possibility that ol' Jim had lied to this dear lady, stayed in town, and murdered some women in his spare time.

"Heavens, no. He wouldn't drive that thing to Los Angeles, let alone Vegas. I'm telling you, it's a heap of junk. He took his other car — his Toyota. He just uses the van for his work. He's a painter, you know. Not the artist kind, the house and wall kind."

"Wait a minute," Savannah said, confused. When she and Dirk had arrived at Oates's house, they had looked through the garage window and found the garage empty, except for a mountain of painting supplies. "If he didn't take the van with him and it isn't in the garage, where is it?"

The old lady smiled, happy to supply the answer. "Oh, that's because Charlotte has it. She borrows it sometimes when he's out of town . . . you know . . . when she's got some furniture to haul or something like that."

"Charlotte?" Savannah felt a prickle of anticipation. "Who's Charlotte?"

"Charlotte Murray, his sister. Such a sweet

girl. I've always really liked Charlotte. Looks just like her brother. Maybe if we win big, we can give her enough money to buy a van for herself, or at least a bigger car. You know, she can't haul a decent bill of groceries in that little Honda of hers. Why, she . . ."

Savannah waved to Dirk, who was halfway down the block, looking dejected as he left one house and headed for another. Seeing her beckoning him, he perked up and joined her beside the Buick.

"Get in," she said.

Once inside the car, she turned to him and said, "Charlotte Murray."

"What about Charlotte Murray? I already talked to her."

Savannah shook her head. "What? You already know about Charlotte Murray?"

"Yeah, I told you. I questioned her already."

"About what? Who is she?"

"She works at the hospital. She's a head nurse, Kevin Connor's supervisor."

Savannah felt a rush similar to the one provided by a hot, strong Irish coffee. It flowed through her body, making her tingle to her fingers and toes.

"Do you mean to tell me," she said, "this Charlotte Murray is the one who gave Kevin Connor his airtight alibi? The one who says he was there at the hospital all day and couldn't have possibly murdered his wife?"

"Yeah. Why?"

Time slowed for Savannah, as it often did at moments of high stress . . . or exquisite delight. She laughed, reached over, and slapped Dirk on the shoulder. "Charlotte Murray is Jim Oates's sister," she said. "He's been on a trip to Vegas this week, and *she's* driving his white van."

"No way!" Dirk's eyes lit up with the light of a man who thought he was drowning only moments before but now sees a luxury cruise ship coming to pluck him out of the cold waters of the Atlantic.

"You got it, big guy."

He grinned — an evil grin. "So, whatcha say, Mama? Is it about time to go to the hospital?"

She placed her hands on her stomach and began to huff and puff. "Yes, sirree, Bob. I feel like I'm about nine and a half months along and finally something's about to deliver!"

Savannah didn't exactly hate the hospital — at least, not the way she hated the city morgue. But it was a close second.

Antiseptic-smelling hallways with highly polished floors and open doors that revealed the unhappy side of living and dying — hospitals reminded her of the fragility of human beings. And in her line of work, she had plenty of reminders of that sad fact already.

But today, as she and Dirk hurried down the

hallway, their shoes squeaking on the shiny linoleum, she was in a far better mood than usual. There was nothing quite like a break in a case to put a spring in a girl's step . . . hospital hallway or not.

And while they were a long way still from figuring out the "why, when, and where" of the case, at least they had a line on "who." And as Savannah's brother, Macon, would say, "That's better than a bite in the ass."

"When you interviewed this gal," she said to Dirk, "did she seem like the type to you?"

"The type?" Dirk shook his head. "No. *Tumblety* seems like the type. Assuming there's a type. And we both know there ain't."

Savannah had to admit it was true. In her years of investigating homicides, she had pretty much concluded that about anyone could commit murder under the right . . . or wrong . . . set of circumstances.

But one killing, done in the heat of passion and regretted a moment later, was one thing. Two, maybe three, murders in a week — that was something altogether different. That took a person of a different mind-set. And it was hard for her to imagine that anyone who had chosen nursing as a profession could do such a thing.

After hiking for what seemed like miles through the cavernous maze of hallways on the ground floor, they came to the surgical unit where Kevin Connor worked. And more importantly, where Dirk said he had last interviewed Nurse Charlotte Murray.

They found her desk at the nurse's station near the elevator bank, but after a look around, Dirk told Savannah that she wasn't among the nurses milling about in their bright blue smocks and heavy white sneakers.

Dirk walked up to a young black woman with copious beaded braids who was sitting behind a desk and said, "Is Nurse Murray on duty?"

Her pretty face lit up with recognition and interest. "You're the one who was here the other day," she said, lowering her voice conspiratorially. "The policeman who was asking about Nurse Connor's wife."

"That's right," he said, dropping his voice to match her whisper. "Is she around?"

"She was. I think she's on a break right now."

Savannah noted the gleam in the young nurse's eye — the sure sign of a dyed-in-the-wool gossip. And when investigating a case, those were Savannah's favorite people. You couldn't trust half of what they told you, but one hundred percent of it was bound to be interesting.

"Where does she usually go when she takes her breaks?" Dirk asked.

"Depends on how long her break is," the nurse replied. "Sometimes she goes to the cafeteria. And since she smokes, sometimes she's up on the roof, having a cigarette." She glanced around, then lowered her voice even more. "And sometimes . . . she takes a nap . . . in there." She nodded toward a door down a hallway to their left.

It was something in her tone and in the quirk of her brow when she said, ". . . in there," that set Savannah's wheels turning.

She leaned onto the desk and gave the nurse her friendliest down-home smile. "What's . . . in there?" she asked.

"It's sort of an unofficial break room. It's where they catch a nap when they get the chance."

"Who's *they?*" Dirk wanted to know.

"The head nurses," she replied, again lifting one brow. "The doctors. The surgical nurses."

For a moment Savannah could see those last three words, like a giant neon sign flashing over the woman's head.

"*Surgical* nurses?" Savannah repeated. "And *head* nurses?"

She nodded knowingly.

"And maybe sometimes they might be napping in there at the same time?" Dirk said.

"They might be in there. They might be napping. Depends on who it is how much sleeping is going on."

"Gotcha," Savannah said. "And do you suppose they're 'napping' in there right now?"

"Naw, don't think so. I haven't seen anybody go in there today yet."

"How about the day that Kevin Connor's wife died?" Dirk asked. "Do you think there were any head nurses and surgical nurses in

315

there napping together?"

"I was sitting at this desk all day. I saw Nurse Connor go in there. He stopped by the desk first and said he was really tired after a long surgery he'd had that morning. Said he was going to get some sleep before a myomectomy in the afternoon. He told us not to bother him."

"And was he . . . bothered, that is?" Savannah asked.

Again, the nurse looked around, but the only other two nurses in the area seemed deeply engrossed in a patient's chart. "Nurse Murray went in there for a couple of minutes. When she came out, she said he was sound asleep and reminded me not to disturb him, to let him rest."

"How long was he in there?" Dirk said.

"About an hour. Maybe a little longer."

"How did he look when he came out?" Savannah asked.

"Look?"

"Yes. Did he look . . . rested?"

She nodded. "He looked fine. I mean, he didn't even look like he'd been sleeping. Usually people come out of there with pillow prints on their faces, their hair standing up, and drool on their chins."

Savannah turned to Dirk. "That sounds like you in the morning," she said. "Or pretty much any time up till noon."

Dirk ignored Savannah's comment and said

316

to the nurse, "Do you think I could see that room?"

"You mean, like go in there and look around?"

"Yeah. Exactly."

"I don't see why not. The door's usually unlocked, and I don't think anybody's in there right now. Go ahead."

"Thanks . . . for everything," Dirk told her.

"Yeah," Savannah added. "And you have a real good day, darlin'."

The nurse's eyes sparkled with good-natured mischief. "I always do."

As they walked away and headed toward the room in question, Savannah whispered to Dirk, "Don't you just love a blabbermouth?"

"I depend on them," he replied. "They're almost as informative as pissed-off ex-wives."

When they reached the door at the end of the hall, they were pleased to find it unlocked. Dirk entered first and switched on the light.

Following him inside, Savannah was surprised to find far less than the five-star accommodations she was anticipating. Although she hadn't expected the nap/break room to have down pillows and Egyptian cotton duvets, she had figured that doctors snoozed on something better than a gurney and a simple cot.

Both "beds" were empty, but rumpled pillows and sheets suggested that they had been used recently.

Savannah shut the door behind her and

joined Dirk beside the large window.

"So much for the idea that Connor couldn't have left this room without being seen," she said.

"Just what I was thinking. Tell everybody not to bother you, hop in and out of the window, and go on about your merry way of murdering your old lady."

"How?"

He gave her an exasperating, weary look. "One thing at a time, if you don't mind."

She turned and glanced around the room. On the far wall was a line of small gray lockers that were secured with assorted padlocks and combination locks.

"Oh, lookie, lookie," she said. "That one there on the end says MURRAY. And it's got a padlock."

Dirk sniffed. "Yeah, but I ain't got a warrant and my butt's still sore from the chief chewin' on it. He hasn't gotten over us breaking into the Montoya chick's place yet."

"Eh, the chief should fall down a flight o' stairs," she said, walking over to the locker and fingering the simple padlock.

He said nothing as he watched her examine the mechanism.

"There's nothing to this," she said. "I had one of these on my high school gym locker."

"I could get a warrant," he said. "Maybe . . . in a few hours. Of course, by then Nurse Blabbermouth back there at the desk will tell a dozen people we were asking about Murray and that we came into this room. And they'll tell Nurse Murray, and she'll get rid of anything in there that might be any good."

"Ninety seconds," she whispered . . . the voice of temptation. "That's all it'd take me to have her open."

"I can't. The chief would be having my oysters fried for dinner."

Savannah reached into her purse and fumbled around, searching for her lock pick. "Why don't you go see if you can track down Murray?" she suggested. "And maybe check with security to see if they keep track of what vehicles come and go out of the parking lot. They might have one of those gates where you have to use a card to get in. Or maybe they have a camera set up, showing who's doing what."

"Good idea," he said. "I'll see if either Connor's or Murray's vehicle left during the day."

"You do that." She gave him a big grin and a wink. "And I'll meet you in the lobby in a while."

"And when we hook up again," he said, "you can let me know if it would be worth my while to get that search warrant."

"Oh . . . let's just say I'll be able to give you an informed opinion."

Half an hour later, Dirk found Savannah sitting on a chair in the lobby, reading a year-old copy of *People* magazine. She had a satisfied smirk on her face that matched the one on his.

"Did you find Murray?" she asked him.

"Nope. Get this: While we were in the locker room, somebody — I can't imagine who — told her we were there, asking for her. She split, said she had a headache and had to go home."

"Are you going to put an APB out on her?"

"Not yet. Let's go by her house and see if she's there. With any luck, she'll still be driving her brother's van."

As they walked out to the visitors' parking lot, Savannah asked him, "Did you get anything interesting from security?"

"Yeah, I did. Murray left the garage at ten forty-nine that morning and didn't come back until eleven thirty-five. Connor stayed here," he said, "according to the cards that they use to get through the gate."

"Or Connor could have left, using Murray's card. The record wouldn't necessarily show what vehicle was being driven."

"True."

"Is there a video?"

He shook his head. "Nope."

"Darn. There's never a video when you need one."

"Unless it's a convenience store that's being robbed. Then there's a camera, but some moron forgot to put in a tape. What did you find in the locker? Anything?"

She suppressed a chuckle. "Oh, I guess it's a matter of opinion. But I think so."

"Talk to me."

"How about a pair of red clogs, exactly like the ones I saw in Kevin Connor's living room?"

"We already figured they're fooling around. That's old news."

"How about a pair of men's jeans . . . about Kevin Connor's size . . . wadded into a ball in the bottom of the locker?"

He shrugged. "I'm not excited, Van. I hate to tell ya, but —"

"What if I told you that those jeans have some suspicious dark brown stains on them?"

"I'm breathin' hard. . . ."

"And some interesting white lines on the knees that look sorta like tic-tac-toe marks."

"White lines? Tic-tac-toe?"

"Yeah. Ring a bell?"

He shook his head. "Not at all."

"You said you bleach your toilet and bathroom floor once a week. Haven't you ever gotten a few drops on what you're wearing and ruined it?"

"Naw, I clean it when I'm naked, just before I get into the shower."

She grimaced. "Gee, thanks for the visual I didn't need. Anyway. . . . Trust me, when you're cleaning a floor with bleach, you don't want to kneel on the floor with good clothes on."

He brightened, stopped, and put his hand on

her shoulder. "Or you wind up with white marks on your clothes."

She nodded. "And remember Kameeka's kitchen floor? It's tile — those little tiles that are about two inches wide."

"Are the tic-tac-toe lines on those jeans about two inches wide?"

"Bingo!"

Before she knew what was happening, he had grabbed her, pulled her to him, and planted a rough, whisker-bristly, hot and hard kiss on her lips.

And he didn't release her all that quickly either. She had plenty of time to savor it, think about it, and compare his technique to Ryan's before he finally let her go.

Her final analysis was: What Dirk lacked in Ryan's finesse, he more than made up in raw enthusiasm.

Not bad, she thought. *Not half bad at all.*

As they continued on across the lot, Dirk chatted on brightly, ecstatic about the case's latest turns — as though nothing unusual had just happened. "I'm gonna get Jake McMurtry to come over here and sit on that locker," he was saying, "so that nobody unscrupulous breaks into it before I can get that search warrant. We don't want those jeans to take a walk."

"Uh-huh."

"And I'm gonna swing by your place and drop you off on my way to Murray's house. I don't want her to see you, face to face, just yet.

We might need to use you in some other 'non-official' capacity later, and we don't want her to know that we're a team."

"Hm-m-m. . . ."

When they reached the Buick, Dirk was still scheming, joyfully plotting the demises of Charlotte Murray and Kevin Connor — a very happy boy.

But for the moment, Savannah had forgotten all about the investigation. She was too busy wondering at the odds of her getting kissed — and kissed very well, indeed — by her two favorite guys in one week.

Gran's right, she thought. *Wonders never cease.*

Chapter
22

"Where's my sister?" Savannah asked Tammy when she walked into her living room and didn't see Marietta attached to the telephone.

"Upstairs taking a bath," Tammy replied as she shuffled a pile of papers on the desk.

"How's she doing?" Savannah was afraid to ask, but even if the news was bad, it was best to be informed.

"She's singing."

"The blues?"

"No. She's actually really cheerful. And I'm pretty sure that I heard her packing in the guest room earlier."

Savannah held her breath, barely daring to hope. "Really? Don't mess with my head, girl. I'm much too fragile right now."

"Really. And I thought I overheard her phoning the airline earlier. I think she's Georgia bound."

"And happy about it?"

As though to answer her question, a voice drifted downward from the upstairs bathroom. It was Sister Mari, in fine form.

"I ne-e-ever got over those blue eyes. I se-e-ee them e-e-everywhere," she wailed, murdering the old Johnny Cash ballad. Splash, splash. "I mi-i-is those arms that held me . . . when a-l-l-l the love was the-e-ere!"

Savannah tried to mentally assemble the puzzle that was her sister and, as usual, couldn't quite put the pieces together. "How can she be this happy about going home?" she asked Tammy. "I was threatening to lock her out the other night, and you should have seen the hissy fit she threw. And now . . ."

"I wo-o-onder if he's sor-r-ry, for le-e-eaving what we'd begun," continued the concert upstairs.

Savannah shook her head. "Go figure. I'm going to eat some lunch, fuel up. I have a feeling it's gonna be a long afternoon."

By the time Marietta had finished her bath and countless verses of her song, Savannah and Tammy had eaten their lunch, and Savannah had filled Tammy in on all the newest developments.

"He's gone out to Murray's house to pick her up if she's there," Savannah told her. "And I think I'll buzz over to Charlotte's brother's place and do some plain, old-fashioned surveillance."

A cloud of jasmine-scented perfume arrived in the kitchen a few seconds before Marietta appeared, wrapped in a red chiffon robe over a black lace teddy. Her carefully poofed hair and meticulously applied makeup hadn't been disturbed during the long bath.

And, as well as smelling like the cosmetic counter of a drugstore, she was beaming from ear to ear.

"Good afternoon!" she said, giving Savannah the full radiance of her smile. "How are you this fine, fine day?"

"O-o-okay," Savannah replied suspiciously. "Boy, aren't we chipper."

"Chipper? My cup of joy is just plain boiling over!"

Savannah glanced down at the teddy's built-in push-up bra and the abundance of cleavage swelling above it. "I can see that," she said. "Both cups, in fact. What's up . . . besides your boobs?"

"I'm going home! This evening!"

"And that's good news?" Savannah asked.

"It's the best! I'm going home to my own true love. I was on the wrong road, but now I've seen the light."

"You have?"

Tammy cleared her throat. "Would you like me to leave? I have some work that I can —"

"No, stay if you wanna," Marietta said. "I've gotta run upstairs and finish packing."

"But . . . but what about What's-His-Nose . . . the chat-room guy?" Savannah asked.

"Oh, he turned out to be such a mistake. What a loser!" Marietta waved one hand, displaying bright red, dragonlady nails with white glitter hearts. "But it's worked out for good in the end. You see, when my darlin' back home found out that I'd come out here to California in search of what he couldn't give me, he called and proclaimed his love to me again."

"Again? Your darlin' back home?" Alarm bells jangled Savannah's nerves. "You don't mean —"

"Yes, my sweet Lester. He's finally come to his senses, and he says if I'll just come back home, he'll leave that worthless Lucille. He's done some soul searching, and he says he's actually getting to the point where he can start to think about dumping her once and for all."

"Oh, Mari, I don't think —"

"He just didn't know what he had with me till he heard I was gone, you know. He called and said that the thought of me being here with another man was just too much for him to bear. It was driving him plum crazy."

"Wouldn't take much," Savannah muttered under her breath. "Lester's always been a little short on smarts where his women are concerned."

"Now don't you even start with me, Miss Savannah Smarty-Pants. You don't know squat about the deep, dark matters of the heart. And you don't know what I should or shouldn't do because you ain't me!"

Savannah stood and scooped up her dishes from the table. "You're absolutely right, Marietta. I'm not you. Excuse me for a minute. I have to go find that tube of Super Glue. I'm going to apply it to my mouth like it was lip gloss. That way I'll refrain from telling you how stupid I think it is for you to go back home and take up again with a married man . . . a man whose wife already tried to blow you up with a shotgun." She stopped, clapped her hands over her mouth, and said, "Oops. Too late."

She tossed her dishes into the sink and went upstairs to the bathroom. She needed to brush her teeth. She needed to wash her face. She needed to dunk her head under water three times and bring it up twice.

But the moment she stepped into the bathroom, she nearly fainted. It had to be over a hundred degrees in there and as humid as a Mississippi swamp in July. The only thing missing was the mosquitoes.

"Good Lord, Mari," she mumbled. "Were you taking yourself a *tub* bath or a *steam* bath? A body can't hardly breathe in here."

It didn't take her long to see the cause of the problem; Marietta had turned on the overhead heat lamp and had neglected to turn it off when she'd left the room.

Savannah quickly switched it off, grumbling under her breath about the electric bill that she probably wouldn't be able to pay. Not even when the bright red alarmist notice came in the mail — the one with all the bold print, exclamation marks, and evil threats.

Needing a quick fix of energy and a feeling of renewal after her latest Marietta encounter, she filled the sink with cool water, pulled her hair back with a headband, and bent over. Splashing the refreshing water on her tired eyes felt great, in spite of the fact that the room was still too hot and humid to breathe.

She picked a white hand towel out of the wicker basket on the back of her toilet tank and dried her face with it. Looking down at the towel in her hands, she remembered the soft, plush, spa-quality towels in Caitlin Connor's bathroom and thought how nice they would feel in comparison to this nearly worn-out rag. Maybe she would treat herself to some one of these days when —

Suddenly, she dropped the towel onto the sink edge and whirled around. She stared up at the heat lamp in the ceiling for a long moment. Then she turned and ran out of the bathroom and into her bedroom.

She grabbed the phone on her nightstand and dialed Dirk.

He answered after five rings. "Yeah?"

"I know how they killed Cait," she said.

She had expected him to be at least mildly enthused after hearing her announcement. But she had forgotten she was talking to Dirk.

"Yeah, well, good for you," he said. "I went by Charlotte Murray's house, and she was gone. Her neighbor was working in the yard, and he said he saw Charlotte run into the house for a few minutes, then leave with a couple of suitcases about five minutes before I got there."

"That stinks," she said, "but I know how Connor did it, he —"

"Connor lawyered up is what he did. I brought him in just now and got all of ten words out of him before he clammed up and called that Marvin Klein dude to represent him. Klein was here in a flash, and I had to let Connor go."

"Hmm, sorry to hear that; Klein's tough, but —"

"So I'm back at square one. I hate this friggin' job. Did I ever tell you that?"

"Yeah, you mention it at least twice a week." She took a deep breath, determined to keep talking this time no matter what. "Cait called Kevin at the hospital and told him she had made herself sick from working out and starving herself. He recognized the symptoms of heatstroke and sneaked out of the hospital. By the time he got home, she was probably already in bad shape, weak, maybe disoriented and confused — those are symptoms of heatstroke. She might have even been unconscious."

She paused to catch another breath. "Go on," he said. "I'm with you."

"So, all he had to do was drag her into the bathroom — that's why her arms were up, also her hair, and her clothes bunched up on her body — and turn on the heat lamps. If I remember, there were two or three of them in the ceiling, over by the shower stall."

"Yeah, I think there were. And those things can really heat up a place fast."

"Tell me about it. You can't breathe in my bathroom right now."

"What?"

"Never mind. Anyway, all he had to do was leave her in there with the door closed. Maybe he waited a while outside the room, and when she didn't come out, he knew he was home free."

She could practically hear Dirk's mental wheels purring on the other end. "And when he got home," Dirk said, thinking aloud, "he could have just turned off the lights, let the room cool down a little, and called 911."

"You got it."

"Then how about Kameeka? If he's so smart, why did he just bash her in the head the old-fashioned way?"

"Maybe he didn't have time to think of anything better."

"And Tesla Montoya?"

Tesla. Even the thought caused Savannah's heart to ache. "We don't know yet that she's dead."

"She's been missing for three days," he said softly.

"I know," Savannah replied, a catch in her voice. "Believe me, I've been counting."

Savannah sat in her Mustang, half a block down from James Oates's house, watching waiting, hoping that Nurse Charlotte Murray would make her brother's house one of her stops now that she was officially on the run.

Detective McMurtry had been dispatched to Charlotte's house, should she happen to return, and Dirk was serving a search warrant on Kevin Connor's beach house. He had sent another detective from the station to serve the one on Murray's hospital locker. Tammy was posted in front of Tesla's place, just in case somebody suspicious decided to visit once more. It wouldn't be the first time a killer returned to the scene of the crime.

Maybe, between all of their efforts, they could come up with something that would lead them to Tesla. At least, that was the plan.

As she sat there in her car, the windows rolled down, she breathed in the fresh, sun-warmed summer air and wondered if Tesla was still alive . . . if she could still breathe, and hear the birds sing, and feel the sun on her face.

She also found herself wondering what Charlotte Murray would look like, beyond the description that Dirk had given her: about five-two, petite, dark brown hair, blue eyes, swarthy complexion.

But other than the driver's license stats, Savannah couldn't help being confused by the idea of a nurse who took life as well as saved it.

Savannah had always had a hard time getting her mind around the idea of a woman committing murder, let alone a professional health-care giver. For Savannah, who thought that the healing arts were the most important calling on earth, it was unthinkable.

She truly hoped that Charlotte would make an appearance while she had the place under surveillance. More than anything, she really wanted to talk to the woman, to find out who, why, when, and, most importantly, where Tesla was.

Sitting there, watching the house, she didn't know what she would say if Murray did show, but she figured she'd think of something when the time came.

She didn't have long to wait . . . or to think of any brilliant strategy. Because she had only been sitting there for twenty minutes — a relatively short time by surveillance standards — when she saw an older Honda pull up in front of the house.

It approached slowly, as though the driver was being cautious, then came to a stop at the curb across the street. No one got out for what seemed like forever and a day to Savannah. Then, the door opened and a woman answering Dirk's description exited the vehicle.

She was carrying a large tote under her arm that appeared to be empty. Small, trim, with short dark hair, wearing surgical greens and a white sweater, she hurried across the street to

Oates's house, unlocked the door, and went inside.

Savannah sat there a few minutes, allowing her to get involved in whatever she was doing inside the house. Then she reached into the back floorboard of her car and rummaged around until she found an empty paper bag that had contained her latest order of Avon.

Opening her glove box, she pulled out a flashlight, a small package of tissues, and a couple of cassette tapes, and she popped them into the bag.

Avon sack in hand, she got out of the car and walked the half block to the house.

After ringing the doorbell, she waited and, as she had expected, no one answered. She could easily imagine the nerve-rattled Charlotte inside, quaking in her nurse's shoes.

"Hello?" she called out cheerfully. "Avon, Mrs. Winterbourne, it's me, your Avon lady. I have your skin softener and your bath gels."

No one answered. She didn't hear a sound from inside the house. But she could instinctively feel the other woman just on the opposite side of the door.

"Come on, Mrs. Winterbourne. I know you're home. You're always home at this time of day." She rang the bell several more times in rapid succession and pounded with the brass door knocker. "You might as well answer, because I'm not going away until you answer this door."

Finally, the door opened just a crack. She could see that the woman inside had put on the chain. One eye peeped out at her, wide and frightened.

"Go away," she said. "You've got the wrong house. My brother lives here, not somebody named Winterbourne."

Savannah smiled and glanced down at the bag in her hand. "Then maybe this is his order." She looked inside the sack. "Yes, now that I take another look, it's some men's shaving lotion and cologne. Is your brother named Jim?"

"Yes, but he isn't here right now, and you should leave," she said, starting to shut the door.

Quickly, Savannah shoved her foot in the crack, preventing her from closing it all the way. "You have to talk to me, Charlotte," she said. "I can save your life, but not if you don't talk to me . . . right now."

The eye that was peeping through the opening widened, then filled with tears. "Who are you really?" she said.

"My name is Savannah Reid," she told her.

"And you don't sell Avon."

"No, I don't. I'm sorry I lied to you, but I had to get you to open the door for me."

"Are you a police officer?"

"No. I'm a private detective. I'm not here to arrest you. I'm here to help you." Savannah's eyes pleaded with the nurse's. And her voice was as soft as peach skin when she added, "Charlotte, if you've ever believed anybody and trusted anyone in your life, girl, you'd better trust me now and open up this door."

"But I can't." Charlotte began to sob. "I can't talk to anybody. I have problems. Terrible problems."

"I know what you mean. So do I. We're both just a couple of women in an awful situation. Let me inside, and we'll talk. We can help each other. I promise you."

Savannah waited, not daring to breathe as the tortured woman weighed her options.

"I don't think anybody can help me now," Charlotte said. "I think it's all gone too far. It's over. There's no way that this can have a happy ending."

"You're right about that," Savannah said. "But maybe if we put our heads together, we can think of something we can do to keep it from getting any worse than it already is. Charlotte, let me inside. Let's talk."

"Move your foot," she said at long last.

Savannah was afraid that if she moved her foot, she would get the door slammed in her face. But she couldn't stand there like that all day. So she did as she had been asked.

The door closed.

But then she heard the chain jangling on the other side. And it opened.

Nurse Charlotte Murray was standing there, tears streaming down her face. "Come on in," she said. "I don't think I really deserve any-body's help at this point. But if you're willing to give it, I'll take any I can get."

"Smart lady," Savannah said, hurrying inside. "Let's make a pot of coffee, if Jim's got some, and we'll have us a good, long, heart-to-heart. Believe me, I just became your new best friend."

Chapter
23

"I never thought I'd wind up in a situation like this," Charlotte said as she cupped her hands around the coffee mug as though drawing strength from its warmth. "I just fell in love with a married man and then . . . got stupid."

Savannah thought of Marietta. At that very minute she was hurrying back to Georgia to be with a man who was *considering* leaving his wife and kids to be with her . . . again.

"Yeah, there seems to be a lot of that 'stupid' stuff going around these days. Maybe it's an airborne virus."

They were sitting in Jim Oates's living room, a bachelor's pad with an enormous television, an oversize stereo system, and assorted gym equipment. The diminutive Charlotte was half buried in a giant beanbag chair, while Savannah sat on a denim futon. And while their surroundings could hardly have been classified as cozy, Charlotte seemed surprisingly open and at ease once she began to confide in Savannah.

"You were at the Connor house with Kevin

the other morning when I came by," Savannah said, not asking . . . just letting her know that she had placed her there.

When Charlotte didn't deny it, Savannah continued, "Kevin didn't tell me your name that day. He said that you were married and he was protecting your interests."

"Kevin was protecting himself, not me. I'm not married," Charlotte replied. "I was for a while. But Mr. Murray and I went our separate ways several years ago. It seems like I've been choosing the wrong guys all my life."

"You aren't the only woman to make some bad investments when it comes to romance. We've all been there."

Charlotte's face fell, and she began to cry, one hand over her mouth. "Not every woman has done what I've done for a man," she said between sobs. "I used to think he was such a wonderful person. Now I know better, but it's too late."

Reaching into her purse, Savannah found some tissues. She left the futon, walked over to the beanbag chair, and handed the tissues to Charlotte.

Sitting on the floor at the woman's feet, Savannah placed a comforting hand on her knee. She knew from the DMV that Charlotte Murray was only in her early thirties. But she looked so much older. She had the sunken-eyed appearance of a person who wasn't sleeping, but suffering enormous grief and guilt.

"You need somebody to talk to about it, Charlotte," she said. "You can't hold something like that inside. It will eat you alive."

Charlotte sniffed and nodded. "It *is* eating me alive. It's like having this huge, black ugliness right in the center of my chest. I feel like I'm going to explode."

"Talk to me, Charlotte. Tell me what happened, and I promise I'll do everything I can to help you."

Savannah felt time slow as she waited for Charlotte's response. The only sounds were those of the nurse's soft weeping and the occasional car passing on the street outside.

She didn't push for an immediate response, realizing that this was probably the most important decision that Charlotte had ever made. Except maybe the decision to help her lover commit murder.

"I didn't kill them," she said finally. "Kevin did. But I knew about it, and I didn't do anything. I didn't even tell him how wrong he was. At first it was because I loved him so much. But then I went along with him because I was afraid he'd hurt me if he had any idea that I wasn't completely on his side."

"I understand," Savannah said. "Did you know he was going to kill them before he did it?"

"Not with Caitlin. He told me about that afterward. He said he did it so that we could be together. But he didn't have to murder her. He

340

could have just divorced her."

"So, why *did* he kill her? Do you know?"

"A few months ago he took out a big life insurance policy on her. And he would get even more if she died from an accident. They were having financial problems. They were about to lose that big house and the cars. Kevin cares a lot more about that stuff than Cait did. He said he didn't think he could stand to lose it all and start over with nothing again." She twisted the tissue between her fingers. "I also had a feeling that Cait might have found out about me. From a couple of little things he said, I think she might have been going to leave him. He wouldn't have wanted a divorce either. Again, losing half of the stuff wouldn't have suited him."

"Did he tell you how he killed her?"

She nodded and dabbed at her eyes. "He said he went home because she said she was feeling bad. But when he got there she was already half dead from all the stuff she was doing to herself to lose weight. She was unconscious, so he just pulled her into the bathroom, turned those heat lamps on, and left her there."

"Did you let him use your security card to come and go that day from the hospital?"

"He asked me if he could use it. I thought it was a little weird, but I didn't ask why. He was always losing things. I figured he'd just misplaced his."

"And how about Kameeka?" she asked.

"Why did he kill her?"

Before replying, Charlotte took her coffee mug from the nearby end table and held it tightly to her chest. "That night . . . after he had killed Caitlin," she began, "he was checking her e-mail on their home computer. He was making sure there wasn't anything there that might incriminate him if the police got suspicious and checked the files. He found an e-mail that Caitlin had written a few days before. She had sent it to both Kameeka and Tesla. She said that she had mailed Tesla a tape that she had made. On the tape she said that she was worried that maybe her husband intended to hurt her. And she told them that if anything happened to her, they should take the tape to the authorities."

Savannah tried to hide her surprise. "Kevin told you all of this?"

"Yes." Charlotte laughed, but the sound was bitter. "Kevin talks a lot when he's drunk. The night after Cait died, he got stinking drunk and came over to my house. He talked to me for hours, told me about how he'd killed her. I guess he felt like he was going to explode, too."

"I suppose so. Did he tell you how he killed Kameeka?"

"He said he got into her house early that morning through a sliding door in the rear of the house that wasn't locked. She was just getting out of bed. When she walked into the kitchen, he hit her. . . ." Charlotte's voice broke

342

and it was several moments before she could compose herself enough to continue. "He hit her with a baseball bat that he had taken with him."

"And then he dressed her body, put it in his car," Savannah said, "took her out to Citrus Road, and dumped her?"

"Yes. He wanted it to look like someone had hit her when she was jogging." She paused to wipe her eyes. "After he killed her there at the house, he cleaned up the blood off the floor, and then he checked her computer so that he could erase Cait's e-mail."

"How did he get her password?"

"She'd stored it. You can do that so that you don't have to sign in every time."

"Okay. I don't know much about that sort of thing. Go ahead. . . ."

"And the sad thing is, she hadn't even opened the e-mail yet. She hadn't read it, so he wouldn't have even had to kill her. He could have just sneaked into the house and erased the letter. She never would have known the difference."

Savannah sat there on the floor, patting the woman's knee and wishing she had one of Ryan's mini-recorders going in her purse. Confiding like this in familiar surroundings was one thing, but would Charlotte deny everything later? She had to get something unique, something substantial that could be used in court.

She asked the question that she had been

dreading. "Charlotte . . . is Tesla Montoya still alive?"

Again, Charlotte covered her face with her hand and sobbed. "No."

Savannah felt something deep inside her crumple and die. And for just a moment she allowed herself to wonder how many more pieces of herself she could afford to lose in one lifetime.

She reached for the woman's hand and clasped it tightly between her own. "Charlotte," she said softly, "you have to take me to her."

She nodded. "I know."

Savannah stood and gently pulled Charlotte to her feet. "Let's go," she said.

As she led the weeping nurse to the door, Savannah felt a sadly familiar rush of bittersweet victory. It was too late to save the beautiful lady with the dark, soft eyes.

But at least she could bring Tesla home. And that would have to be enough.

The road to the little town of Oak Grove was picturesque with its woods of gnarled oaks, the creek that meandered alongside, and the occasional scenic mountain view. But it was one of the deadliest stretches of pavement in the country.

White crosses, bouquets of artificial flowers, and ribbons decorated the spots where drunken teenagers had missed sharp curves and struck the ancient, unyielding oaks, ending their young lives far too soon. More than one driver had nodded off for only a second or lost their concentration while changing a CD, and plunged over one of the road's many cliffs — not to be found for weeks or months.

And, according to Charlotte Murray, Tesla had met her end at the bottom of one of those cliffs.

Savannah navigated her Mustang around the winding road as they climbed higher and higher into the mountains. Sitting beside her in the passenger's seat, Charlotte had gone from crying to a stoic silence that troubled Savannah.

She was afraid that at any moment, the woman might realize how candid she had been and regret it.

More than anything, Savannah wanted to give Dirk a call and tell him what was happening. But she didn't dare do anything that might break the connection between herself and Charlotte — a bond that seemed to be growing tenuous at best.

"Are we getting close?" she asked as the road became even steeper, and she shifted into a lower gear.

"We're almost there," Charlotte replied, her voice so low it was barely audible.

Savannah looked around at the wild hillsides. One looked like the other, adorned only with rocks, scrub brush, and the occasional patch of prickly pear cactus.

"How are you going to know when we get there?" she asked. "Is there some sort of landmark?"

Charlotte nodded woodenly. "A bridge."

"Okay."

"She's in the van."

Surprised by this new, volunteered tidbit, Savannah decided to press for more. "Your brother's white van?"

"Yes. It broke down just as we got to the bridge."

"You and Kevin were driving in the van with Tesla?"

"Kevin was driving. I was following in my car."

Savannah tried to swallow the knot in her throat, but couldn't. "And Tesla was already dead?"

"Just about. Kevin had hit her in the head, like he did Kameeka."

"At her house?"

She nodded. "He was trying to get her to tell him where the tape was. She wouldn't; she kept saying she didn't have it. And we couldn't find it."

Savannah made a mental note of the "we," but decided to let it pass for the moment, because Charlotte was still talking: "Tesla gave him her e-mail password, though, and he was able to erase Cait's letter."

"She had read it then?"

"Yes."

"So why hadn't she gone to the police?"

"Kevin said he thought it was because she was here in the U.S. illegally. If she went to the authorities, she might get investigated herself. Caitlin had told him that she was an illegal, and at first he felt safe, that she wouldn't turn him in because of that. But then he got to thinking about it, and he didn't want to take the chance. So he asked me to help him pick her up that day at the coffee shop."

"You were driving the van when he grabbed her in the parking lot?"

She nodded. "Yes, and I'll never forgive myself. He said he was just going to take her back to her house and make her give him the tape. Then he was going to threaten her, scare her into staying quiet. I had no idea what he was really going to do."

Savannah found it hard to believe that, since he had already killed two women, it would never occur to Charlotte that he might kill a third one. But this wasn't the time to speak her mind.

"At Tesla's house," Savannah said, "after he struck her and erased the e-mail, he put her in the van and you guys drove up here?"

"Yes. He wanted to take her way up into the hills, where nobody ever goes. Then he was going to take the plates off the van, remove anything inside that might lead back to Jim, and then drive it over a cliff with her inside."

So he thought he'd remove the plates, huh? Savannah mused. Obviously he didn't know about vehicle identification numbers, permanently placed inside all automobiles by the manufacturer.

"And you two would drive back in your car?" Savannah said.

"That was the plan. But that damned van . . . it was always breaking down on my brother. It died, just up there —" She pointed to a small bridge ahead that crossed over a narrow arroyo about forty feet deep. The creek ran through the valley below, its bed a maze of rocks, worn smooth by the constant flow of water.

Savannah pulled over to the side of the road and switched off the Mustang's engine, giving it a rest from the climb.

She turned to Charlotte, who still looked stoic, but was trembling. "Let's do it," she told her.

"We're not going to be able to go down there," Charlotte said. "The cliff's too steep."

"We'll try anyway," Savannah replied as she got out of the car and tucked the keys deep inside her slacks pocket . . . just in case Nurse Charlotte decided to take a drive back to San Carmelita and leave her out here with the coyotes and prickly pears.

And Tesla Montoya.

They walked toward the bridge and just before they reached it, Savannah could see for herself the place where the van had left the road. Crushed sage bushes and a fresh slide in

348

the dirt and rocks at the precipice edge marked the spot with sickening clarity.

Savannah approached the drop with caution, watching her step while keeping an eye on the woman beside her. She still hadn't decided how much she truly trusted Nurse Murray, and she had no intention of taking any unplanned trips over the edge herself.

"There it is," Charlotte said, pointing to a patch of white amid the brush and stones below them. "It landed down there on the rocks next to the creek."

Savannah could see the van; she could also see that without some sort of rock-climbing gear, there was no way anybody was getting to it.

"See," Charlotte said. "It's nearly straight down."

"Uh-huh." Savannah left her and walked across the bridge to the other side. Charlotte followed.

"Where are you going?" she asked.

"There's more than one way to skin a cat," Savannah replied, "but don't ever say that around Diamante or Cleopatra."

"What?"

Savannah didn't answer. She had found what she was looking for: a way down that was less steep, a challenging path, but doable.

"Come on," she told Charlotte as she began her descent, hanging on to thorny bushes for balance.

"I'm not going down there," Charlotte called after her. "I . . . I just can't."

I wouldn't want to either if I were you, Savannah thought. *Reality checks can be pretty painful.*

"Yes, you can," she yelled back. "Just take it slow and easy like I am. You'll be okay."

"I mean . . . I can't see *her.*"

Savannah stopped and looked up at Charlotte, who was leaning over the edge watching her. "I know exactly what you mean, Charlotte. Come along now."

Charlotte shook her head. "I'll wait here for you." She glanced around her at the wilderness on either side. "Where am I going to go? You've got the keys in your pocket."

"Yes, I do. And we didn't have anybody following us this time to give us a ride back, did we?"

Charlotte winced, then withdrew from the edge. "I'm going to sit right here," she said. "Be careful, because I'm not going to come down there to rescue you if you fall."

"I wouldn't expect you would," Savannah mumbled as she continued on down to the crashed vehicle below.

She made it down the cliff in less than two minutes, reminding herself that the trip back up would be tough without the aid of gravity.

When she reached the bottom, she still had to navigate her way across the creek to the other side. Halfway over, she decided that she

350

would add the price of her loafers to Leah Freed's bill. After slipping and sliding among the wet stones and wading in the foot-deep creek, they were bound to be a write-off.

Her feet were nearly numb from the cold water by the time she reached the other side and the van.

She had seen worse wrecks in her life. At least the van still looked like a van. But it was badly twisted, the front crushed so badly that she was dreading the sight she would find inside.

Metal and glass could do such horrible things to the human body. She wished that people realized that fact when they went hurtling down the freeway at breakneck speed without wearing their seat belts.

She found the side door ajar. Being careful not to cut herself on the broken glass and jagged metal edges, she climbed inside.

The smell of gasoline was so strong it nearly gagged her, and the interior was so dark that she couldn't see anything at all until her eyes adjusted to the gloom.

One of the van's front seats had been shoved into the rear of the vehicle. The headliner had torn loose and was hanging down, a dirty, ragged curtain. Shattered glass sparkled everywhere, like a shower of rough-cut aquamarines.

But there was no body.

No Tesla.

Savannah jumped out of the van, her heart racing. She began to run up and down the creek's edge, stumbling over the rocks, searching, and trying desperately not to hope.

"What is it?" As though from far away, she could hear Charlotte shouting down to her. "What are you doing?"

But Savannah ignored her as she looked behind every bush, every boulder.

And it was behind one of those large rocks that she found her.

Tesla was lying, face down on the stony ground, only a few inches from the creek's edge. She was still wearing the jeans, T-shirt, and sneakers that she had been wearing when she left the photo shoot that day . . . so many years ago, it seemed.

Savannah ran to her, knelt beside the motionless form, and reached to turn it over. She was expecting to find a cold, lifeless body, as empty and soulless as all the other corpses she had seen in her career.

But the flesh of Tesla's arms when she touched her was warm. Not as warm as it should be, but living.

And once the body was turned over, Savannah could see an ever-so-slight rise and fall of the chest.

Pressing her fingers to Tesla's jugular, Savannah could detect a faint, erratic pulse.

"Tesla!" she shouted, gently jostling her. "Tesla, wake up, honey."

The closed eyes didn't open. They didn't even flutter.

Savannah looked at the wound on the side of her head that was so horribly similar to the one on Kameeka Wills. Dried blood had matted her beautiful hair to the side of her face, and her left arm was bent at an awful angle, obviously badly broken. Her jeans were torn at the knees, and her right leg had bled profusely in the shin area.

"But she's alive," Savannah whispered. "Thank you, God."

She stood and looked up at Charlotte Murray, who was standing on the edge, watching, trying to see around the rocks and vegetation.

"Get your ass down here, Nurse Murray!" she yelled up to her. "Right now! And don't give me no lip. You've got a patient to take care of."

Under her breath she added, "The most important patient of your career, gal."

Then she fished in her jacket pocket for her cell phone. She dialed and a few seconds later she heard Dirk's gruff, "Yeah?"

The sound of his voice had never been more welcome, and she nearly burst into tears. "I'm in the mountains behind Oak Grove on old Camino Road," she said. "Charlotte Murray is with me. She led me to Tesla."

"Are you serious?"

"She's still alive, but barely. Get the paramedics up here, a chopper if you can."

"How do I find you?"

"I'm about ten miles east of Oak Grove. The pony's parked on the side of the road. Shake a leg, buddy. I don't think our girl's got long here."

Click.

Once again, Dirk hadn't bothered to say good-bye, kiss my tushie, or toodle-ooo.

But this time, Savannah really, *really* didn't care.

Chapter
24

"She's not completely out of the woods yet," the doctor at Community General Hospital told Dirk when they cornered him in the emergency room waiting area. "And she's not going to be for a while. But we're getting her rehydrated and she's stable. Considering that she was out there, injured and exposed to the elements, for three days, she's doing remarkably well."

"Do you think she'll make it?" Savannah asked.

The doctor pushed his glasses up onto his head and rubbed his hand across his eyes. "I'm pretty sure she will," he said wearily. "We're going to have some problems with that arm. It's got a compound fracture, and even if the surgeons can save it, I don't know if she'll regain any substantial use of the limb."

"Is she awake?" Dirk asked.

"She's in and out, but that's to be expected, considering her physical condition and the head injury."

"How bad is that?" Dirk asked.

355

"The CAT scan looked pretty good. I think she'll have a full recovery, mentally at least." The doctor turned to Savannah. "She says she was able to pull herself out of the van and down to the creek for water. If she hadn't been able to drink, if the weather hadn't been mild these past few days, and if you hadn't found her when you did, she never would have made it."

"Nurse Murray helped," Savannah said. "She treated her at the scene as best she could and then assisted the paramedics on the way here."

The doctor nodded. "Murray's good," he said, then added, "Why was she out there in the mountains with you? I thought she was on duty today."

Savannah glanced at Dirk. "A long story," she said.

"I'll call later to check on Montoya," Dirk told the doctor. "Take good care of her and let me know when she's well enough to talk to me. I have some important stuff to ask her."

"I'll bet you do." He nodded thoughtfully. "Yes, I'll just bet you do."

Savannah and Dirk were leaving the hospital when she got a call on her cell phone. Looking at the Caller I.D., she said, "Oh, dad-gum, it's Tammy. I forgot all about her. She doesn't even know we found Tesla."

She punched the TALK button. "Hello, sugar. Guess what."

"What?" Tammy said.

356

"We found Tesla Montoya. She's in bad shape but alive. We got her to the hospital in time, and she's stable."

"That's great! Good work! I've been working here myself."

Savannah had to think hard to even remember what the kid was doing. "Yes," she said, stalling while she thought, "and how's it going?"

"Ve-e-ery interesting," she replied with her not-so-good Bugs Bunny impression.

"So, what's up, doc?"

"I was sitting in front of Tesla Montoya's house . . ."

Oh, yeah, Savannah thought. *That's where we sent her.* "Okay, and . . ."

". . . and Kevin Connor came by."

Savannah stopped in the middle of the hallway and grabbed Dirk's arm. "Connor dropped by Tesla's place while you were watching it just now?"

"About half an hour ago."

Dirk was instantly alert. "What was he doing there?"

"What did he do?" Savannah asked her. "Did he go inside the house?"

"Nope. He got out of his car, looked around, then hurried up to the front porch. He took the mail out of the mailbox next to the door, shuffled through it, and shoved it back in."

"He went through the mail," Savannah relayed to Dirk.

"And," Tammy continued, "he stuck one piece of it, a small manila envelope, inside his shirt."

"I'll bet you dollars to doughnuts that it's the tape," Savannah told Dirk. "The one I told you about, the one Cait sent to Tesla. Connor's got it."

"Do you want to know the rest?" Tammy said. Savannah could practically hear the self-satisfied chuckle in her voice.

"Do bullfrogs croak when you goose 'em?"

"What?"

"Yes! I want to know the rest. Give it to me."

"I followed him when he left Tesla's and guess where he is now."

"Where?"

"Leah Freed's house."

Savannah stared at Dirk for a moment, then said, "Oh, Lord. He's at Leah's house. Do you figure he's gone there to kill her, too?"

"I wouldn't put it past him," Dirk replied. "What's one more victim when you're on a roll?"

"We'd better get over there right away." To Tammy, she said, "What's the address?"

"Heron Lane, number 138."

"Stay right where you are, darlin', and we'll be there in ten minutes. Call me if he leaves."

"Ten-four."

Savannah laughed when she hung up. "The squirt's getting the lingo down," she told Dirk.

"And she's getting pretty good at tailin' the bad guys, too."

Savannah and Dirk spotted Tammy's hot-pink Volkswagen Beetle parked a few houses down from the address she had given them.

"If she's gonna do a lot of this surveillance work for us," Savannah said, "we'll need to get her a blue Ford sedan . . . or something that doesn't stick out like a sore thumb."

"Yeah, really," he replied. "Cars shouldn't be painted girlie colors."

"Girlie colors?"

"You know — nail polish colors. Except for red. Red's good, for cars or fingernails. Toenails, too, with those little strappy sandals you gals wear."

The slightly lecherous gleam in his eyes warned her not to pursue the topic any further.

She looked into the Beetle as they drove by. It was empty.

"Hey, where's the kid?" she asked, suddenly alarmed. "I told her to stay put."

"Oh, man," he said. "That's just want we need now, for Miss Nancy Drew to get herself in trouble."

"No, wait a minute. . . ." Savannah caught a glimpse of shining golden hair sticking above a star jasmine bush next to Leah Freed's modest beach cottage. "There she is. What's she doing?"

"I believe she's peeping in the window."

Savannah laughed. "One of these days I'll have to mention to her that it's a crime."

"Like you don't do it."

"Not for fun . . . not like your buddy Tumblety."

"Eh, don't bring up a sour subject. I'm still pissed that I can't bust that creep for these murders."

"Well, now you can arrest Connor." She pointed to the silver Maserati parked across the street. "That should make it up to you."

"Barely."

He parked the Buick a little farther down the block, and they got out.

Avoiding the front of the house, they sneaked around to the side of the building, where Tammy was hiding in the bushes.

"Ps-s-st. Hey, Sherlock," Savannah said.

Tammy whirled around, her eyes wide with excitement. She looked enormously relieved to see them. She beckoned vigorously.

"Take a look," she whispered, when they ducked behind the jasmine with her. "They're . . . you know . . . doing it."

"Doing *it?*" Savannah thought she must have heard wrong. "Leah and Kevin are doing it?"

"Big time. Look!"

Dirk sniffed. "I don't wanna look. I'll barf."

"Well, *I* wanna look! Move over," Savannah said.

She peeped through the window, and even though the partly drawn curtain concealed much of the scene, she could see enough out-flung, bare limbs and piston action to know that Leah wasn't getting murdered. Quite the contrary, in fact.

"I don't believe it!" she said. "I could've sworn those two hated each other!"

"And you know what else?" Tammy said, practically dancing in her shorts.

"What else?" Savannah asked her.

"Before they started, you know . . . that . . . they opened the envelope, the one he took out of Tesla's mailbox. Inside was a cassette tape. They listened to it, and they were laughing."

Savannah's eyes narrowed and her face hardened. "Oh, they did, did they?" She turned to Dirk. "Let's bust these bastards."

"How do you wanna do it?" he asked her, his eyes as cold as hers. "One in the front, one in the back, or both of us through the front?"

Savannah stepped back and surveyed the exterior of the cottage, trying to guess at the interior layout. "If we break in the back door, we can probably nail him before he can get out of the bedroom and out the front door."

"I'll go to the front, just in case he runs out that way," Tammy offered.

"He might be armed, Tammy," Savannah said.

"Hell, Van," Dirk said, glancing in the bedroom window. "I can bust a door down faster than that. If he bolts out the front, he'll be lucky to be dressed."

"That's true. Let's go."

Savannah had to give Dirk credit for one thing: He was excellent at breaking in doors. He had it down and they were inside in four seconds.

In another two, they were standing at Leah Freed's bedroom door, looking at the startled, horrified, and quite naked couple on the bed.

"Now there's a sight that'll haunt my dreams," Savannah said as Dirk rushed forward, grabbed Kevin, and shoved him face forward onto the bed.

"You're under arrest, Connor," Dirk told him. "As I'm sure you know, you have the right to remain silent. And we both know you've already got yourself a fancy-dandy attorney who ain't gonna get you off, 'cause I've got you good, buddy. *Real* good."

Savannah walked into the room and picked up a silk robe that was lying on the floor. Tossing it in Leah's direction, she said, "I want you to know, in spite of this new development, you're still gonna pay me every penny you owe me."

"What is this?" Leah exclaimed as she climbed into the robe. "What's going on here?"

"Like you don't know," Savannah said. "Like you didn't help him set this whole thing up."

"What thing?"

Savannah gave Leah a long, hard look, then shook her head. "Boy, a model decides to leave you and you take it really personally, huh?"

"I don't know what you're talking about."

When Dirk had Kevin cuffed, he pulled him to his feet, where he stood in all of his naked glory.

Savannah averted her eyes, but not before noticing that Kevin Connor had at least one quality that women might have found desirable.

"So, Kevin," she said. "Exactly how many of your girlfriends did you involve in these murders of yours?"

His face, already crestfallen, fell a few more notches. He didn't reply.

But Leah did. "What do you mean?" she said, bristling. "What do you mean by 'his girlfriends'?"

"That's right, Leah. Plural," Savannah answered. "He's been playing hokeypokey with a little nurse at the hospital. She even helped him dump Tesla off a cliff, and she hid his bloody jeans after he killed Kameeka. She says they were 'in lo-o-ove'." She gave Leah a tight smile and cocked her head sideways. "Tell me, Leah . . . are you two in lo-o-ove, too?"

Leah jumped off the bed and landed in front of Kevin. "Is that true?" she shouted in his face. "Have you been screwing somebody else? Have you?"

Kevin didn't say a word.

"I think he's exercising his right to be silent," Savannah said.

Leah's face went from red to purple, her eyes practically bugging out of her head. "Answer me, Kevin." She slapped him hard across the cheek.

Dirk made a movement toward her, as though to stop her, but Savannah shook her head, and he hesitated.

"If you have been," Leah was saying, "I'll find out and then I'm going to tell them everything. I swear, Kevin, I will!"

Kevin's face flushed as dark as hers as he glared down at her. "Oh, yeah?" he said, his voice low, his tone ominous. "Well, if you do, I'll tell them how you knew all about it long before I did it, and you didn't do a damned thing to stop it. That would make you an accessory."

Kevin turned to Dirk. "It would, wouldn't it?" he said. "Wouldn't that make her an accessory?"

"No way!" Leah shouted. "I didn't know about Kameeka or Tesla until afterward. I thought it was just going to be Caitlin. I . . ."

Suddenly, both Leah and Kevin seemed to realize what they had just said. Their faces went from purple to white.

What a colorful couple, Savannah thought. *And chatty, too.*

Dirk looked across the room at Savannah, and they both started to laugh. "Don't you love it?" he asked her.

"It's what I live for, darlin'," she replied. "It's what I *live* for."

Dirk and Tammy sat on Savannah's sofa,

watching the eleven o'clock news. Next to them, Savannah was relaxing in her easy chair, one cat on her lap, the other keeping her feet warm on the footstool. The bowls of popcorn in their laps were nearly empty, but their cups were overflowing with satisfaction and more than a little plain old conceit.

"Did that sister of yours find her way home?" Dirk asked, kicking off his shoes and propping his feet on her coffee table.

She didn't object. At least he was taking off his sneakers first these days. There was hope for him after all. "Yes, Mari called half an hour ago. She made it home in one piece. Lover Boy Lester didn't pick her up at the airport like he said he would. Seems his wife wouldn't let him out of the house."

"Doesn't sound good," Tammy said.

"Never does where Marietta's men are concerned." She glanced at the TV screen and saw a familiar face. "Hey, hey," she said. "Here we go."

"Kevin Connor" — the Los Angeles news anchor was saying — ". . . arrested today for the murder of his wife, the plus-sized supermodel, Caitlin Connor, and her friend, another model, Kameeka Wills. Although he will be represented by famed defense attorney, Marvin Klein, the district attorney says he has an excellent case against Mr. Connor, which includes both forensic evidence and witness accounts. He has also been charged with the attempted murder of a third model, Tesla Montoya, who remains in the hospital in stable condition after being rescued from a mountain road above Oak Grove. It is alleged that Connor dumped her there after a brutal attack."

"Ah . . . Kevin's not looking too happy there," Tammy said as they showed the standard "perp walk" footage.

"At least he's got his pants on," Dirk said. "I hate havin' to arrest naked guys. Girls, I don't mind, but buck-naked guys give me the heebie-jeebies."

"Hey, listen," Tammy said, pointing to the TV.

"A second suspect, famed talent agent Leah Freed, is also under arrest," the female anchor continued. "Authorities believe she and Kevin Connor were romantically involved and that she was a co-conspirator in the Connor murder.

"Caitlin Connor was originally believed to have died accidentally from an extreme diet and exercise program. She was attempting to lose a large amount of weight in a brief time to fulfill a contractual agreement between herself and Wentworth Cereal. We now go to Dr. Jensen at the worldfamous Malibu Weightloss Center for a story on the dangers of crash dieting. . . ."

Savannah's living room was silent as the TV physician issued his warnings, including a brief editorial on society's pressure on women to remain unnaturally slender, no matter what the cost to their health.

"Gee, you've gotta be pretty happy with that, Van," Dirk said, when the story was over.

"It's a start," Savannah said. "Not exactly a Cape Canaveral blast-off start, but a step in the right direction." She reached over to her end table and picked up a copy of *Real Woman*. It was the latest issue. On the cover was a picture of Caitlin Connor, her red hair spilling over her shoulders, her skin glowing with health, her eyes alight with the joy of living.

"Caitlin had thousands of fans who loved and admired her," she said. "If even a few of them learn from her example, maybe she won't have died for nothing."

She laid the magazine aside. "But either way . . . we did right by her, didn't we?"

"We did, Van," Dirk said. "We sure did."

Savannah wiped a tear away with the back of her hand, reached down, and stroked Cleopatra's black, satiny fur. She sniffed and said, "Anybody for a bowl of Chunky Monkey?"

"With chocolate syrup and whipped cream?" Dirk asked.

"Always, sweetcakes. Always. We don't want nobody around here blowing away in a stiff wind."

"Not likely," Tammy said. "Not with you around to feed them."

Savannah looked at her young friend and gave her a soft smile filled with affection. "You did great job on this case, kiddo. We couldn't have done it without you. You want some carrot sticks with whipped cream and chocolate on top?"

Tammy beamed, basking in the praise. "I'll take some ice cream, too. A big bowl. After all, we closed a case. We caught the bad guys. Several of them. It's a special occasion, right?"

"Special, indeed," Savannah said. "Let's celebrate!"